WITCHMARK

9/8 $15.88

WITCHMARK

C. L. POLK

A TOM DOHERTY ASSOCIATES BOOK

New York

This is a work of fiction. All of the characters, organizations, and events portrayed in this novel are either products of the author's imagination or are used fictitiously.

TO AJ AND TOM,

WHO WERE THERE EVERY DAY

WITCHMARK

ONE

An Emergency

The memo stank of barrel-printing ink and bad news. Oh, it began with the usual hurrahs, our boys victorious and finally coming home, but it ordered me to banish sixteen patients from my care by week's end. I didn't have ten men who were safe to send home to their families. This could not stand, and I'd tell Mathy to her face.

Green-tinged gaslight in the stairwell gave way to the lobby's white-gold aether lamps, and I suppressed a wince at the familiar prickle and whine of modern lighting. The clerk at reception waved me over, but I ignored the message slips in her hand.

"Have you seen Dr. Matheson?"

"Good evening, Dr. Singer. She left twenty minutes ago." She nodded her head leftwards.

Matheson had sent her memo late to escape before the news spread. She wouldn't be the one to send veterans home before they were ready. That responsibility was on me.

"You aren't the only one to ask." The clerk thrust messages into my hand. "They all left early. Department heads, board members . . . It's a bad one this time, isn't it?"

"Mandatory patient discharge." My fingers barely grazed

hers, but the old wound to her shoulder joint throbbed a dull red to my talent. My fingers itched to heal it. I drew away.

She curled message slips into tubes and slid them into labeled cubbies. "Well, it's to make room for the soldiers coming home, isn't it?"

It was. The war in Laneer was over, and as predicted, Laneer surrendered to Aeland's might. A happy event, to be sure. But when I thought about the fifty thousand soldiers on their way home, the chance they shared my patient's problems . . . I ignored the sick feeling in my gut, stuffing the messages in my coat pocket beside the crumpled memo. "What about Robin?"

"Haven't seen her. The nurses are in a meeting."

This damn memo, and no Robin to commiserate. "Thank you. Have a quiet evening." I gave her a polite nod and headed for the exit, faltering as I pushed the heavy door open.

It's perfectly safe out there. I knew it, but I still had to scan the trees when I stepped through the hospital doors. Their branches bent heavy with ripening apples, not the weight of enemy snipers.

Perfectly safe. Laneer's everlasting summer and gunfire were an ocean away. I was home in Kingston, where carriage wheels and bicycle tires hissed along rain-dampened streets, the air crisp with a streak of winter. I patted my pockets, searching for cigarettes I didn't carry anymore. Maybe Robin would let me have one. Solace knew I needed one, after my day.

Brass carriage bells, trilling bicycle bells, and shouting sounded, not far away and coming closer. A carriage careened around the corner. Cyclists scattered like startled fish. The driver hauled on the reins, putting his weight against the carriage brake. "Emergency!" the driver cried, stilling his agitated horses.

Cold pooled in my gut. We weren't an emergency hospital. If they needed a surgeon, I'd have to take up the scalpels I hadn't touched since I came home from the war.

The coach door banged open, and a broad-shouldered gentleman leapt out, bearing a sick man in his arms. The patient's face rolled toward me, and my heart kicked against my chest. Not just sick; by the waxy look of his skin, this man was dying. He lifted his trembling hand to claw at my coat lapels.

I put my arms under the patient's shoulders and knees. "I'm Dr. Singer, sir. I'll take it from here."

"I found him in the street." Instead of letting go, the gentleman grasped my arms, and between us we made a carry chair. He nodded to me over the patient's head. "I'm Tristan Hunter."

He adjusted his grip on my sleeves and ran like we had to outpace a tin grenade. Where had he learned to move casualties like that?

The sick man groped for me again.

"Sir? Can you tell me your name?"

"Nick Elliot," the sick man said. "Help me, Starred One. I am murdered."

I stumbled. The gentleman glanced at me, wide-eyed.

"He's raving." My excuse was feeble.

We rushed past the crowd huddled around the lobby wireless, their faces pop-eyed and staring at us. A competence of nurses strode out of Audience Hall A. Robin—thank the Guardians—broke from their midst, following us to an empty treatment room. Mr. Hunter handled the turn and dump in the dark as competently as any medic I'd worked with in the war.

He stepped back to snap on the light. The harsh white glow of aether prickled over my scalp and blazed over Mr. Elliot's pale face, the bruised hollows around his eyes deep violet.

Robin stretched a pair of rubber gloves over her hands, but I didn't bother. She caught my overcoat as I shrugged it off, her hand already out for my bowler.

"Poison," he gasped. "In the tea. Please, Starred One. Help me."

Don't say that out loud. I tore his vomit-stained shirt open. Abalone shell buttons plinked on the tile floor. I planted my bare hand on his chest and choked down a gasp.

Mr. Elliot's aura was the green of new spring leaves. A stranger with a witch's aura, dying on my table? This was a disaster.

Robin handed me a stethoscope. Mr. Elliot's pulse tied a stone to my hope of saving him, his labored breathing an off-time rhythm shuddering in his skinny chest.

"Is there an intravenous kit left?"

Robin threw open supply drawers. "No."

"Find a kit. Find two. Run."

Robin dashed out of sight. I spread my fingers over the stranger's chest. The deep scarlet light of his heart faltered. Gray particles gathered in his stomach and kidneys: dull, but with a feeling of metal. He had been poisoned, and not by bad food or filthy water. I couldn't save this man without magic.

Tight muscles in my arms and legs quivered. I could save him. Then he would talk. Then I'd wind up in the asylum . . . or worse, my family would save me from the asylum.

Mr. Elliot dragged in a tattered breath. "I got too close. They needed the souls. The war—"

He gagged and rolled away from me, retching. I held him steady. "Don't try to talk."

He dragged in ragged breaths and kept talking. "Find my murderer, Sir Christopher."

I froze. "I'm Dr. Singer."

He groped for my arm. "Promise me."

A crackling line of static rushed over me. Tendrils of green light shot from his fingers and twined up my arm. I fought his grip, but the vines held fast, stretching from his grasping fingers.

I lurched backward, trying to break free. He held on and top-
pled from the exam bed, landing on the tiles with a cry. The
light-vines constricted, sinking under my skin.

Nick Elliot raised his head. He was on his last shreds of life,
his grip on my arm trembling.

"Take it," he said. "Please. Use it to save them."

There was no time to ask who I was saving, or from what.
The souls, he said. And he knew my real name.

"Please, Sir Christopher," he panted. "The soldiers . . . they
deserve the truth."

The truth about what? The war? I wasn't sure the soldiers in
my ward could handle any more truth. I tightened my grip on
his hand. "I will."

Nick's power wound around me, trying to connect with
mine. He needed my help to do this. I stopped fighting the vines
for one breath and reached out.

I hadn't linked with anyone for years. I had thought I never
would again. His agony shuddered through me, his desperation
closed my throat, and his power filled me as he yielded every
speck.

The treatment room faded as a vision took me. I stumbled
on worn carpet patterned with pink roses, tripped on my way
down the stairs. My insides felt shredded, and I lurched over tiny
black and white tiles to a glass-fronted door. I had to get help. I
had to live.

The light-vines faded and his body went limp. I was Nick
Elliot no longer; his last urgent memory faded with his life. I felt
for a pulse, for breath, but it was merely ceremony. He was dead.

"Miles!"

Robin stood in the doorway clutching an IV kit. She dropped
it on the counter and knelt next to me. "Are you hurt?"

Robin stared at me, raising her gloved hand to hover next to
my temple, as if there was something there to see. Hot and cold

raced over my skin. Pins and needles spread from my fingertips, crawling up my right arm. "Am I bleeding?"

"No." But her brows were bunched together. "Are you sure you're all right?"

"I'm all right," I said. "Help me get him on the table."

His power welled inside me. I had to check to make sure I wasn't spilling light every time I moved. What had he done to me? I scrambled to my feet and tried to lift Nick Elliot's body.

Robin stared over my shoulder. "Sir? What are you doing in here?"

Cold fear prickled down my back.

Mr. Hunter stood behind me, tucked into the corner where he'd seen and heard everything.

My hands turned to ice. He would tell Robin as soon as he worked past the denial. He'd tell everyone in hearing range a witch had worked a spell on me, that the witch had called me Starred One and worse, Sir Christopher. But how had I failed to notice him?

"Forgive me," he said. "I didn't want to be in the way. One never knows quite what to do in these situations."

"I'm sorry you had to see that," Robin said. "He was in a lot of pain. Would you like to take a moment in the hospital lobby? Or I can find an empty treatment room . . ."

Yes. Get him out of here.

"Thank you, I'm quite well." He gave her a slight bow, his smile polite before he regarded me. "Doctor, do you need to sit down? You look shaken."

Blast this man. What was his game? He'd seen everything, but he looked at me with polite concern. I stood up straighter. "I'm fine, thank you. I hate it when I can't save them."

Robin and I laid Nick Elliot on the table and straightened his limbs, closed his staring eyes.

Mr. Hunter stood at the foot of the examination table, hands behind his back. "He said he'd been murdered. Had he?"

"It'll take a death examination to find out," I said. "The police have to be notified, in any case."

The cabinet on the left held sheets. I unfurled one over Nick Elliot's body, draping him in white-laundered linen. "You said you found him in the street."

Mr. Hunter tugged a corner of the sheet so it fell evenly. "At West Fourteenth and Wellston."

"West Fourteenth? Wakefield Cross Hospital is closer." Robin bent and picked up the buttons.

"He asked to come here."

My heart thumped hard—once, twice. A witch had passed the best hospital in Kingston to come here. To come to me. I shuffled to the treatment room's stone sink and turned on hot water. I wet a scarlet bar of soap and used the circling of one hand ringed around the other to calm down and think. Mr. Hunter had seen. He'd seen it all. And he hadn't said a word.

"We need to report it," I said.

"I'll get him sent downstairs." Robin had the beginnings of a medical file piled up on the counter. "You'll handle the exam?"

The antiseptic scent of carbolic acid rose from my soap-slippery hands. "I'll do it tomorrow."

"We have the luncheon fundraiser tomorrow."

"Guardians, save me from that waste of time."

Mr. Hunter stood up a little straighter, frowning at my language. I dried my hands on a linen towel. "I'm sorry, sir, but I must attend this. If there's nothing else I can do for you?"

"Actually . . ." Mr. Hunter took my Service coat and my second-best hat. He presented them as if he were my footman.

I draped my coat over my left arm, caught the brim of my hat in my hand. Paper crinkled in the pocket—the damned memo.

"I'd like a private word. I won't take much of your time."

Here it was. Threats. Blackmail. Whatever he wanted for his silence.

"We can talk in my office."

TWO

Negotiation

I climbed the eighty steps to my office with a quivering stomach and trouble on my heels. I willed my feet to move, kept my head high, and tried not to betray my lack of advantage or leverage. Mr. Hunter could report that a witch had called me Starred One, and I would wind up in an examination. I'd never get out.

Mr. Hunter kept pace with me up all four flights of stairs. "You climb these stairs every day?"

"More than once," I said. "Come in."

He took it all in at a glance. I scarcely had enough floor for my desk, and the guest chair folded flat to lean against the deep windowsill until someone needed it. He'd have to sit sideways, or there would be no room for his knees between my desk and the ceiling-high wall of shelves.

He bent over to peer at paper-bound penny novels, stood straight to inspect my small collection of medical journals. He eyed the distance from wall to wall and grimaced.

"It's minuscule."

His scorn stiffened my spine. I had a fine view of the south garden. Plenty of doctors envied my view. "You wanted a private place to talk."

"I don't imagine you'd want this conversation overheard any more than I do."

He removed his gloves and hat, and in other circumstances I would count the sight of him as a moment of joy. His hair was long enough to braid into a single golden rope. The plait lay on his shoulder, hanging over the lapel of his coat. His formal clothing was unmarred, as if Nick Elliot's sickness hadn't dared smirch his appearance. He dressed in the latest fashion, and his face belonged on the cinema screen—golden-skinned symmetry, with graceful bones and keen blue eyes. Lines around his mouth indicated a mirthful nature, and the light in his eyes suggested that he found something amusing without seeming cruel. It added up to the handsomest man I'd seen in years. It was a shame gentlemen didn't become actors.

Because he was a gentleman. His coat was good cashmere, his gloves fine kid, but there was more to him than money—ease and privilege rested in his manner. So when he put out a hand, I took it. His face rippled as if I saw him through old glass. I kept my expression pleasant with years of training. But the wavering distortion over his features . . . What was that?

"So. You saw everything," I said.

"Yes."

"Heard everything."

"I'm afraid so."

"And you'll keep silent, if—"

His mouth curved, and he was dazzling. "This is where I threaten and extort, is it? Shall I ask you for money, or demand wicked deeds?"

My head came up and I faced him square on, uncurling my fisted hands. "Get on with it, will you? It's late."

His smile faded. "Forgive my jest, please. I don't want to be connected with a witch any more than you do, Doctor. If anyone hears he tried to touch you with his power . . ."

"I'll be ruined," I sighed. "Tell me what you want."

"I wanted to find someone like you."

He knew. Did he know what Sir Christopher meant, too? My stomach quivered, and I tried to calm it with a slow breath. He thrust straight to the gut, his honesty a blade. He was looking for a witch. He was going to get in my business and stay there. I had to get rid of him. But I knew in my bones that this good-looking bit of trouble was going to stick.

I said nothing. People speak to fill a silence, to seek a connection. I stood patient and attentive and waited.

He smiled at me. Not placating, not a hint of uncertainty in it. "I want to know who killed Nick Elliot."

He did? I put the desk between us and aligned the reports on my desk blotter. "Why? You didn't know him."

"Call me an altruist."

If I hadn't been raised so well, I'd have laughed in his face. Altruist. Indeed. "There must be more to it. Why do you want to know who killed Nick Elliot?"

He tilted his head, and I fancied his eyes reflected the lamplight the way a cat's would. "Interesting. You don't deny he *was* killed, Doctor."

Oh, rot. "I won't know until I do the exam."

He leaned toward me. "Will you do it now?"

"I have to get home before my landlady locks the doors."

"Ah. You want me to get to the point." Mr. Hunter leaned on my filing cabinet. "I need to know why magic is dying."

I stilled. Magic dying? It wasn't. He was wrong—

Blast! He'd shocked me with his pronouncement. I scrambled to make up for it.

"I see," I said. "How am I supposed to know the answer?"

"I want you to help me find it. You and Nick Elliot are the

only witches I've met in Aeland. Mr. Elliot is dead. But here you are, alive and free."

And I had promised Nick, hadn't I? He had given me his power so I could find the . . . truth. About the war, I guessed. The war I had come to loathe, the war that had left so many men shattered inside. Mr. Hunter wanted to help, but he knew too much about me already, too many of my secrets. I had no choice but to deny it. "You want my help in finding out who poisoned Nick Elliot, and knowing will lead you to— No, it's insane. I can't help you."

"You can, Sir Christopher. And I can help you."

My breath caught in my throat. This was worse than blackmail.

I had been found.

Run, I told my useless legs. Run!

"You're afraid," he said. "Don't be. I'm in as much danger as you." Mr. Hunter raised one hand clenched in a fist. The edges of his fingers glowed red, and he opened his hand to show me a tiny light. The core of it glowed brighter than a candle, brighter than gas lamps, nearly as bright as aether.

If he told the truth, it could only mean two things: He was a lowborn witch in fine clothing, or he was a runaway mage like me. He offered me this show of magic as a token of trust. He could report me, but I could report him back.

If he wasn't lying. But I should report him, if I knew what was good for me.

I tried for one last bluff. "I'm sorry. How are you making that light?"

"Like this." He lifted the light and touched it to my hand.

"What—"

Another sense of self touched mine, tense and hopeful in the instant before the sensation of power linked with my own. I snatched my hand away. The light stuck to my fingers, wavering without his touch to steady it, fading, dying without him.

"Link to it," he said. "Touch it the way you would a heart."

The light steadied, a little dimmer than it had been. It balanced on my fingertips and my blood rushed, the magic making me feel taller, clear-sighted, powerful.

I'd missed this so much.

He touched me again, guiding my efforts. "You're alive. You're free. But you're untrained."

The little light glowed. I had the trick of holding it, of feeding it droplets of the power to burn.

I lifted my gaze from the light to Mr. Hunter's face. His warm smile reflected the wonder I felt. I couldn't see the link between it and me. I tried to coax it into brightening—

A breeze rattled a loose windowpane. A draft made my gas lamp flicker, the cold trickling into my thoughts: Could someone see us? I closed my fist. My bones were shadows bathed in scarlet before the light extinguished, leaving me small and cold. I'd completely fallen into his hands.

"Help me find out who killed Nick Elliot, and everything I can teach you before Frostnight is yours." He propped his chin on the pad of his thumb and the second knuckle of his index finger, examining me again. "Starting with how to hide your true nature, I think. You shine, Starred One, to anyone with the power to see."

Possibilities lay outside the door he'd cracked open. If I could appear mundane to highborn mages with the trick of seeing magical auras, Kingston could be mine to walk again. "What happens then?"

He hesitated. "I have to go home."

Only until Frostnight. How much trouble could he be, if he would be gone in eight days?

Too much trouble, and I knew it. "I can't help you. I have

patients to tend." But Nick Elliot had bypassed a better hospital and tried to tell me something about the war and its soldiers before he died. What did he mean? And who would want him dead for it?

"I'd never ask a healer to abandon his patients," he said. "But if I can teach you something you can use to help them, wouldn't it be worth it?"

If he could help me do something about what I saw when I touched them—

No. No more miracles. But whatever Nick Elliot knew, it had died with him, unless someone worked to find it out. If Nick had known what troubled my patients, why they suffered, if their worst fears of violence would come true . . .

The third stair from the top creaked. Mr. Hunter's eyes widened in alarm, and we sprang into action. I took my seat as if we had been chatting over my desk. He unfolded the guest chair and slouched in it. No footsteps sounded in the hall. Rubber-crepe shoes. A nurse.

I relaxed.

The silhouette in the frosted window was dark and short, the knock familiar. Robin pushed the door open and sidled halfway through. "You can leave the reports until tomorrow. The police aren't coming."

"They're not? Why?"

"Everyone's at another murder. Killer's a veteran, like the last one. Horrible, from what I gather."

Robin caught sight of Mr. Hunter and ducked her head. "I'm sorry, I didn't mean to interrupt."

He stood up. "Please don't worry, Mrs. . . ."

"This is Miss Robin Thorpe," I said. "Robin, meet Mr. Tristan Hunter."

"Delighted, Miss Thorpe." He offered his hand, but converted it to a more formal half-bow when Robin bent her head in greeting.

"My apologies, Mr. Hunter, but I've just been handling the body. A pleasure to meet you," she said, and turned her attention on me. "Miles, didn't you hear me? You don't need to do that report now."

"I should take my leave so you can go home, Doctor. I hope you will consider my offer. May I have your answer tomorrow?"

I wavered. It was unwise to step outside of the anonymous role I'd fashioned for myself, to get involved, but whatever Nick had known, if it would help my patients . . . I needed it. Damn it.

"Come in the afternoon. I'm off shift at four, and I have a luncheon to attend."

"I look forward to seeing you then." He left with a touch of his hat. My skin tingled as if he still touched me, guiding me in keeping the light ablaze.

Robin waited until Mr. Hunter's footsteps took him to the first landing, her hands on her hips. She turned to eye me once the sound of his departure faded.

"What offer?"

My pens lay askew on the blotter. I laid them out in parallel lines, tidied the reports in front of me. "He wants to know if Nick Elliot was murdered. May I have a smoke?"

She grinned. "No. Bad days only."

"I lost a patient. Is that bad enough?"

"No. Why would Mr. High Hat care if it was murder?" Robin asked, eyes narrow. "Didn't he say he found Elliot in the street?"

"He did."

"What if he killed Nick Elliot himself and wants to snarl up any investigation?"

Clever Robin. But if he had, why didn't Mr. Elliot accuse him? "I didn't think of that."

"I suppose you can tell the police he's a little too interested," Robin said. "They're the ones who'll be doing the investigating, after all."

"I can do that." I had no intention of doing that. All Mr. Hunter had to do was report me, and I was done for. "What are you still doing here? Aren't you supposed to split your shift for the luncheon?"

"You need to go home too. I need you to be extra charming to a rich dowager at the luncheon tomorrow. They're cutting laundry again."

So the board's savage little economies had struck Nursing this time. Beauregard needed money, but it was trying to eat itself. "I'll ask her for five thousand marks."

I had expected her to smile at promising such an outrageous sum, but she stuck her hands in the pockets of her heavy gray skirt. "There's something else."

"What?"

"I gave my notice. I'm going to medical school."

I caught my breath.

Robin was the best nurse in the hospital. She was my friend. Everything would go to shambles without her. She'd have patients waiting a year to see her the moment she became Dr. Robin Thorpe. She was leaving the hospital . . . leaving me.

A good man would be happy for her. "Excellent. Congratulations. Queen's University?"

"Yes. I start with the Frostmonth term."

"General Medicine?"

"Surgery."

The waiting list in my head doubled. "Those tiny hands of yours are perfect. You'll need to stand on a box."

She laughed. "I could use stilts."

The ache curled around my heart. She'd be the best. "I'll miss you."

"No, you won't. We'll stay in touch. Though you should leave here." She described the hospital with a sweeping gesture. "You're a better doctor than this."

"They need me." None of the other physicians in Mental Recovery had seen the war. They didn't know how the "hopelessly outgunned" Laneeri had fought back with surprise, silence, and savagery. The men here needed me. After everything I had been forced to do in Laneer, I could never abandon them.

Robin sighed. "Okay. I'll let it go for today. But you need to go home."

"I should write my reports—"

"They can wait, Miles. Go home. Sleep in your own bed, and let's have fun at the fundraiser tomorrow."

"What would I do without you?" I would find out, wouldn't I? She would be gone right after Frostnight.

"You'll manage." Robin handed me my hat, determined to see the back of me.

I was nearly home when I smelled fire. The sight of it soon followed: A narrow wooden house burned in the middle of the block, its gables ablaze. A soot-streaked woman stared numbly at the furniture her family had dragged out of the house, piled on the street as onlookers brought blankets, water, and prayers.

I was off my bicycle in a moment. "I'm a doctor," I called. "Is everyone all right?"

A big man in a leather welder's coat brought me a little girl, pale and crying. "She won't stop."

"Are you her father?"

"Neighbor. Father's on shift at the presses. Everyone got out, but the closest fire wagon's on Trout Street."

The heat of the flames made my face feel tight, while the night breeze blew cold on the back of my neck. Clouds crowded the sky, joined by black smoke rising from the burning house. "Are all the neighbors out?"

He waved at the collection of people in the street who carried furniture, toolboxes, uniforms, and food out of their homes. The wind was on our side at the moment, but the tall, narrow houses on the nineteenth block of East Raven Street jostled each other's shoulders. A gust could set the next roof burning, and the next, and one fire wagon against a block ablaze would be pissing on a campfire.

The cold breeze on my neck crawled, and a high whine sounded in my ears, the way aether felt, only moving closer. The crowd parted for the long nose of a sleek, fabulously expensive black automobile.

I shrank back, holding the crying girl in my arms. She'd inhaled a little smoke, but being out in the fresh air would cure her. I shielded my face behind her as the heavy doors of the car opened and a man emerged.

He was dressed for an opera premiere. He rounded the nose of the car and opened the passenger side, bowing to the woman who exited the vehicle in a cloud of lavender cigarette smoke. A sparkling black gown draped over her elegant pale limbs, and a snow fox stole embraced her shoulders. I knew her family by the patrician sweep of her long nose and the icy paleness of her hair. She was a Carrigan, a Storm-Singer, and if she looked my way it was all over.

My heart battered against my breastbone. She didn't look at me or any of the crowd in the street, choosing to focus on the bank of cloud above the fire, amber light glowing on her skin. The man waited two steps behind her. She stood with her head thrown back, her fur looped around her shoulders, and did magic right under the noses of the people standing in the street.

She gave no outward sign of her effort, but her Secondary's knees sagged as she took as much of his strength as she pleased. I shuddered. That would have been me, if I hadn't escaped. Nothing but a Storm-Singer's minion, my own gifts dismissed as useless.

I turned my face away when the Storm-Singer and her lackey returned to the car. They drove out of sight as clouds billowed overhead, huge and dark with water. Droplets landed on the upturned cheeks of the onlookers. The little girl in my arms stopped sobbing as a raindrop splattered on her forehead, and she scrambled out of my arms crying, "Rain! Rain!"

Soon the nightgowns of the evacuated neighbors stuck translucently to their skin. They praised the rain as a miracle, hugging each other in relief. It was a miracle, for them. They had no idea that the wealthy woman in shiny beads and fur had saved their homes with magic; how could they? Magic was rare, a dangerous curse. It brought no one good fortune. I mounted my bicycle, heading east as fast as my legs would take me.

I had to be small, as unremarkable as a mouse. If Mr. Hunter could teach me to shield my power, I could stop riding along back streets from home to work. I'd have to stick to the East End, but I could enjoy a restaurant, attend the cinema, socialize outside of the hospital without worry. And if Nick held the key to the nightmares and urges that troubled my patients, I couldn't turn that aside.

When I crossed the intersection of East 32nd and Magpie Road, the pavement was utterly dry. My near discovery and the overflowing feeling of Nick's power made me sick. I'd only escaped because I was beneath their notice. I only survived because I was supposed to be dead.

I tightened my grip on the handlebars and pedaled harder.

THREE

A Humble Mouse

I scared sparrows off the high iron fence around the Beauregard Veterans' Hospital gardens at half past six in the morning. I fumbled the bicycle lock with my gloves still on, but my fingers still tingled with Nick's power and the need to use it.

The heels of my best shoes echoed through the lobby. The seats collected around the silent wireless set sat vacant. I said good morning to a pair of surgeons in scarlet officer's tunics. Their medals swayed as they gave my gray flannel suit disapproving stares. Disapproval, not horror or revulsion. My secrets would have been all over the hospital if anyone knew. Breathing came easier.

Half the aether lights were still off at the nursing station for the Mental Recovery Unit. Smiles greeted me, but the unit nurses kept working, undisturbed by my presence.

No one knew, then.

I shivered and retrieved my white doctor's coat from a hook, wishing I had a cardigan to wear underneath. One of the nurses laid newspapers at the best-lit desk in the nursing station for me while the coffee burper finished brewing.

"Thank you, Kate."

Kate nodded. "Will you change into your uniform later, Doctor?"

"I didn't bring it." Would she understand? "It doesn't feel right."

She studied me. "You were at Kalloo."

I'd spent my whole tour there. "Mobile Hospital 361," I confirmed. "Beauregard Battalion."

The doubt in the set of her mouth eased. "I had three brothers in Princess Anna's."

Had. "Did any of them come home?"

"Albert's coming home right now."

"I'm glad."

Her smile faltered.

I offered my handkerchief, but she had one. All her brothers gone to die in Sir Percy's War. Lost siblings left a gap that hurt to touch, and I couldn't help remembering my own as I patted Kate Small's hand. She collected herself and moved to gather the night logs, leaving me with the pair of papers that represented the two sides of Kingston.

The *Herald*'s front page bore a photograph of Dame Grace Hensley cutting the ribbon for Kingston's newest aether-powered battery exchange depot. *A Hensley Triumph,* the headline read, followed by *300 New Jobs in Time for Soldiers' Homecoming.*

I ran my fingers over Dame Grace's face and shoved the *Herald* aside.

The *Star* had stopped the presses in favor of printing a screamer, the paper's stark, huge headline only a single word: *Horror!*

Some bold photographer had risked arrest for the photo sprawled across the front page, and they had to have cast-iron nerves to have stepped into that abattoir. I knew what those black streaks on the wallpaper had to be; the forms under the white covering sheets were too small, too still.

I read the story of Cpl. James Badger, who had taken up a kitchen knife to stab his wife and children before turning the blade on himself. Neighbors had reported he became silent and withdrawn after his return from the war. A poisoning had nothing on this. Nick's story would fill a space between competing ads for aether-powered wireless receivers and telephone service.

"How awful." Kate set the logbooks down and read over my shoulder. "Do you think—?"

I caught her eye, and neither of us dared say it. I pushed the *Star* off my station's blotter. "Do you want the paper?"

She folded it closed. "The patients shouldn't see this."

"You could try holding it back." The men would hear the story on the wireless. They'd tell each other, and stories grew in the telling.

The burper stopped gurgling. I pushed my chair back, but she said, "You take it black?"

"I do, thank you."

A copy of yesterday's memo lay on the counter, reminding me that I had to discharge a third of my patients. In all the excitement of yesterday, I'd given it little thought.

"Has anyone seen Dr. Matheson?"

"Not this early. The memo?" Kate gave me a steaming cup to cradle in my hands.

"Of course."

"No one wants to send so many home, Doctor."

Not without a cure, or even confirmation of what I hardly dared think: that the veterans in my hospital unit and Cpl. James Badger had more in common than their combat service. If I sent a man home to bloody results, I'd never forgive myself. I had to find Nick Elliot's secrets. I hoped they would tell me what to do. "I know. But they're not ready."

Kate patted my shoulder and left me to read last evening's paperwork. The duty logs were a chronicle of frustration: Patients wouldn't sleep. Patients wouldn't take their tonics. Patients were resistant.

Dollars to buttons Dr. Crosby had had the night shift. A glance over my shoulder confirmed it—he sat inside the call office with his lips crushed between his teeth, shedding miles of ink from his glass-barreled pen. I went back to the logs and learned who lay sleepless in the dark, who had nightmares, who shuffled through dim corridors unable to let the night go by without someone to stand watch.

The morning murmur between the nurses on shift change stilled. I ducked.

You're perfectly safe, Miles. Don't be a fool.

I tugged at my shoelaces before I raised my head, following the path of craned necks and turned heads to the unlit north corridor.

Young Gerald was out of bed. He swept his crutches ahead of him, and they landed with a muffled thump, rubber feet against wooden floor. He swung between the crutches' legs, the whole lurch of his body landing on one bare foot. The *creak-thump!* of his crutches put a shiver down my spine.

I halted a nurse who moved to chivvy him back to bed. "It's still the blue hour, Young Gerald."

"Morning, Doc. You're not wearing your uniform." Plowlines of worry lined his forehead. "Is something wrong? Aren't you going to the lunch with the others?"

"I am." I crossed my arms in a posture of sternness, but winked at him to soothe his worry. "What's got you up and bothered?"

"Old Gerald, Doc." His face was pinched up, his dark hair pillow-rumpled. "He's got the morbs."

"He talked?"

"To me. He wouldn't talk to Dr. Crosby last night." Gerald's crutch creaked under his shifting weight as he avoided Dr. Crosby's eye. Another shiver dug tack-tipped fingers into my back.

"Well, let's see if he'll talk to me."

We kicked up the dust heading back to Ward 12, a high-ceilinged room with north-facing windows showing a coal-dust sky. No gas lamps shone here to disturb patients with a fragile hold on sleep. Seven men lay on their beds.

In the fourth bed from the door, Old Gerald lay on his back and stared at the ceiling. Weariness lined his face, but he dug his fingernails into his palms. His lips moved in soundless speech, the shapes of his words a short phrase muttered again and again.

Young Gerald thumped over and settled in his own bed, covering his leg with gray woolen blankets. "The doctor's here."

Old Gerald turned his head, catching the younger with a look. "You told."

"Had to," Young Gerald said. "You'd do it too if it were me."

"You're young," Old Gerald said, as if the distance between their ages were more than ten years.

"You've got a family," Young Gerald said. "I don't even have a sweetheart. What about them?"

Enough. I leaned between them and poured them each water to drink. Old Gerald went quiet. Young Gerald's lips pinched together, frustrated at the interruption.

I offered Old Gerald a glass. He eyed it, but took a wary sip.

"I know you're feeling under the weather today. We don't have to talk about that." I didn't want to. If Old Gerald talked to me of setting off to the Solace by his own hand, I'd have to section him. I hated the rule that stripped patients of their right to despair. I'd been there and knew all too well what it felt like.

So I pushed the conversation onto safer paths. Dr. Crosby had already complained about this, but I asked. "Did you sleep, Old Gerald?"

"Can't," he said. "*He* dreams when I take the tonic."

Ah. Pieces of the picture came clearer. "What does *He* dream of?"

"Killing," Old Gerald said. "And the fierce terrible joy *He* takes in it. Kills everyone on the ward. Young Gerald, Sniffy, Nurse Robin—horrible, the things *He* smiles at. I can't sleep, Doc." Old Gerald clutched at the blankets. "You don't know what *He*'ll do. If I sleep—"

I snatched back my urge to reach out, to comfort him. Full of Nick's power as I was, it would be too easy to use it. His brown eyes were wide, and his gaze darted all around the room. He breathed in tight gasps through his mouth. If I took his pulse, his heart would be racing. Had he been in this panic all night?

Gerald Grimes wasn't even my worst case. How could I thrust sixteen of these men into the street with nothing and no one outside the hospital to help them? Blast this war, and a curse on those who thought battle fatigue was a myth and an excuse. I shoved my anger aside. If Gerald thought I was angry at him, that would just make it worse.

"I can give you a tonic for sleep, if you want it." Stupid question. But I had to ask.

"No."

"Please try a tonic, Old Gerald," Young Gerald said. "I'll sit up. I'll watch."

"Can't. *He*'ll—" Old Gerald's shoulders slumped. "I can't."

I wasn't surprised by his confession. Many of the men here shared Old Gerald's delusion. Right now he needed to feel safe enough to sleep. Not a miracle. No one would even notice. My fingertips tingled with Nick's power, impatient, barely contained.

No one needed to know what I'd actually done.

"I have an idea. You can go to sleep, if I put *Him* to sleep."

"Can you do that?"

"Let's see, shall we?"

I fumbled around in my pockets and unhooked my fob watch. A few hours of sleep would go unnoticed. It would sink into the routine of the morning. I took his wrist. His heartbeat fluttered, exhausted but still running for its life. Crescent-shaped welts reddened the palm of his hand. My vision slid out of ordinary focus and locked on the glowing paths of life inside Old Gerald's body: the rush of air as he breathed, the pulse of blood as his heart beat, and the red-brown muck concentrated in Old Gerald's head.

I raised the watch. "Keep your eyes on the watch. Follow it, and listen to my voice."

I'd never seen anything like it until I'd come here. Some of my patients had it whirling in their head, like a mass of tiny insects raging over the humped wrinkles of their brains. This could be my patients' madness. It could be the source of the worst patients' nightmares and horrific temptations. I'd been too afraid to touch it. But Gerald was getting worse, and I had to send men home.

It's only one patient. I touched the writhing edge of the mass with my overflowing power.

"Imagine a box," I said. "A nice, strong box, and *He's* inside it. The box is sealed, and *He* can't get out."

Old Gerald breathed slow and deep. I took the mass of red-brown energy and contained it.

"Now picture the box getting smaller. Smaller and smaller. *He's* still trapped inside, but the box shrinks smaller, so *He* shrinks smaller. Tinier. Less important."

I forced it to fold up small. It lurked underneath the twin lobes of his brain, tiny, but refusing to disappear.

"You've done it," Old Gerald said. "That's put *Him* away."

It had bled off the feeling of being too full with power. I breathed more freely. "Sleep, will you? Even a nap. I'll send a nurse to dose you if you need it."

Other patients were awake, waiting their turn to speak to me. I would miss the shift meeting if I stayed. If I walked out now, soft lines of trust between me and my patients would break, lines that would take more work to knit up.

The choice was no choice at all.

I sat down next to Bill Pike, who'd been Prince Richard's First Cavalry of my own Beauregard Battalion. He had the same kind of nightmares as Old Gerald, of killing and murder and sick, dark glee. I thought of Cpl. Badger in the paper this morning as Bill grabbed the sleeve of my white coat and levered himself upright.

"Help me, Doctor. *He* wants to kill you."

Eleven o'clock saw me trying to write up all my notes. My last entries had little more than a line or two, smudged with my haste. The Kingston Benevolent Society was hosting this luncheon, and Mr. Hunter's words lingered in my mind. I shone to anyone with the power to see.

How important was this benefit? It was important to us, but was the cause worthy enough for the attention of any of the Royal Knights? An awful vision of a Stanley or a Pelfrey's eyes widening as they recognized a dead man from across a crowded room made me nauseous. I imagined running from the hotel, being caught, being taken back home to give up my power to a Storm-Singer.

That shut it completely. I couldn't chance it. I had to get

caught up in something and miss the coach. Paperwork. Reports. Nick Elliot.

Perfect. I hadn't done the urgent care assessment.

I headed for the Urgent Care ward and collected blank forms, squirreling away a few extra copies to hoard in my office. I had to telephone a request for a death examination file. When it arrived, I would have lost track of time.

"Miles!" Robin called.

Drat. There she was, and she was picture perfect. She wore her long, braided hair in a net that shone with tiny, colorful stones that matched the ones dangling from the beaded shoulders of her sea-blue dress.

"Robin," I said. "You look splendid."

"You need to hurry; the coaches are here."

She led the way up the stairs to my office. The soles of her shoes tapped against the rubber stair treads, scuffed on the tiled landings, each noise grating on my ears.

"I'll meet you there. I just—"

"Miles Singer, I know you," she said. "You have forms in your hands. You'll think, *I just need to note this down so I don't forget.* Then the next thing you know all the coaches will be gone and you'll have missed the whole luncheon."

Double drat. "I wouldn't."

Robin dismissed my protest with a wave. "You've never been invited to a benefit, Miles. This is important. Don't sabotage your career."

She stood in the doorway, waited for me to put on my coat, and escorted me out into the street where the coaches waited. Robin picked a coach and set her satin-gloved hand in mine when I helped her inside.

Doomed. I nodded to the doctor across from me, one of the fellows not garbed in a scarlet officer's tunic. "Is this lunch a fuss and production? I've never been to one."

"Don't worry," he said. "Lunches aren't as important as dinners. Wait until someone asks you what your department needs before talking about it. What's your specialty?"

"Psychiatry."

He chuckled. "Enjoy your lunch and relax." He looked out the side window, ending the conversation. His dismissal comforted me. I was on the bottom rung. I could stay out of sight, unnoticed, unknown.

We traveled to the Edenhill hotel, a finger of steel and glass challenging the silver-clouded sky. Our parade of twenty-four doctors and nurses in sack suits, day gowns, and dress uniforms multiplied in the smoked glass mirrors on the walls, and we poured into the Starlight ballroom.

Two dozen round tables for eight gathered on one side; a sitting area for the movers and shakers lounged on the other. The mass of us mingled under hundreds of glass globes suspended from the ceiling. Each was its own gentle aether light, bathing the crowd in a glow meant to mimic a nighttime sky visited by a wink of fireflies. Drafts made the globes sway and click, nearly unheard in the buzz of conversation and the high-pitched whine of aether.

Some of the champagne the waiters had served to the aristos managed to trickle over to us groundlings. Robin caught two glasses of the stuff, and we stood still for the first fizzy sip. It was sweet, with green grass and meadow flowers on the nose—Miss Vanier's Deer Valley? Perhaps it was. I stole a bit of the ballroom's wall, keeping the crowd between me and the wealthy, seated hosts.

"You can't hold the wall up, silly. Look. There's a wealthy dowager now."

I spotted the butterfly pin on the lapel of her smart day gown. "She's still mourning."

"Gray is just the fashion now—oh, wait. Sharp eye, Miles."

Dr. Matheson stepped out of the crowd. She wore an hourglass of a day gown the color of a midnight sky. It suited her golden skin and dark hair, but the set of her face was impatient.

I tried my best to smile. "Dr. Matheson. You look lovely."

She eyed my flannel suit. "You're not wearing your uniform."

"I need it ready for the Homecoming," I said. "Imagine if I spilled crab chowder on it." As if the Edenhill would stoop to serving crab chowder to members of the Benevolent Society! I had to fight a smile at the idea. "I need to talk to you. About the memo."

"I can't exempt your patients from the discharge order. You're straight out of luck."

"Mathy."

"No."

"They're not well enough."

"No. Sixteen beds won't even be enough for the men coming home. Now chin up." She tweaked the lay of my necktie. "You've never come to a benefit."

"I can duck out and go back to the hospital, if you like."

Robin kicked me in the ankle.

Mathy worried at my pocket square. "Relax. Imagine they're your patients. You're a wonder with your patients. You can talk to them. Don't worry."

Maybe this was how your mother treated you, even when you were a grown man. Maybe she would have fixed my tie and asked if I were all right.

I smiled around the ache. "Thanks, Mathy. You better get in there and start the speeches—"

"Actually, I was looking for you," she said. "Come with me. I've been asked to make an introduction."

Doomed. "Me? Who would want—I mean, who are we meeting?" Another doctor. Another psychiatrist. No one important. Please. I tucked Robin's hand into the crook of my arm. She squeaked in protest, but walked with us through the crowd.

Dr. Matheson dragged me to the velvet rope separating us from the wealthiest and most important of the attendees, the hosts. My hope thumped to the parquet floor. I kept pace with her, but every step made the band around my chest tighten a notch, and then another.

She shot us straight toward a clutch of posh young people dressed in the highest of daytime fashion. They wore sack suits and sinuous silk gowns in the non-colors of the cinema, all fog and smoke and deep coal shadows, their hair combed back in shiny, careful ripples. Their leader lounged in the center of a lily-back settee, listening to the man perched on the arm of her seat. She threw her head back and laughed, echoed by her entourage.

Dr. Matheson lurched to a stop, anchored by the bolt that had passed through me and fixed me to the floor. Robin halted by my side, standing as tall as she could. My throat squeezed shut as the leader stared at me, her mouth open, her posture as still as mine.

We both saw a ghost standing before us.

"Chris," my sister said.

"Grace," I replied. "It's Miles, now."

Doomed.

For a few whispered moments, the Starlight Room held its breath.

"Miles." All at once she stood eye to eye with me. When had she grown so tall? I thought I'd never see her outside of newspaper photographs again, but here she was, watching me with whiskey-brown eyes so like our mother's. Like mine.

"I thought you were dead."

Traces of the girl I knew lived inside the woman—her jaw

more pointed, the soft cheeks melted away, the dimple in her chin identical to mine. Grace, who had been painting butterflies the morning I climbed down the elm tree next to my bedroom window and left her life forever.

Or more accurately, until now.

My heart raced. I couldn't run, couldn't cause a scene. All these eyes and respectability jailed me, forced me to smile as if this were wonderful.

"That's because I didn't write."

"You bastard." She seized me in a tight hug.

My sister. I raised my arms and hugged her back. She crushed me close, and she muffled a sob next to my ear. It wouldn't do to rock her as I had when she'd come to her brother in tears. It wouldn't do to wrest myself free and run, run until my legs gave out.

My sister had found me, and my freedom was at an end.

FOUR

Promises

M y name sat before the place setting at Grace's left hand. Fast work. Robin had a table in the center, not bad for getting courses at the proper temperatures. I held out the chair on my left for the woman with the butterfly pin. I leaned to my right and kept my voice low. "Did everyone else get bumped down like dominoes, or is there a board chairman sitting in my place next to the kitchen?"

Grace clapped me on the shoulder and laughed. "I'm sorry I separated you from your friend, but I couldn't resist having you with me. Will she be cross?"

Robin was already enchanting the gentleman on her left with conversation. "If I bring back a good donation to the hospital, she'll consider it a boon."

"Oh. Well, let me take care of that."

Grace opened a purse covered in silver beads and produced a checkbook. She blew on the drying ink and tucked a check for five thousand marks into my breast pocket. "I think she'll forgive you now."

"Grace, you're a brick."

She rolled her eyes at my worker's slang, but she still smiled.

"We're all dreadfully curious, please forgive us," the woman at my left hand said. "We couldn't help but notice your reunion with Miss Hensley."

My reunion. I held up a quirk of my lips, showed her the right face. "It was quite a surprise," I said. "I hadn't seen her in years."

"Miles and I grew up together," Grace said, and sniffled. I tried not to melt in relief as she told incomplete truths that supported mine. "We were inseparable as children, but he joined the army to become a doctor."

True, as far as it went. She was keeping my secret. Why?

"This is wonderful." The widow picked up her glass. "Here's to the two of you finding each other again."

We lofted glasses and drank. My wine tasted bitter.

Small courses came one after another, calling for salad forks, a fish knife, red and white wineglasses. I fell into the smiling countenance I'd learned as a young man, but Grace was smooth as a still pond. My tempestuous sister had grown into a woman who steered a conversation where it pleased her, and it pleased her to bless Beauregard Veterans' with her approval and our family's money. Would it please her to leave me where I was, doing what good I could for the world?

It wouldn't. She would take me back into the clutches of family. She wouldn't ever let me go.

A witch who knew my name had died in my arms last night, and today I dined next to my sister for the first time in thirteen years. I didn't like coincidences. Nick had known my true identity, had died while trying to tell me secrets about the war—

I fought to keep from choking on roasted lamb. If there were secrets about the war, the Invisibles knew them. That included my sister. She would lead the Queen's secret mages one day.

"Are you all right, Miles?"

I reached for my water glass, forestalling an answer. My

sister was an Invisible, but not yet one of the Queen's Ministers. Besides, the image of Grace feeding someone poison was ridiculous. A bolt of lightning, perhaps. Or a sword to the heart. I nearly smiled at the thought.

"I'm fine."

Grace sniffled. "Skip dessert, will you? I want a private word before you go."

Every eye at the table was on me. "Oh, Grace. You know how much I enjoy dessert. And I should get back to my patients." And Nick Elliot, waiting for me in the hospital morgue.

"Please, Miles?"

Manners wouldn't permit me to refuse, not in such polite company. We bowed to our table before she led me to the lift, where a couple in silk and cashmere waited. She pressed a button, and our gilded chamber rose the eighteen floors to the top, all of us staring at the pointer clicking to each floor number.

The well-dressed women went right; Grace turned left to an ebony-paneled door. She led the way through a luxurious, modern suite colored black and silver, smoke and glass. My steps sank into the carpet, and the view from plate-glass windows went for leagues, all the way to the ocean.

Grace reached for my shoulder. "I thought I'd never see you again—"

I moved away from her hands. "Don't touch me."

Grace froze, staring as if I'd slapped her. "Do you honestly think I would—"

"I can't risk it." I had to get out of here before she wound a linking spell around me and locked it down. After that, she'd own my power as if it were hers, to use as she wanted. She would be able to find me no matter where I hid.

I would belong to her.

She reached for me again. "You have to consent to binding."

"I know that's not true, Grace."

"I just want to talk. I haven't seen you in so long. . . ."

I had thought I'd never see her again. "Stay back."

"Whatever you say." She backed up. "I'm so glad to see you. Let's not talk about binding. When did you get back? Were you hurt?"

Five feet separated us, and when I didn't reply she retreated again. I found my tongue. "Months ago. I . . . they captured me."

"I know," she said. "I wanted a funeral. Father wouldn't allow it. He said it was too much like giving up."

"Father never liked to bow to anything that interfered with what he wanted."

Grace's clamped lips pulled back. "Chris—"

"Miles." I couldn't breathe properly. "Who did you bind? Anyone I know?"

"No one," Grace said. "I never bound anyone."

I was at the door in a heartbeat, fumbling with the locks.

"Miles! Please don't go."

I threw open the door and looked for the stairwell.

"Miles! My blood on it!"

I looked back. "Swear it."

She had a blade out of her pocket in a heartbeat. I shut the door but kept my hand on the lever. She drew the white-handled blade across her skin. "I bind my power to this promise: I will not bind your power to mine without your consent."

Blood welled up in her palm, and she drew a stylized G that carried the suggestion of a bolt of lightning. "By my oath, my mark, and my blood, this is true."

She used the strictest of vows. A tripled oath was impossible to break. It was old magic, older than Link Circles, older than storm-singing, and she'd done it without hesitation.

She held her hand out. The blood seeped back into her skin, the spell a part of her forever.

I could trust her.

I took her hand and traced my finger over it. A thin scar crossed her palm, a new line of fortune to join the rest.

"You have a cold."

"You have a new witchmark." She flexed her fingers. "Did you get it in the war?"

"A what?"

"A witchmark. You've always had the pink one, but the new one's green. Just there, and there." Her fingers hovered over my head: one near my temple, the other at the back of my head. "You can't see auras without touching someone, still."

I shrugged. "Plenty of things I can't do."

Grace covered her mouth, chagrined at her rudeness. "You survived the war."

Not that I deserved to. "I did."

"We knew you'd gone there. Father found out you were at medical school."

"Why didn't he haul me back?"

"He thought you'd come home. We kept your disappearance a secret for months," Grace said. "Then you shipped out. He was devastated. When the telegram came to tell us you were missing . . ."

"He what? He cared?" I barked out a laugh that had no mirth in it. "He probably started parading potential Secondaries in front of you before the message hit the desk. How did you say no to him for this long?"

Her mouth thinned. "When you went missing, he went wild. He made the army go after you."

"*Father* pushed General Johnston into raiding Camp Paradise?"

"Awful name." Grace's face pinched as if she smelled something bad.

"We had to call it something," I said. "Bitter irony seemed best."

Grace hunched her shoulders and watched the sky. I marveled at her face—she was older, a woman now. And yet she was just the same, as if she had been there all along. "Was it— was it bad?"

A cold, round pressure nudged at the back of my skull. A ghost. A memory I brushed away with my fingers. "You wouldn't happen to have anything to drink around here, would you?"

"Of course."

I took a velvet-covered seat at one end of a glass-and-wrought-iron coffee table. Grace poured me a deep glass of whiskey, diluted with a dropper of water. I drank more in my first sip than was strictly polite and set the empty glass on the table between us.

Grace took the seat to my left, setting the cut-crystal bottle at the corner. I shifted to the right and turned my face to the highest view in the city.

Ships sailed out of the mouth of the Blue River in the window to my left. The Ayers Inlet framed the other side of the westward-pointing finger housing the oldest, wealthiest parts of Kingston, from the bone-colored banks and trading houses to the pale green domes that roofed the palace. Gold and scarlet-leafed trees lined all the streets I could see. It was greater than when I left it, the buildings taller and more prosperous. I should have left it forever. I shouldn't have loved Kingston so much.

People moved along the grid lines of the roads, the pulsing life of Kingston, so small and busy-seeming below us. Some of them had sisters. What would they tell me to say to mine?

I missed you. We can't meet again. It wasn't your fault. "I thought I'd never see you again."

"Why did you leave?"

"I wanted to heal people." I poured us both a finger's-breadth of whiskey.

"I know. I wouldn't have stopped you."

"I wanted to be free."

"I would let you have your freedom—"

"Then why bind me at all?" I asked.

"Because I need you," she said. "None of the other Second-aries want liberty the way you do. They bend their necks and dismiss their own talents as worthless tricks. None of them is someone the other Secondaries can look up to."

"I want freedom, and so you want to chain me, to teach the others they should be like me."

"I need you because Storm-Singers and Secondaries should bind as partners. Because Secondaries aren't failures. That's a lie. It's only because we need the power."

"You'll always need more power, Grace." I didn't want this argument. "However nobly you intend to use it, you'll always need more. I can't believe you went this long without binding anyone."

"No one felt right. No one felt like you, or had your power, or knew what I was going to do before I knew it myself. You and I, we're hand in glove—"

"And I'm the glove." But together, we could do anything. We'd stopped a deluge of rain on our land to save the beauty of spring flowers when I was only eight. I could ken the winds and know the patterns of air and water when we linked, but alone I couldn't even whistle up a breeze. Together, we were invinci-ble. Without her, I was a disappointment with nothing but second-rate tricks. No. I saved lives. I had purpose. I was worth more than a mere power reserve, and I wouldn't become less, even for Grace.

"We could make this work," Grace said. "I don't have to draw on you in Circle. I already Call without you."

"So my slavery would be just for appearances?"

Grace pressed her lips together. "I already promised, Miles. Don't insult me."

"All right. Tell me what you've been doing."

"I'm getting married." Grace's smile was soft and warm, the wonder of it still fresh. "My fiancé designed this building."

"Edwin did this? He never."

Grace's face fell. "Edwin was years ago, Miles. I'm engaged to Raymond Blake."

"Of the Grand Lake Blakes?" Nothing less than the most powerful of the Hundred Families for the scion of the Hensley legacy. I had another sip of whiskey and left some of it in the glass. "But you were devoted to Edwin."

"Miles, I was fourteen."

I cocked my head and took aim. "Father didn't want you marrying a Secondary."

A muscle in Grace's jaw jumped. "Ray's wonderful. He plays the harp. He designed this hotel. He's handsome, talented—"

"And Talented? He's a Storm-Singer."

Grace shifted in her seat. "He's in the Circle with me, yes."

"Caller or Link?"

"He's the Caller for his Station in the Second Ring."

That made him a skilled weather manipulator, far better than Links who had the power, but not the finesse. His position in the Second Ring could be talent. It likely was. But his name certainly had something to do with it.

"A union between the Hensleys and the Blakes would give you a stranglehold on the Invisibles."

Grace looked away. "Say a firm grip."

The last swallow of whiskey shivered in my glass. "How bad is it?"

"It's been difficult, since you left."

My rebellion had consequences. I reckoned the costs—the inconvenience, the loss of power, the embarrassment to the family—and I could see which way the wind had blown. "Father's power eroded. You never bound a Secondary. But if you had your prodigal brother at your side—"

Grace sighed. "Yes."

"And you vowed on your blood not to bind me?" I sat back in my chair, wondering. "Why?"

"None of that matters as much as you," Grace said. "You're alive. I can have my brother back."

"Christopher Miles Hensley died in the war."

"No, he didn't." Grace raked her fingers through carefully dressed waves, and mahogany hair flopped into her eyes. "I missed you every day you were gone."

"I'm sorry, Grace."

"Don't be," she said. "You're here now."

But I wasn't going back. Cover it in satin and silver, but a cage is still a cage. I rose, buttoning my jacket, and crossed the room to where she sat. "Do you have any appointments this afternoon?"

"No."

"Then let me heal you." I traced over her face with my fingers. She'd been battling congestion with saline, but the virus was still there, irritating her nose and throat. I knew the shape and attitude of cold germs, and I soon had a picture of this particular virus. She sat still and let me cure her, though she'd burn with fever for half an hour and sleep exhausted for the rest of the afternoon. But she'd be up and hungry in time for supper, cured.

When I took my hand away, she caught it. "Thank you, Miles. I hate colds. I never learned to endure them. What would you like from the kitchens? There's a menu by the telephone—"

"I have to go."

This was the price I paid for freedom and medicine: seven years' service to Her Majesty, and my only sister. I couldn't look at her face, couldn't see what I'd put there. A tearing ache in my throat kept me silent as I walked away.

She waited until my hand touched the door. "Miles."

I barely missed resting my head on the paneled black surface. "What?"

"I'm not giving up. But I'll keep you a secret from Father."

Hope trickled over the ache. Enough to swallow and say, "Good."

I pushed down on the scrolled iron lever.

After making sure my handkerchief wasn't waving a damp crumpled corner out of my jacket pocket, I assumed a pleasant expression and walked out of the lift. Guests still lingered in the lobby, but I ignored their attempts to speak with me. I hurried out to the apple-scented air of the street.

If I craned my neck to peer at the topmost windows of the Edenhill, would I see my sister watching me leave her again? I kept my focus on the street around me, walking with the fashionable crowds of the Wakefield business district. Money movers and deal makers strode with purpose on their way back from luncheon meetings, uninterested in the bounty of fruit overhead.

I wove around a trio of teenage girls filling pails with apples to take home. The girl who had climbed into the branches yelped a warning. I caught a gold-and-scarlet fruit out of the air.

"Sorry, Mister."

"No trouble." I offered it to a girl in a knitted cap and a striped sweater.

She shook her head. "You caught it. It's yours."

I took my prize away and jogged across the street, dodging drafts of bicyclists. The apple was round and firm, a little cool from hanging in the autumn air. Grace had loved apples. She'd eat them until she had a stomachache, especially at the beginning of Leafshed when they weren't quite ready yet. She'd first gotten drunk on hard cider she'd stolen from the servants' larder, and even the unhappy result didn't break her steadfast devotion to her favorite food. I swallowed a lump in my throat and dropped the apple in a litter bin.

I couldn't have my sister back. Even if I learned to mask my magical aura, we couldn't be seen together in society. She couldn't visit me, and I could never go home again. With care, we could meet in secret.

If I was careful, I could draw stories out of Grace about what her friends and associates were doing, collecting information on those who might be connected to Nick's murder. No Minister would be cast down for less than treason. If they learned I was hunting them, I could be next to Nick Elliot in the morgue.

Grace would talk, if I asked her about it. Grace had a free tongue around people she trusted. As children, she had trusted me most of all. I could ask her nearly anything. Was she the same woman? I had to wonder.

A draft of cyclists in ready-made tweed suits waited for the long parade of pedestrians to cross. I hurried my steps to catch up with the tail end of the pack, startling a woman in a fox-trimmed coat. She looked over her shoulder at me, and my apology for disturbing her dried in my mouth.

Clara Sibley met my eye, and she stared, round-eyed and shocked, at the boy who had competed against her for top marks in Life Science. There was no way to deny it, no way to pretend she was mistaken.

Coming into the business district with all its respected banks and firms had been a risk. Bound Secondaries often took care of their Storm-Singer's mundane affairs, managing the legwork required to grow their finances. Blast! I would have been safe inside a hired carriage, but now I was sunk. She'd tell her

Storm-Singer she saw me, and the rumors would fly straight for my father's ears.

I shouldn't have stayed in Kingston. I was lucky to have lasted this long.

"Forgive me." Clara's expression was smoothed into polite reserve, suitable for addressing a stranger. "You look very like someone I went to school with, but I see you are not him."

It was a lie, and I could have kissed her for it.

"No harm done," I said. "Perhaps he'll be amused to hear he has a double."

"I wish he could be amused. He died in the war. But I remember him as a friend."

"I'm sorry for your loss and grateful for his sacrifice." Oh Clara. You're a brick. "He was lucky to have such a friend."

"Thank you," she said. "I must go."

She gave me one last look as we parted ways, and I hurried toward the hospital, head down.

FIVE

A Miracle

Beauregard Veterans' was a building in half-mourning, fashioned from gray stones and black-framed windows, the kind with many panes pieced together to make a larger whole. It was the old site of Wakefield Cross before they moved into a larger, grander building farther uptown and kindly donated the land to a then-sleepy and ceremonial army. It was never built to shelter so many battered souls, but the calm gravity of its proportions shouldered the burden with grace.

The black iron fence bordering the grounds was some of the finest wrought work in Kingston, cluttered with employee bicycles locked around its posts. A shiny black carriage stood by the walk. The coachman crooned to four satin-groomed black horses as they ate the apples from his hands. I returned his nod and walked to the front door among the swirling of fallen leaves, dried and crunching under my shoes.

Warm air rushed through the opened door, patting my cool cheeks. Patients gathered around the wireless in the lobby, those not lucky enough to claim a chair standing behind, all heads leaned toward the amplifier. They smiled to hear of the last ships launched from Mostway Island, crowded with soldiers returning home. The newscast ended. Some gave up their seats to those waiting behind. Strings and horns played upbeat dancing music, and patients nodded in time or patted the tempo on their knees.

One of the men who rose to give up his seat was Old Gerald. I blinked at his presence in the lobby. The wireless was a patient favorite, but the men with that peculiar cloud in their heads avoided it and all the modernized parts of the hospital. But here he was, taller than I expected, of broader shoulder, and the lines around his eyes deepened with a smile. He looked vital, despite the uneven gait of a badly healed leg. He'd found brilliantine somewhere, shaved his cheeks and chin, trimmed and waxed his mustache.

We met with a handshake. "It's good to see you up and about, Old Gerald—you don't mind the name, do you?"

"I'll answer to it." He fell into step beside me.

"You're looking much better," I said.

"It's a miracle, Doc."

I'd done it again, damn me. "I'm glad rest made you feel better."

"You lifted a weight off me. It almost doesn't feel real."

"Do you mean *Him?*"

Gerald nodded. "It wasn't real, though. Was it?"

This was tricky ground, best explored in privacy. "I know it felt real at the time."

"But I was mad," Gerald said. "I went mad, because of what I'd done—"

He shut up tight, checking to see if anyone could hear him. He glanced back at me, the question clear on his face: He was free of his nightmare. But would it return?

Not if I could do anything to stop it. Nick's body waited for me downstairs, and Mr. Hunter probably expected me above. I would find out what Nick knew and what he'd died for, whose secrets he'd been killed to protect. But patients came first, always.

"Let's go out to the garden, Old Gerald. Likely the air will do you good."

We visited a stone bench by a fish pond, and he sat down to tell me what haunted him. He confessed the days and nights of helpless fear and the battles where he learned what a man would do in the midst of war. I knew what a man would do, if it meant living through it.

Then he told me when he'd first started thinking a killer lived inside him. "I was coming home, Doc. I had my ticket on account of falling for a pit trap. Wound got infected, but I pulled through. But then *He* came, and I knew it would never be over."

"And you still feel this way."

I'd struck the target. He sucked in a breath. "What if it comes back?"

"If it comes back, you'll know this time it isn't real."

"If it comes again, you can help me. Right? With mesmerism." He hunched his shoulders against the breeze and watched the silvery shapes of fish nosing up to catch insects skimming on the pond's surface. "If it comes back. Maybe it won't."

"I used the mesmerism to help you sleep. It made you feel better."

"It's more than just sleep. But . . ." He screwed up his courage and asked. "Would I have wound up like the fellow on the news?"

So it had come out. "We don't know why James Badger did what he did. It's a horrible business. Did you hear he'd had no work since he came home?"

"Hard thing, to serve your country and come back to nothing." Old Gerald patted his breast pocket and grimaced. "D'you mind if I smoke, Doc?"

"Even less, if you'll give me one."

He offered a cigarette with some surprise. "You smoke gaspers?"

"The front," I said. "Trying to quit."

"Can't see why. It's relaxing." He lit his cigarette with a cupped hand, snuffing the match with a practiced speed. He held it between his thumb and forefinger to hide the glow of the burning end behind his palm. He'd seen some of the same land I had.

The cigarette was acrid, the smoke barbed as I sucked it into my lungs, but the rush, the calm, swept over me. I'd gone three weeks without one, and I was dizzy with it.

We studied the pond and the speckled silver bodies of fish, endlessly hunting. "I want to go home, Doc. Marie needs me. She got on without me, but it's shameful to not be there for your family. And here I am—"

Golden leaves dripped from a white-barked birch tree. One tatter-edged leaf landed in the pond. Fish nosed it, mistaking it for food.

"I can find work. I'm a gardener."

It was too soon. "You've been up and about for a few hours."

He waved it away, smoke trailing around his fingers. "You know what I heard on the wireless? Our boys are coming home. How many will need my bed? And Young Gerald's?"

No one had told the patients, but they read a shift in the wind, sensed what we tried to hide. "Young Gerald doesn't have any family to—"

"He's got me," Old Gerald said. "Send him with me. We can make room. We can take care of him. He's cheerful. His leg doesn't pain him. He hasn't had a nightmare in a week."

I needed to watch Old Gerald. I needed to monitor the progress of the miasma clouding his brain, to see if it would spread again. I couldn't discharge him. He was my subject.

He was a grown man, and I couldn't keep him here against his will.

"Parade Day," I said. "It's only three more days."

"It's a deal, Doc."

We shook hands on it.

I'd done a miracle, all right. Old Gerald wasn't the silent, closed-off man I'd met two weeks ago. He strode into Ward 12 with a grand wave for everyone and sat next to Young Gerald, intent on sharing his news.

"Dr. Singer."

I turned. "Dr. Crosby."

"Did you enjoy your luncheon? You're back later than the rest of the doctors."

"Personal counseling session," I said. "Mr. Grimes needed to talk to me."

"Ah. Your miracle cure."

The hair on the back of my neck prickled. "Not really," I said. "He responded well to mesmerism this morning. Was there something you needed?"

"I saw a gentleman waiting outside your office. You haven't yet made it that far." He said this last with a nod for my coat and hat, the red scarf around my neck. My palms itched. Dr. Crosby wasn't widely liked—not by his fellows, not by his patients—and I didn't count among his defenders. But if Crosby had set his sights on me, I would have a miserable month until he decided to pick on someone else.

"Thank you. I had better see to him. Good afternoon, Doctor."

I wasn't running away. I was in a hurry to meet Mr. Hunter. I took the stairs two at a time, ignoring the stitch in my side around the sixty-fifth step. Mr. Hunter waited for me on a wooden bench across from my office. He read a book with astonishing speed. His hat sat next to him on the bench, and a lock of hair had slipped out of his queue. He put one finger between the pages, then rose to his feet.

"Dr. Singer." My blackmailer bowed to me, an elegant dip of his head and shoulders. I almost returned the gesture, all the ceremony and manner of the aristocracy waiting just under my skin, but stopped myself and stuck out my hand.

"Mr. Hunter. I've kept you waiting." My heart rushed as he took my hand to shake. "My apologies. I was with a patient."

"Not to worry." He held my hand for a heartbeat longer than custom, and his fingertips slid along my palm as he let go. My skin held the sensation, clung to it.

"Have you been here long?"

"I've been reading this book." He held it up so I could see the title. "I found it sitting on the bench."

I groaned. "That one's popular on the unit." All the gloriously morbid stuff was.

"Have you read it?"

"No."

Mr. Hunter patted the book cover. "It's about a woman who is in love with a man haunted by the ghost of his first love."

"What rot." I unlocked my office door. "Come in."

He let me get my coat off before he shut the door behind him. He slipped the book into its place with the other penny novels before untying his scarf.

"I would have thought it ridiculous if I'd heard it before coming here." I took his hat. He unfastened his coat with nimble fingers, and I hung them on the hook next to mine. "I'd wonder why they didn't go to a witch to take care of the problem."

I winced. "Because it's just a story."

"You and I both know that's not true."

A frightened quiver shot through my chest. "Mr. Hunter, please."

"How did it come to this?" He wiped a hand over his forehead as if he could erase his vexation. "Every single spirit speaker I've visited is a fraud. Every building reputed as haunted is just drafty and old. Every true witch I've seen in a trial has no hope of freedom."

"They don't try you until you fail the examination."

"And they'll arrest someone on the barest suspicion, so long as they're poor. Did you know that?"

"I do," I said. "Which is why I would like you to *please* stop speaking of it."

"But you know it's real." He spoke in a low voice.

I turned to my window. "It doesn't matter. What matters is what the people believe."

"And they believe witches are—"

"Almost wiped out, and those who bloom with the power inevitably go insane," I finished. "It could be worse. A hundred years ago, they were considered evil and had to be killed. But how do you not know this?"

He scowled. "I suppose lifetime imprisonment is an improvement. How did you survive, your family of witches?"

He didn't know who I was. Nick had called me Sir Christopher, and he had just repeated it. Mr. Hunter didn't know anything an Aelander witch would know, and he wasn't a runaway Secondary if he didn't know that witches and mages were different. But what was he?

He spoke into my silence. "You're not the only witch I've seen."

"What? You said—"

"You and Nick were the only witches I've met," he clarified. "But I have seen others. Wealthy and powerful, and therefore dangerous. Why do wealthy witches walk free?"

"I've no desire to wind up in a trial." He asked a dangerous question. I didn't dare answer it. "And neither should you. Please let's stop talking about this."

He cocked his head, his eyebrows hunching together, then shrugged and leaned against my filing cabinet. "I won't tell anyone your secret, Doctor. Will you accept my offer?"

"I will examine Nick Elliot," I said. "I will share everything I discover. I need to know what he knew about the war. If it can help my patients . . ."

Mr. Hunter plucked a book from the shelf I kept full of novels for the patients, flipping pages. "I want to be present while you perform the examination."

"It's a grisly business, Mr. Hunter."

He shrugged. "What's inside a man is much like what's inside a stag. If I faint, you may mock me."

I couldn't help smiling. "If you faint, I promise I will."

"So you'll let me attend?"

"If I didn't let you attend, would you pester me for the report?"

He laughed, and I caught my breath at the sound. I wished I was funny, just to hear him laugh again. "Definitely."

"Then I may as well let you stay for it."

Mr. Hunter followed me down the long flights of stairs to the morgue. I kept our pace swift. Was he here to block the investigation, or did he really want to know the truth? Where had he come from? He was no Aelander, from his ignorance.

I slowed our pace down the last flight of stairs, ready to ask, but he spoke before me.

"What can you tell me about asylums?"

I blinked at the unexpected question. "I suppose they're much alike," I said. "What do you want to know?"

"Why do you send the mad to live so far away from their families? They can't visit easily."

"That's the point, sometimes." I rounded the banister and tried to keep my steps from echoing. "Sometimes solitude from your family is part of the cure."

"Because your family is the illness?"

"I didn't say it." I laid my finger alongside my nose, and he flashed a grin at me.

"Mr. Hunter," I said as we came to the bottom of the stairs. "I can't help but notice you aren't from here. Not from Kingston. Farther away."

"Very far," he agreed. "This is the morgue, isn't it?"

The door was marked so, in black painted letters. His origins were off-limits. What was he hiding?

I found the correct key, and the door swung open to darkness.

"Odd," I said. "There should be an attendant."

I snapped a switch, and the morgue filled with cold white aether light. Long stone examination tables lined up two by two in the green tiled room. I set my medical bag down at the nearest table.

Mr. Hunter followed, hands behind his back. "Which of these drawers holds his body?"

"I'll have to look him up." I found the clipboard on the wall. Nick Elliot's name was the last on the list. He'd been signed in at eight. But there were entries next to the sign-in boxes. The body had been signed out.

Signed out?

"What is it?"

I shook my head. "There's been a mistake. It's probably nothing."

He'd been checked into drawer 12. I moved across the room and pulled it open. "What the deuce."

He followed me over. "Was Nick Elliot supposed to be in there?"

"Yes." The drawer was buffed, and the corners were still wet. This drawer had held a body today.

Maybe he had been moved. I opened each one, looking for Nick Elliot. The smell of bleach wafted from most of the drawers. We'd been cleaned out of cadavers.

"They're all gone," I said. "Every body. What the *deuce*." I unclenched my fists and tried to breathe. The morgue empty, all the bodies gone . . .

Mr. Hunter leaned on an examination table. "This is unusual, I take it?"

I slammed the last drawer and it bounced back, catching me on the elbow. "Yes. I don't know." I squeezed my arm, pressing the outraged hurt away.

"Let's go through it step by step," he said. "What are the most common reasons for a body leaving here?"

"Family, claiming the body for burial. Perhaps the police came for him."

"How would you determine that?"

Would he help me like this, if he were responsible? He was so calm, reasoning the problem out, waiting for the answer. "Paperwork."

I opened the clerk's office and found the outgoing files for Notes of Transit. "Oh no."

The police hadn't come, but Kingston Civic Burial Services had. I found Nick Elliot's name on the bottom of the pile of transit notes.

I handed the file to him and stuffed my clenched fists into my pockets. He pressed his lips together in a thin angry line. "This says—"

"That Nick Elliot's body was sent out for cremation."

SIX

The Tyranny of Paperwork

There was a chance Nick hadn't been cremated yet. I dashed for the phone. "Operator, I need a line to Civic Burial. The crematorium."

I waited through clicks and tones as my call connected to the office. The phone rang six times before a voice answered. "Crematorium."

"This is Dr. Miles Singer from Beauregard Veterans'. I'm calling about a body transported to burial services this afternoon. There's been a mistake."

"What kind of mistake? They were all dead when they got here." He congratulated his fine joke with a wheezy chuckle.

"I meant to do a death examination on one of them. Nick Elliot."

"All the bodies from Beauregard came in hours ago. Your patient's probably ash by now."

The wooden receiver grew slick in my grasp. "Are you sure?"

"I ran the bodies myself. They're all in there. Bad luck."

"Bad luck," I echoed. My insides felt hollow. "Thank you for your time."

Mr. Hunter came to the doorway of the attendant's office. "Too late?"

"Too late." I pointed at the papers in his hands. "I shouldn't let you sort through those. They're confidential."

"You do live a life of secrets." Mr. Hunter went back to his perusal of the day's files. "How did Elliot's body wind up at the crematorium?"

"The hospital runs on paper. Someone writes his drawer on the right form; somebody with no knowledge of Nick gets the form; Nick's body gets transported." I moved to the sink and washed my hands, using the ritual of soap and water to calm down.

"By E.M., whoever that is." He walked out of the office, still holding the transport file. "Or J.R."

"Who's J.R.?"

"I'm not sure, but they left an angry message about not being able to wait around when children needed to be taken home and fed."

"Hold on." I dried my hands and went back to the hanging clipboard, the first signpost on the paper path taking Nick Elliot's body from the morgue to the crematorium. "Six bodies signed out by E.M., here."

He riffled the transit slips. "Six bodies taken by the city, the forms initialed J.R." He read the names to me, and I checked them against the records. Some of them had rested in aether-cooled drawers for longer than two weeks—about how long we kept an unclaimed body before sending it off to civic burial. Most of them would be cremated and interred in the veterans' wall, their names and dates of service to the country etched over their seals.

Nick Elliot wasn't a veteran. But there was a reason why someone would send his body off so quickly. "Is there a 'D' in box nineteen on Nick Elliot's note?"

"There is," he said. "Don't tell me. Diseased?"

"His symptoms looked like cholera, or some other flux," I said. "Some people prefer to err on the side of caution when it comes to diseased bodies."

"Thanks to E.M." Mr. Hunter flipped through pages of the duty log. "The one who left the angry note is J.R." Pages shushed against each other as he read back. "No E.M. in the duty log."

"Blast it."

We searched, but there was no E.M. on the sign-in sheets, or in any of the files on the desk.

"It's as if he—or she—walked in, signed out corpses, and then walked out again," Mr. Hunter said, long fingers sorting through forms.

"Every doctor has access to the morgue. I have an idea." I reached for the telephone and lifted the speaker to my ear.

"Operator."

"Hello, Miles Singer again," I said. "I'm looking through a duty log and I'm trying to read an illegible entry by someone with the initials E.M. Can you tell me of any doctors with those initials?"

"Well, there's Dr. Matheson," the operator said, and sniffed.

"Sniffy! Is that you?" I asked.

"Afternoon, Doc. I got my promotion," he said. "No more mopping for me."

"Good man, Sniffy. Congratulations. Anyone besides Mathy?"

"I could look up nurses. Could it be a nurse?"

"I believe it's a doctor. Anyone else?"

"Who has any business writing in duty logs? None besides her," Sniffy said. "Shall I ring her? She might be in her office."

"I'll find her myself. Thank you, Sniffy."

"Who is Mathy?" he asked after I hung up.

"My boss, Eleanor Matheson."

He winced. "No one else with those initials, I take it?"

"No one. But it couldn't be her."

"What makes you so certain?"

"The form specifically ordered the body be held. She wouldn't make a mistake like that." I pawed through paper, trying to make sense of this disaster.

Mr. Hunter sat on the corner of the desk. "Is your opinion born of sentiment or evidence?"

"The sign-out time was ten past eleven. She would have been getting ready to leave for the luncheon then."

"Did you see her at ten past eleven?"

"No," I admitted. "I was updating patient files. Then I had to meet up at the front for the ride to the hotel."

"How many of you met there?"

"Two dozen." I scratched my jaw. Prickles of beard stubble grazed my fingertips.

"And you don't recall seeing her."

I closed my eyes and thought back. She hadn't been among those shuffling around for a carriage seat. "I didn't see any of the department heads. They must have traveled separately from us."

"When do you remember seeing her?"

"At the luncheon," I said. "She was already there when I came in. So she didn't have enough time."

"When did you arrive?"

"Ten past twelve."

He borrowed a pad of paper, making notes. "So you can't account for her whereabouts at ten past eleven. She could have come down here, initialed all the bodies for release, then gone to the hotel in a private coach."

"But why would she?"

"I've no idea," Mr. Hunter said. "Nor am I saying she did."

"Hey!" A woman dressed in the sturdy gray cotton coat of hospital clerks stood in the doorway, her eyes wide with outrage. "What are you doing in here, mucking with my papers?"

We had invaded her domain, pawed through her records, and did the gods knew what to her filing system, but you never let a clerk see you falter. I turned, my posture square to hers.

"You're Slater, I presume? You're late."

"I am not." She thrust her chin out. "I start at five. It's not five yet."

Mr. Hunter picked up the duty log and paged through it. "The morgue was empty when we arrived."

"So you thought you'd go flinging my papers about, because there was no one to stop you?" She marched in and took the duty log from his hands. "These are confidential. Where's Riggins?"

"Riggins left a note in the log saying they had to fetch their children," I said.

"I'll report her," she said. "I've had all the headache I can stand. Now what are you two doing in here?"

"I'm Dr. Singer from General Medicine," I said. "I will write in this log that I arrived here at twenty past four and found the morgue empty, if you'll answer a few questions."

"It's a deal." She thrust the book at me and turned an expectant gaze on Mr. Hunter. "You're not a doctor, are you."

He handed me his silver pen. "Mr. Tristan Hunter."

She knew a fine coat when she saw one, and slid one foot back to bend her knee in deference. "Sorry for barking at you, sir."

"No apology needed," he said. "I was here to lay hands on a body, and it's already gone." How elegantly he skated past the truth.

Slater reached for the sign-in sheet. "Whose?"

"Nick Elliot."

"Oh, he was a mess when he got here," she said. "Begging your pardon, but he died of a flux. Terrible."

I stopped writing to flip back a page in the log. "You were the attendant on duty when he came in. What's your first name?"

"Louisa. It was an awful job, cleaning him up. You say he's gone? His belongings too?"

Hope flared in my chest. "We haven't checked."

Slater opened the lower right-hand drawer. "All I could save were his keys—you wouldn't want the clothes he died in, sir. You really wouldn't."

I could have used those clothes. "They're gone?"

"Incinerated," Slater said. "Didn't think you'd need 'em."

"Blast."

Slater ducked her head. "Will you write me up? I didn't know; the form didn't say to keep the clothes."

"Who brought the body last night? Was it a nurse, about this tall, Black, with her hair in lots of braids and in a knot?"

She waved the description away. "Everyone knows Nurse Robin. She didn't come down. Orderlies brought him."

Robin wasn't stationed on Urgent Care. She'd probably had to go back to Surgical Recovery. I wished she had come down, though.

"May I see the sign-in form? It wasn't on the desk."

"I filed it," Slater said. "I do my filing, unlike some people I could mention."

Mr. Hunter produced a second pen and wrote down another note, borrowing the same scratchpad he had before.

Slater brought me the file, opened to Nick Elliot's sign-in form. "Here. See? It said 'hold body for examination.' Nothing about the clothes or effects. It should have said. I wouldn't have burned them if it had."

"So it does. But the body wasn't held."

"That's not on me," Slater said. "Riggins never checked the form. Did you need the clothes? I'm sorry. I didn't know."

"The keys will suffice, Miss Slater," Mr. Hunter said. He didn't have a right to them, but I held my tongue with a little disquiet.

"There's paperwork for 'em." Slater sat down at the desk. She pulled a green form from a desk drawer and turned it toward him. "Sign here. I'll fill out the rest and send the finished form to Dr. Singer. You can deliver it to Mr. Hunter, can't you, Doctor?"

"I can." This was a festival of rule-breaking. "Let me write this bit in the log. Who is J.R., by the way?"

"Julia Riggins," Slater said.

"I'll want to talk to her tomorrow."

Slater smirked. "Wish I could see that."

I wrote a quick note detailing my arrival at twenty past four to an empty morgue. Mr. Hunter accepted a ring of keys with a smile. Slater blushed, dropping her chin so she could look up at him with big eyes. I stepped out to fetch my medical bag.

He came out after me. "There's a lot of stairs to climb."

"Eager to leave?"

"We have a trail to follow." He threw a companionable arm around my shoulders. "Let's get on it."

Mr. Hunter sidled past my desk and shook the keys on their ring to make them jingle in celebration. "I hate picking locks," he said. "This is wonderful."

"What are you going to do with those?" I asked. I'd helped him . . . not steal them, precisely, but he didn't have them through honest means.

"Investigate Nick Elliot's home," he said, inspecting each one.

"You can't do that," I said. "It's a job for the police."

"Have you heard from them?" He tossed the keys in the air and caught them, the brass and iron barrels clinking together. He leaned against my bookcases, disturbing the skeletal hand I kept in a glass dome next to *Bones of the Body*.

"Not yet. I'll have to ring them."

He took the folding chair. I snapped the telephone on, and waited for Sniffy to answer.

"Operator."

"Sniffy, put me through to the Pickton Street Police Station."

"Right away, Doctor. Did you find Mathy?"

She couldn't have done it. It didn't make sense. "I expect she's gone by now."

I waited ten minutes before I finally spoke to someone in uniform. By the time I finished explaining to Police Sergeant Couchman I couldn't believe my ears.

"We can't investigate without an examination to determine cause of death," he said.

"I treated him last night," I said. "He told me he'd been poisoned."

"I'm sorry, Doctor. Without the body, we can't examine. If we can't examine, we can't determine."

"This man died horribly. Are you telling me you won't do anything?"

Mr. Hunter gave me a shrug and a sympathetic look.

"We can open a file," Couchman said. "But getting evidence without a body—it would have to be airtight."

"I can't believe this." It was everything I could do not to raise my voice. "You're telling me if I hide the body well enough, or if I dispose of it, I'll get away with murder?"

"I don't advise you try it," Sergeant Couchman said.

"That's absurd."

"We hang murderers," Sergeant Coachman said. "Would you want to convict without the strongest possible evidence?"

I rubbed the bridge of my nose. "What would it take to convince you Nick's death was a murder?"

"Evidence," Couchman repeated. I was getting on his nerves. I didn't care. "We usually start from the results of a doctor's investigation into—"

"Cause of death." My bruised elbow landed on the desk. I longed to know who'd torn away Nick's chance at justice. "Can't you try to find evidence?"

Couchman tried to soften his tone into sympathy. "I know this is hard to accept, but we have to follow the law. Without evidence there was a murder, we can't go on. We've tied up the line long enough. I'm sorry, Doctor."

He rang off. I slammed the receiver back in its cradle. Bad luck. I rested my forehead against the heels of my hands and tried to breathe.

"The police aren't coming, I take it?"

"They won't do anything," I said. "The body's gone. The clothes are burned. There's no evidence."

"There might still be something to find." He shook the ring of keys.

"You propose breaking and entering."

He waved the criminal notion away. "Investigation."

"I'm no investigator."

"Doctors investigate all the time," Mr. Hunter said. "You gather the evidence of illness and diagnose. You can do this."

Realization lifted my head from my hands. "I can."

He grinned. "That's the spirit."

Infected with his approval, I smiled back. "No, I mean I officially can. Environmental inspection. It's part of diagnosis. Where's the form?" I opened the stiff drawer on the left and sorted through the spare copies of obscure hospital forms I hoarded, just in case.

"Do you have a form for everything?"

"The tyranny of paper." I found a copy and put it on my desk blotter. My tortoiseshell pen sat nearby. "Half my day is filling out forms."

"I'm surprised they don't have a form for when you go to the lavatory."

"Not so loud, they might hear you."

He smirked, head canted in an attempt to read what I was doing. "So you fill out the form and then we can go to Nick's apartment?"

"I fill out the form, twice. I send the original to my boss—"

"Your boss who is the only person in the hospital with the initials E.M. who has the authority to release bodies to have them destroyed? You need her approval?"

I set my pen on a felt pad. "You think she wouldn't approve it? It wasn't her handwriting."

"I don't know if she would or if she wouldn't. But will you chance it?"

"It's the rules," I said. "I'm sure it wasn't her. She'll stamp all the copies. We keep the originals and file the rest. Then I'm authorized to do the environmental inspection."

"Today?"

"She's probably already gone," I said. "Tomorrow."

"We can't wait until tomorrow. If she says no—"

"Mr. Hunter." I picked up the pen and wiped the nib clean. "What are you suggesting?"

"Fill the forms out, send them to your boss. Come with me tonight. If she says no, we'll not lose the information we'll gain going tonight. If she says yes, we're fine."

"I'm sure she'll say yes."

He huffed and looked at the ceiling. "Pretend two possibilities exist and you aren't sure of the outcome. What do you do?"

I grimaced. "You are a bad influence, Mr. Hunter."

He grinned. "Thank you. I try."

I checked boxes and wrote terse answers in the spaces provided until two copies lay on my desk, the ink drying on each. "I'll leave these until morning."

"This is where you will find me a useful individual," he said. "I know a thing or two about ferreting out the truth."

"You know a thing or two about bending it, too." I nodded to the keys he spun around on his finger.

He tossed the keys in the air and caught them again. "People lie, Doctor. They fib. They omit. They smooth matters over with the easy thing to say. You know this."

How easily he talked of laying the truth aside, as if it were a tie in a color that didn't suit. "Have you lied to me?"

He took a moment to think about it. "Not that I recall."

I set my pen down. That's what a liar would say, isn't it? "You're smooth. You ask questions like you have a right to the answers, and I go along with what you want, without knowing why you want it."

Mr. Hunter put the keys on the desk where I could take them away. "Only you can decide if I'm trustworthy, but I'd like you to think so. What can I do?"

"Tell me where you're from."

He glanced away, shoulders rising. "A long way from here."

"Another country?"

He looked back at me. "Yes."

"Which one? The Republic of Edara?" By his coloring, he could be Edaran, but they had closed their borders nearly two hundred years ago. There weren't many Edarans anywhere in Aeland.

He shifted in his seat. "Interesting you assumed Edara."

"So it's true?"

He winced and shook his head. Not Edara, then. Laneeri nobles wore their hair long. My heart kicked at the idea of him being a spy, and my enemy. He couldn't be.

I liked him.

"Mr. Hunter, where are you from?"

He glanced away, fingers covering his mouth. "I don't think you'd believe me."

"Is it so unbelievable? Why does your face waver when I touch you?" I pressed on.

He blinked and raised his head. "You can see the veil?"

He was using magic to mask himself without even testing his limits. "I'm asking the questions. Is it power? Like your light?"

"It's the same," he admitted. "The face you see . . . resembles mine."

"So you disguise yourself. With the power, which should be impossible to do for long." I fought to breathe against the heaviness in my chest. I wanted to go back and forget I'd said anything about the truth or lying, but I had to go on. "Why?"

He shifted uncomfortably. "My natural appearance attracts a great deal of attention. I need to blend in."

"And you're not a gentleman."

He combed the escaped lock of hair back into his queue. "The truth is, I'm not a gentleman. But you are."

I shut my mouth. When things decide to fall apart, they crumble on all sides.

He crossed one leg over the other. "People bow to me. They curtsy, touch their hats, show me deference. You never do. You're perfectly polite to everyone, including your equals."

"This isn't about me," I said. "I was asking you."

"I told you I've seen wealthy witches here. In the box seats at the cinema, at concerts. In dining rooms and fine hotels. I kept my distance from them."

"Mages. We're mages." I swallowed the lump in my throat. "Have you—seen them in pairs?"

He nodded. "Where one walks enslaved to the other? It's vile. It's perverse to take a bond and use it for—" He shuddered.

"They don't do bindings where you're from?"

"They don't," he said.

That hurt my chest. He came from someplace I could be free. "Do you have to hide your magic?"

"No. You'd be well-respected there," he said. "Healing is a vital talent."

"But you won't tell me where you're from." I didn't know this man. The face I saw was a mask, constructed from the power. He was no Aelander. I needed the truth even if I had to take it.

I seized his hand. He yanked at it, but I held fast. "I want—"

I pushed past the ordinary, nondescript, too-regular aura as if it were a layer of skin, and my words died in my throat.

Mr. Hunter had told the truth. His mask did resemble his true face, but it was a blunted, crude thing compared to the truth of him. He was finer, more ethereal . . .

Eternally beautiful.

"Amaranthine," I whispered.

"Starred One," he answered, his expression resigned. "Hail, and well met."

An Amaranthine had visited the legendary painter Briantine in his studio, disrobed, and asked him to paint her. Briantine had picked up his brush and fallen into an ecstatic haze he described as the best hours of his life. He'd awakened to an empty studio. The painting had vanished, paid for with a sack of oak leaves turned to solid gold. He toiled for years trying to recapture her on canvas until he finally put his eyes out. His failures rest in the Royal Gallery, considered masterpieces.

Stories about the Amaranthines had a lot of endings like that.

"Forgive me. Please." I wanted to touch him, glide my fingers over the planes of his face, and to even think of such a thing made my nerves jangle at the impertinence. "I didn't know your kind were real."

"We are." His power rubbed gentle ripples over my scalp, down my back, over my skin. "Once my kind and yours were true friends."

I wanted to be his friend. I wanted him to smile at me. I wanted—

My knees hit the floor. His life was so vibrant. Health and power radiated from him, welcoming as a hearth fire. I could kneel here and bask in it all day. I wanted him to want something of me, so I could do exactly as he asked—

I shut my eyes. "Stop."

I snatched my hand away, eyes clamped shut. I had no grave dirt, no copper, none of the herbs that protected against them. In this tiny space he could touch me again and make me his creature. He could make me his slave and make me love servitude. I scrambled backward, falling against the corner of my filing cabinet.

"I apologize," he said. "But you see why I aimed to keep it secret."

His *voice*. I flung out one hand, eyes still screwed shut.

"Don't touch me." I demanded. I begged. I hoped he would laugh and ignore me.

"I will not bespell you again."

Amaranthines had no choice but to speak the truth, so they lied with honest words. I could see no hole in the statement to wiggle through.

"Please, Miles. I am sorry." That resonance was gone from his voice, the power that could leave me rapt to hear it once more. This was why Briantine had never painted another model again, why he couldn't stop, why he ended his torment.

I hadn't lasted five seconds.

"I didn't think you could break my veiling spell, and I hoped . . ." He faltered. "It doesn't matter. It's safe. You can look."

I kept my eyes shut.

"Miles, please."

There was no command in it, no enchantment. He sounded regretful.

I opened my eyes.

He appeared mortal again, merely handsome. It was a relief. I could have wept. "You will never bespell me again?"

"I don't want you as my thrall. I won't enchant you and leave you broken."

Sincere-sounding, but the words had too much room to twist. "That's not a promise I can accept."

"I might have to use magic on you. To teach you, or protect you, or simply to amuse. I can't promise to never use magic on you, but this I swear: I do not want you as my minion."

I saw the hole. "Do you need me as your minion, despite your wishes?"

"No."

I could trust his answer, though I shouldn't trust him. The Amaranthines used to walk the world with us, amused by us, if we were fortunate enough to be amusing. Then they'd left the world to guard the dead, and no one could agree on why. Some said it was a punishment for troubling mortals so. Others claimed they had taken the place of the gods, who had abandoned us to chance. More said they had never been real at all and were just made-up stories to explain what we now understood as mental unreason, or more rudely put, madness.

But Mr. Hunter was real. I could have offended him, and then my life would be worth nothing. I could be offending him right now. I bowed my head. "I apologize."

"Please don't—" He helped me to my feet. "Don't defer to me. Don't behave as if I'm more of an authority, or infallible, or whatever the stories tell you I ought to be."

"But you're—"

"Vain," Mr. Hunter said. "Prideful, arrogant, easily bored, prone to mischief. And there's about as much naked honesty as I can stand. Let's find Nick Elliot's flat."

SEVEN

W. 1455 Wellston Street

I held my tongue all through the ride up to Wellston and West 14th. Fashionable tailors and dressmakers kept their shops on Wellston, their plate-glass windows dark for the evening. Horse-drawn vehicles dotted the streets, delivering laundry, groceries, and evening mail. Once we left his fine coach I kept two paces behind Mr. Hunter, whose unbuttoned overcoat flared in the wind. Dead leaves skipped over the smooth black road. He paused between apple trees on the median and let bicyclists struggling against the headwind pass. All those people passed him with no idea who walked in their midst, that the good-looking man in the fine coat and the anachronistic plait was a legend.

The legend scanned the doors parked discreetly between shops, the entrances to apartments above. I punched my hands deeper into my pockets and waited for his decision.

"Straight out the door and into the street," he mused. "I'd do that, in a panic." He turned eastward into the wind's face and chose his destination, a brick building hosting a Martin & Gold bookseller on its first floor.

Mr. Hunter stood on the black and white tiles spelling out *1455* and tried a black iron key in the lock.

I surveyed the street. "You think it's this one?"

The lock tumbled open. He held the door for me with a little grin. We stood shoulder to shoulder, reading the names on the brass-doored mailboxes mounted on the wall.

"Elliot." I laid my finger on the engraved plate. "Three-oh-one."

The stairs groaned under our feet, and I had another surprise—the worn carpet running down the hallways was covered in pink roses.

He took two steps and turned back, peering at me. "What is it?"

"I've seen this place before."

"Do you know someone who lived here?"

"No. It was when . . . when he died." I couldn't talk about this in the open.

He patted my shoulder. "I understand."

I wanted to lean into it. I wanted to flinch away. Instead I asked, "Is that supposed to happen?"

He cocked his head. "Yes. Don't you know?"

It had been ages since witches had claimed to guide the dead. "I don't."

"I think so. But let's find three-oh-one."

"Right." *Act like you belong here, Miles.* I squared my shoulders, prepared to smile at anyone we met.

A woman in a velvet coat met us on the landing, and we stepped aside to let her pass. She stole a look over her shoulder at Mr. Hunter, my surplus Service coat beneath notice. A snatch of music played on the second floor—someone with a violin, not a wireless or a phonograph.

He paused to listen. "They're quite good."

"Morbid subject matter, sir."

He flicked a dissatisfied glance at me. "What do you mean?"

"It's the last aria from *The Revenge of Lucus.*"

The violin's voice rose in attack, the sharply played notes bitter laughter as Lucus watched the bewitched underlings of his enemy Corian rise up and stab their king-general to death. I shivered.

Mr. Hunter climbed the stairs to the third floor. "Lucus the Justice Bringer?"

"Lucus the Destroyer," I corrected. "Lucus the Witch-King."

"The Witch-King," he scoffed. "What of Lucus's rule? Forty years of law reform, the tradition of education for girls as well as boys—"

"Pardon me, sir, but can you do evil and erase it by doing good with the result?" I asked. "Lucus brought reform, but he bought it with blood."

The look he turned on me was skeptical. "So the good he did . . . was evil?"

"No," I said. "It's complicated. Here's three-oh-one."

Mr. Hunter tried a brass key to match the battered keyplate. I scanned the hall. Someone would come out and see us breaking into their neighbor's flat.

"No luck?"

"It has to be one of these—ah."

The door swung open to reveal a small but tidy kitchen, the window above the sink nearly obscured by shelves holding potted herbs. I slipped inside after him and shut the door, snapping the lock back into place.

He stood in the center of the kitchen, eyeing a collection of expensive, aether-powered gadgets. "What do you think of those?"

A floorboard creaked under my foot. Mr. Hunter smiled at my wince. "Sir? Er, my general opinion?"

He waved at the gadgets. "I mean, what does it say about Nick Elliot, having all those?"

I set my medical bag on the baking board and unwound my scarf. "He had money. A cookit, a fast kettle, a mixer, and a coffee-burper? They're expensive." I drew closer, brushing the sleeve of my coat against his. "Maybe he worked for the company. These are all from Sunlight Appliances."

"None of them are connected to the power plate," he observed. "What do you make of that?"

"There's only the one plate," I said. "This place is too old to be full aether."

He nodded to the coin box on the wall. "What else?"

I looked around. What was out of place, what was wrong? What did I see?

A tidy kitchen with expensive gadgets. A window full of green herbs, screening the room from the unglamorous view of the back alley. Everything clean . . .

Everything put away.

"He said there was poison in the tea," I said. "Where's the teacup? Where's the teapot?"

He opened a cupboard. A plain whiteware teapot sat in its place, next to a sugar bowl and tea-tins. Every hook held a white teacup hanging from its handle.

I shivered, the implication crawling up my back. "Someone was here. They cleaned up after murdering him."

"You have the right mind for this, Doctor."

The compliment left me feeling an elated warmth. "Thank you, sir."

He sighed.

"Mr. Hunter," I corrected.

His pained look persisted. "I'm exactly the same person you knew, Doctor. Nothing about me has changed."

"But you're—"

"Foolish," he said. "Socially clumsy. I'm still rather ignorant of your world. Impatient."

"Are you going to rattle off your faults at me every time I remember you're a legend?"

He snorted. "I'll fall off the pedestal sooner or later, if I let you keep me up there. I need you to forget."

"How can I forget?" I came perilously close to laughing, the kind of laughter you can't stop. "How can I forget you're—"

"I am not a story, Doctor." The shoulders of my coat crumpled in his grip. He startled and let go, smoothing them back into place. "I want to go back to how we were before. Friends. Or becoming so."

"We can become friends." Friends, with an Amaranthine. I was a fool.

"Call me Tristan," he said.

My pulse thumped in my ears. "It's not proper."

"Miles," he said. Warmth spread across my chest. He leaned closer. Too handsome, and his face was only half of the truth. "I want to call you so. Will you forbid me?"

I shifted back and bumped into the baking board. "No."

"Miles." The word made my insides leap. "Say it. Call me Tristan."

My lips tingled. My tongue tapped at the back of my teeth. *Tristan.*

"Mr. Hunter," I said.

"Stubborn." One side of his mouth curled up. Cool air rushed into the place where he stood. "There might be more to learn, even though the tea things have been cleaned up."

"Let me look at the teapot." I needed to do something to come back to normal. "If it hasn't been scrubbed clean, I'll need it."

Tristan reached for the door as I did, and our hands collided.

"Rather close quarters in here." He set the teapot on the counter. "What do you want with the teapot?"

"I can test it for arsenic."

"That's what he died of?"

"It's my best guess. He held on long enough to get to the hospital. Arsenic tastes slightly sweet. You'd miss it in tea." I lifted the lid and smiled at what I found inside. The interior was dark from years of brewing, the patina undisturbed by scrubbing.

"Here's our first piece of evidence." I set the teapot next to my medical bag.

"Excellent. Help me search the rest." He moved into the dining room, shuffling aside to let me in. A table for six stood draped in a crocheted lace tablecloth. I put my hand on a delicately stitched fan-tailed bird, found another in a slightly different pose, a third near to the second.

Tristan leaned against the back of a lyre-backed chair, tracing a path along the cloth's peaked netting. "What is it?"

"Expensive, is what it is," I said. "You can't make crochet lace on a machine. It has to be done by hand." I touched the five birds I'd found. "Every single one is different, and they're not arranged on a grid to a pattern."

"How do you know this?"

"I once stared at a tablecloth like this one at mealtimes," I said.

I had kept my eyes down while Father used suppers to praise his precocious daughter and recount my failures—of the day, of the week, of the year, those disappointments never left to scab over and heal. I fought the tears I couldn't shed by counting the fan-tailed birds on Mother's favorite tablecloth. Grace would be a Storm-Singer; I was a Secondary, destined to become my sister's thrall.

"Miles," Tristan touched my shoulder. "What does the tablecloth tell you?"

I shrugged. "It might not mean anything. Regarding his death, I mean."

"But it tells you something about Nick. Why does he have this tablecloth?"

"He didn't buy it. Too expensive. It's from his mother," I said. "She probably made these for extra money."

"How do you know?"

"The kitchen." I waved in its direction. "Expensive gadgets and cheap whiteware. A rich man would have porcelain and a housekeeper, even if the servant didn't live in."

"So, a poor man come to fortune is poisoned. This is the beginning of his story. Let's find out the rest."

Nick Elliot's front room boasted a view of a brick wall and a record collection. The trumpetlike flare of a phonograph's horn pointed to an easy chair, a pedestal ashtray resting beside it. Another aether meter mounted on the wall provided power for a wireless.

"He enjoyed music."

"Enough to endure the wireless," I agreed.

"Hate the stuff. It's a midge buzzing in your ears and the taste of copper on your tongue," Tristan said.

I shuddered in visceral sympathy. "Aether runs on copper wires. Maybe that's why." I opened the hall closet. "He lived alone. The other bedroom's a study, and no women's things in here."

"Miles," Tristan laughed. "I'm surprised at you."

I studied five pairs of men's shoes on the floor of the closet, my face hot. Mr. Elliot could have preferred the company of men. He was at the age where tolerance of the practice would start fraying, but the pressure to marry was not yet unbearable. "You have a point."

"But I think you're right. Nothing is paired. The furniture in here isn't arranged to suit a pair. His bedroom . . ." Tristan turned the faceted glass knob. "Oh. He had a lover."

A pale rose silk dressing gown swung next to a heavier bronze and green brocade, both hanging from hooks on the door. Tristan closed the door again.

"One room at a time. What's this?" He lifted a photo album from the coffee table. "Newspaper clippings."

I pawed through overcoat pockets and found a press license. "He was a newspaperman."

"I think he wrote about gardening."

"Gardening?" I came over to peer at the pages. Tristan turned the page to a newspaper photo of a tiny garden of flowers dancing at the feet of a concrete Summer Maiden.

I covered my mouth. "He was Mr. Greenthumbs."

"The lovely garden of the week?"

East Kingston competed every week for the honor of their six-foot-square plots being named in the *Star*. My landlady had won once, and the clipping sat framed in her front hall.

Mrs. Bass would mourn Mr. Greenthumbs.

"Nick Elliot wrote one of the most popular columns in the city. Who would want to kill him?"

"Perhaps someone knew his secret," Tristan said.

"But they could report him. He'd never pass the tests. He'd be in an asylum before you could blink. Why murder?"

"Rivalry at work? Trouble in the family?"

"His lover? Someone managed to slip poison into his tea, and then clean up—Mr. Hunter." I groped for his sleeve. "He was alone when he had his tea. The murderer wouldn't let him run out into the street. Did you see anyone when you stopped—"

Tristan lifted a finger to his lips.

The floorboards in the apartment hallway creaked. A key slid into the front door lock.

Tristan clamped one hand over my mouth and dragged me into the corner.

EIGHT

Illusion

"Nick?"

A woman entered. Sunk, we were sunk. She'd scream when she saw us, call the police. Could we explain?

She walked into the front room. "Nick?"

She didn't react to us at all.

She shrugged out of a fur-trimmed cocoon of a coat and flung it over the sofa. "Don't tell me you're sick, Nicholas Alva Elliot, and you need someone to wait on you."

Tristan kept his hand on my mouth, one arm wrapped tight around my ribs. Don't speak. Don't move, those hands said, his fennel-scented breaths calm against my ear.

She stripped off slim black leather gloves, and her fashionably short hair curled around prominent cheekbones. Bottle-black hair, by the slight blue sheen of it, making her pale skin seem even milkier. She wore wide-legged charcoal trousers, a cream silk shirt, a slate-and-silver striped tie.

The woman crossed the front room and opened the bedroom door. "Nick?"

She couldn't see us. Tristan had hidden us from her view, a power from legends and stories I'd scoffed at even as I eagerly read those childhood tales. His hand on my mouth gentled, slid down to wrap around my waist.

We were touching from neck to knee. His breath flared warm over my ear, and I didn't dare shift so much as an inch away from him. What if the boards creaked under our feet?

The woman returned to the front room, wine-painted lips pursed. She paused, thoughtful, and then a decision smoothed the lines around her mouth. She tiptoed into the study. Six wooden drawers scraped open and shut, four metal drawers echoed, and the woman shut the last one with frustrated force.

"What are you doing, Nick?" she asked the air. "And where have you gone?"

She came back to fetch her cocoon coat and shrugged into it with a discontented haste. She checked the dining room, the thud of her heeled shoes muffled against the carpet.

My shoulder itched. I was too warm inside my felted wool. Tristan's breath on my neck traveled along my limbs in waves of gooseflesh. In my imagination, I could taste the fennel on his mouth, feel the cool silkiness of his hair tangled in my fingers. Too vividly, with him pressed up against me and a floor creak away from discovery. I shouldn't be thinking of kissing anybody, let alone a half-divine, heartless Amaranthine.

The woman opened her purse and pulled out an engraved silver flask, drinking from it before she put on her gloves and left the flat empty-handed. Tristan tightened his grip, and we stood there until the stairs creaked under her feet.

I tore out of his arms and twitched my coat closed, fastening the buttons at my waist. "What did you do?"

Tristan shrugged. "I'm an illusionist. We're lucky I managed to hide both of us. What was she looking for in the study?"

I was breathing too fast. "You made us invisible?"

He gave me an unsteady smile. "I did."

The power he must possess . . . "Amazing."

"Thank you." His smile widened. "It took a great deal to hide us both. I'm hungry."

He'd performed a feat out of a legend, and he was just hungry? "I'd be on my back seam."

"I can hold on until we're finished searching." Tristan led the way to the study. "Whatever she wanted, she didn't find it. Interesting."

"Whoever came in here and cleaned up already searched the study?"

He stood in the middle of the room, turning a slow circle. "A poor man come to fortune is poisoned . . . for something he wrote? Ah, splendid. I hoped for this."

"For what?"

Tristan slipped on his gloves and lifted the cover plate of an upright typewriter, and the satisfied look slid into vexation. He opened drawers just as the woman had.

"What is it?" I came over to inspect the typewriter.

"The ribbon's new," he said. "But look at this."

He set a box on the desktop. The legend read *Snyder's Best Re-inking Kit*. I opened the lid; the cranking machine was stained with use. No ribbons sat in the compartment meant to store them.

Tristan opened every desk drawer. "No spare ribbons. No boxes of new ribbons. Evidence Nick Elliot reused his old ribbons. The reason why Nick Elliot is dead was in this room, but it's gone now. There's nothing left."

He checked the filing cabinet. "All the drawers are empty."

"The evidence is gone," I said. "It's all gone. We didn't learn anything."

He rocked the filing cabinet. "Help me move this."

I squeezed in on his left, and together we walked the cabinet away from the corner. We found a pile of dust. Tristan rocked the cabinet back into the corner, and we each took a side of the desk.

"Lift with your knees," I warned, and we moved the thing a few inches. Lying in the dust was a scratchpad, probably one that had rested next to the telephone.

"It's blank."

Tristan snatched it up and held it to the light. "Not quite. Hand me a pencil."

I opened the drawer and found soft sketching pencils. Tristan rubbed one over the pad. He glanced at me with wide eyes when he read the message. "You say you didn't know him?"

"No."

He handed me the pad and I read the letters exposed by the rubbing:

CMH=Dr. Miles Singer

Psych, BVH

—permission to interview patients?

—don't spook him!

"BVH is Beauregard Veterans' hospital," Tristan said. "What does CMH mean?"

"It's me," I said. "He knew my name. Christopher Miles Hensley."

"Ah. Any relation to Chancellor Christopher Hensley?"

"You could say that." It was hard to breathe around the icy, shuddering sickness. "He's my father."

"So. You're a gentleman after all."

I nodded and tried to swallow. "I ran away to join the army."

He tilted his head. "You came back earlier than most. You were wounded?"

I closed the door on those memories. I was in Aeland, in Kingston, and Camp Paradise was in the past. "Technically, yes."

Tristan's face pursed up in thought, and smoothed out to polite concern. "I won't pry."

"Thank you."

"I'll even change the subject." He led us through Nick's flat to the kitchen door. "Nick was murdered by someone who had a lot to lose if whatever he was writing came out into the open."

"But he writes about gardening," I said. "Who would kill over gardening? Wait. What if that's not all he wrote about?"

"What else would he write about?"

"The war. He said the soldiers deserved to know the truth."

"Who would kill him for being anti-war?"

"Nationalists," I said. "But not with poison. They'd beat him to death in the street, half of them drunk."

"They deserved to know the truth behind the war," Tristan mused. "What truth?"

"I don't know," I said. "He didn't make a lot of sense. He said something about souls, too."

This arrested Tristan. He grasped my arms. "Yes. Nick had said 'They' needed the souls? He was on the same trail I am."

"You're looking for souls?" I asked. "I thought you were looking for lost magic."

"Souls power magic."

I stopped, openmouthed. "They what?"

"You're a witch because you possess a peculiar strength of soul-energy. Don't you know this?"

"No." It was really that simple? A dozen thoughts whirled in my head, but this wasn't the time or place to demand explanations. "So it's true. The dead do go on to the Solace."

"Of course it is. Why would you think otherwise?"

I should be sitting down for this. "Because the stories about ghosts are just stories. There's no such thing."

"You think ghosts don't exist because Aeland doesn't have any."

I wanted to argue, but I couldn't. Amaranthines were real. The Solace was real. I had a soul. I would go to the Solace when I died . . . and perhaps when I did, Tristan would be there, like the lone acquaintance in a distant town.

"All right. Souls are real, and a sufficiently strong soul makes you a mage, or a witch. Do you have any more shattering revelations for me?"

"Given how little you Aelanders know of magic, we don't have time to go into the rest. Now make your best guess about what Nick meant. Who needed the souls?"

"If anyone would, it's the Invisibles. My people. But you can't get near them. And I won't."

"You're right, I can't." Tristan released me, smoothing my rumpled sleeves. "I have to know what Nick learned, Miles. Will you help me?"

"He knew something about the war. Something the soldiers needed to know. I'm with you. What should we do first?"

"Perhaps a visit to his workplace would bear fruit."

"I don't know if my inspection form would stretch to cover the trip."

"No one has to tell us anything, but it can't hurt to try." He locked the door and motioned for me to follow him. The stairs complained at our passage. "Let's find something for dinner."

Dinner with Tristan. Knee and elbow around a little table in a dining room, or served in the cozy privacy of his home? My fingers flexed. I couldn't be alone with him. I knew how stories of the Amaranthines ended. "I should get home."

He straightened up and composed his features. "I'll call on you tomorrow, after work? I'll have my housekeeper prepare an early supper—"

"I'll have the results from the teapot," I promised.

I unhooked my bicycle off the back of his carriage, and we parted ways on Wellston Street.

I traded a fine meal in Tristan's home for five and a half miles of headwind up the gradual uphill climb to East Kingston. The teapot bulged inside my medical bag as I guided my bicycle off the curb, the sight evoking a guilty little thrill. We'd broken and entered. If we'd been caught . . .

I stood on my pedals and bent over the curve of my handlebars against a force pushing me westward. I crossed train tracks with teeth gritted against the aether wires strung overhead. My legs quivered by the time I reached the wide gray house with white windowsills and the dead heads of autumn's flowers in Mrs. Bass's prizewinning front garden.

A carriage stood in front of Mrs. Bass's front walk, the crest bearing the three boars of the Hensley family.

Flee, Miles. Get out of here. But my legs never obeyed me in Kalloo, and they didn't obey me here. I straddled the crossbar of my bicycle, frozen.

The carriage jolted as a footman in livery—*livery*—hopped off the step and advanced toward me. "Dame Hensley awaits you inside, sir."

He grasped the handle of my medical bag and lifted it out of the basket mounted over my front wheel.

I stirred, finally. "Don't—"

"Sir? If I may assist you?"

He hefted my bag, its pleated leather sides swelled to fullness by the teapot resting inside it. He looked toward Mrs. Bass's house, where my sister probably sat drinking broken-leaf tea in the aroma of boiled cabbage and minced mutton, eating carefully hoarded cookies from a tin.

He held my bag and in it the teapot, an assortment of medicines, my syringe case, and the scalpels I hadn't used since I saved Pvt. James Wolf's life and limb back in Mobile Hospital 361. I could give all those up, and everything in my room. I could ride to break my neck down the King's Way and—

And go where? Grace had sworn on her blood. Whatever she was doing here, she wouldn't walk away with me as her slave.

So I put my chin up and swung my leg over the bike's saddle. I let him take the handlebars, and he walked two paces behind me as I took thirty steps to the front door.

I handed the footman my key. He locked my bicycle, gave me my bag, and took a place by the front door, immaculate in his orange coat and uncaring of the patch behind him where the house's gray paint had chipped away.

Bells from a nearby clock tower sounded the hour. The front door snapped open before the first tolling faded. The pipefitter who snored in the room next to mine stepped outside.

"Doc."

"Arthur. Is everything all right?"

"Fine, only—" He turned his neck slowly, wincing at the movement. "I think I slept wrong. Would you have a look? After your fancy caller."

My fancy caller. Not *my sister*. A small mercy. I made my way to the back of the house, past the dramatic voices on the wireless muffled through the front parlor doors.

Grace relaxed on a cushion-covered wooden chair in Mrs. Bass's homely green kitchen with one of the good teacups in her hand. Mrs. Bass rose from the table to serve me supper, expecting me to fall on a plate the way working men did while women visited in the kitchen.

"Just tea, Mrs. Bass—"

"Go on and eat, Miles," my sister said. "You need feeding up."

Chopped cabbage and mutton shoulder chops braised in wine gone half to vinegar steamed on my plate. A fellow with tar burns on his forearms stepped inside from the washing room and raised his hand. "Missus, Your Ladyship. And—"

"Dr. Singer, this is Douglas. He's in the back bedroom," Mrs. Bass said. "Douglas Fox."

"Road-worker?" I asked, and shook his soap-clean hand.

Stomach acid boiled in his gullet, trying to dissolve a lump that wouldn't give way.

"I hear you're a doctor," Douglas said. "What's a doctor doing living here? Beg pardon, Mrs. Bass. Are you one of them trainees?"

"I'm not an intern, Mr. Fox."

"You're a real doctor? Huh." Douglas swiped his damp brow with his forearm. "I get a pain in my stomach after I eat. Why's that?"

"Could be a few reasons." It was a bezoar, and that meant surgery. I'd have to convince him to take time off work. A hard thing, when getting sick could mean your job. "I can have a look."

"Tomorrow. You've got an important guest." He bowed his head at my sister and stepped out, leaving me to my dinner.

Grace watched me take the first bite of my chop with barely a shiver. Mrs. Bass followed Mr. Fox to join the others in the front parlor, where they'd feed the aether-meter pennies and listen to the evening's audio theater, full of unlikely plot twists and thrilling music meant to heighten the atmosphere. Once we were alone the look on Grace's face writhed from politeness to scandalized ire.

"Birdland? You live in a single room in a boardinghouse in *Birdland*?"

She was as I remembered her, making an awful face at a supper she didn't like or a notion she wouldn't abide. The years melted away as I winked at her. "You're sounding better. Cold cleared up?"

"After I nearly burned to death with your cure. I'm perfectly well." She glanced around at the kitchen. I was glad Mrs. Bass's enameled iron pots were free of stains and she'd never let a speck of dust settle anywhere. But Grace looked as if this kitchen were a pathetic hovel. "How much are they paying you?"

"Enough." The meat had surrendered to hours on the simmer. "I could afford a flat, if I could find one."

"Leave it to me. Birdland. Indeed."

"Why are you here?"

She looked down at her cup before answering. "I came to see you."

"Why?"

"Because you're my—my friend. And I missed you."

I rubbed at the center of my chest, at the warm glow spreading to my limbs. It had been years. "I missed you too."

"And I wanted to talk to you—" She shook her head. "Never mind. This place, you can't live here."

My sentimentality crumpled. She couldn't make decisions for me as if I were her Secondary. "No."

One eyebrow went up. "No?"

"You're not finding me a flat," I said. "You'll pick out a ten-room folly. How did you find me?"

"I telephoned the hospital. Dr. Matheson was most helpful."

"Oh, indeed." The meat was sour.

"Don't be sulky, Miles. Six rooms."

"No."

She rolled her eyes. "Do they even make flats smaller than six rooms?"

"Grace, do you know the cost of a loaf of bread?"

"Are you calling me a snob?"

"Can you deny it?"

She huffed. "What kind of flat do you need, then?"

"You didn't come here to offer to find me new lodgings."

Grace glanced off to the left. "You left work hours ago. Where have you been?"

I couldn't tell her the truth. She'd call down the whole Circle against an Amaranthine. The cinema? She'd ask me what picture I saw. Dinner? I was eating like a starving man. The library? What books did I borrow?

"Miles."

Lie. "I called on a friend."

"Who?"

I looked away.

"Oh. Still sharing the company of men? Aren't you a bit old for that?"

"Grace."

She sipped her tea. "I suppose it's better than shackling yourself to a laundress."

"Grace."

"I'm joking. A secretary, surely."

I stared at her, and she gave me an apologetic look. "I'm sorry. I'm glad you have a friend. Mrs. Bass said you kept to yourself."

"I'm sure she told you everything."

Outside the kitchen, a board in the hallway creaked. I stuffed my mouth with mutton. Grace drank her tea. Mrs. Bass knocked on the door before coming in. "Beg pardon, Dame Hensley, but I don't allow guests after nine, and it's ten past."

"Of course." Grace pushed back her chair. "Thank you for the tea. Miles and I will go—"

"You will go, Grace," I corrected. "I will remain here. I can't tell you what a surprise this visit was."

Mrs. Bass and Grace looked down their noses at my remark.

"Indeed." Grace pulled on a glove. "Surprises are rather the theme of our reunion, aren't they? Goodbye, Mrs. Bass."

She kissed the air next to Mrs. Bass's cheek, and damn if my landlady didn't beam like the sun. Grace glanced back at me before she left, the footman's steps echoing hers on the porch.

Mrs. Bass turned on me. "Dame Grace is a fine lady. You had no call to treat her poorly, however she jilted you."

"It wasn't—" I shut up, started over. "It's been a long time."

"You finish up your meal." She took the tea things away, glancing inside my sister's cup. She went still, and her eyes widened.

"What is it?" I asked. "Didn't she finish?" Grace would no sooner leave the insult of a half-drunk cup of tea than she would dance through Wellston Triangle naked.

"It's nothing," Mrs. Bass said, but her lips were white as she picked up Grace's cup, taking it not to the stone sink but out the back way, the door to the yard creaking open. Then came the sound of bone-clay smashing on pavement, followed by Mrs. Bass spitting three times.

I'd nearly forgotten my dinner. My jaw hung open, but I shut it before Mrs. Bass could see. She flushed when she found me staring.

"I know, it's nonsense." She tried to laugh, as if destroying one of her most precious teacups were nothing to worry about.

"You can read omens in tea leaves," I said.

Her shoulders rose. "Just a bit of lore. It's not *witchcraft*."

"Of course it isn't," I soothed. "But what did you see?"

"I have to chivvy the men off to bed. If you want a bath, the tank is heated." She walked out.

I counted three and consulted the cup left on the table, the one Mrs. Bass had drunk from. A wheel clung to the left side, meaning someone near her would be leaving, not herself. Closest to the arc of coral lipstick was a cross, meaning be cautious, save money, take no risks. The rest of the leaves pooled in the red-tinged brown liquid at the bottom.

She had seen something in Grace's cup. So bad she tried to break the omen. If I took down a cup and drank my own share, what would I read clinging to the inside?

Maybe I didn't want to know, but I already had a good guess. I wished I had my collection of Senecal's *Stories of the Amaranthine*.

Childhood memory would only serve me so far about the lore of the Solace's guardians.

I took my plate to the sink and scrubbed it clean. A draft from the kitchen window wrapped a chilly arm around me. What did I remember? Gaining the enmity of an Amaranthine would mean poetic levels of disaster. Menas the Just had punished them when their tricks on mortals had escalated too far for his patience, and cursed them to speak only the truth. Their vengeance was the stuff of legend, and their mortal lovers died of grief.

Tristan had bargained to teach me, and he would do exactly as he promised. Anything more would be walking on treacherous ground. Especially accepting his invitations to be in more private surroundings. It had been a long time since I had enjoyed the close company of a friend. I was too busy. I had too many secrets. Tristan already knew a good many of them.

But I knew the plot of *A Strand of Stars for Your Hair*. When Helena's ghost rises from her bloody bathtub and into the sky toward the Solace, play-goers wonder if she reunited with Heilyn in the end.

I couldn't let him get close.

Mrs. Bass bustled into the kitchen bearing a small stack of mail. "Your quarterlies came today," she said. "There were so many they couldn't fit in the mailbox."

The envelope crackled under my fingers, my name and address neatly typed with the logo of my bank in the upper corner. The postmark read Leafshed 20, the day Nick Elliot had died. My fingertips tingled. I patted my trouser pocket and assured myself the keys were there.

"Mrs. Bass, can you knock on my door at five?" I asked. "I have an errand to run in the morning."

NINE

To Sing Winter In

Nick's mailbox held a thin letter from Gold & Key Publishing, but no oversized envelope from his bank. I made it into the hospital mess room in time to grab the last sticky bun and a lidded mug of scorched coffee to take upstairs. Porters wheeled trolleys loaded with patient breakfasts, dodging mail clerks who pushed files between departments. The letter poked my ribs, resting inside my jacket pocket. I'd stolen a dead man's mail—to get justice, I reminded myself.

It would all come out right once Mathy authorized my environmental inspection report and filed it with the police. Still, I wouldn't like to have anyone notice the fiddled timelines, and so hid the letter inside the sticky drawer on the left. The teapot rested on a bookshelf as if it were a curiosity. The ink on the inspection forms had long since dried, so I tucked them into my clipboard before heading downstairs to read logs.

Young and Old Gerald trooped out to the garden after I'd spoken to them. Young Gerald sat beside garden plots and crab-walked on gloved hands and one foot to bury bulbs in black earth. Old Gerald raked leaves, filling loose woven sacks. More of my patients worked with them, tending shrubs and picking apples as if Old Gerald's transformed mood had infected each of them.

Those who had followed for fresh air and sunshine were my most recovered patients, but could I send them home? Thriving in the calm of an institution wasn't the same as facing the stresses of the world. But more were coming. More than would fit in our beds even if we discharged every man here. I retreated to the indoors to lay my eye on those who hadn't recovered as well as the gardeners.

Bill lay in his bed, eyes flaring with hope as I came in.

"Can you mesmerize me?" Bill clasped my hand with both of his. "Can you, Doctor? Please."

A dried-blood-colored cloud whirled furiously in his head. I didn't dare touch it. But I brought out my watch and spoke quietly, a trickle of power enough to help him sleep. He'd wake to the same nightmare, but for now he had rest.

At half past eight I purloined an unburnt cup of coffee from the doctor's lounge, sneaking out before anyone could catch me in conversation. Up three flights to fetch the teapot, down five to reach the basement, and I took a place in the lab to test a potsherd for the burnt iridescent sign of arsenic trioxide. I was doing this rather backwards, but I watched the flame wash over the concave surface with a little pride. Nick Elliot would get his justice.

I turned the flame off and turned the clamped shard expectantly, peering at the soot-black surface.

The test was negative.

I lifted my goggles and turned the shard toward the light. The curved chunk of Nick Elliot's hammer-struck teapot didn't leave so much as a sparkle. No arsenic had ever touched it.

Was I wrong about the poison? The symptoms seemed to fit. In a dirtier, less knowledgeable time, Nick's illness would have passed for cholera. He'd said he was poisoned. "In the tea." Those were his exact words. We weren't any closer than before.

I swept the pot's remains into a bin. I turned my back on the cooling apparatus I had assembled for the test and went to the morgue.

I opened the unlocked door. The clerk looked up with alarm, eyes widening when I asked, "Julia Riggins?"

She nearly popped out of her seat to curtsy. "Can I help you?"

"I'm Dr. Miles Singer." She'd seen the note. She knew who I was.

"Have you come to write me up?" Her voice was small, frightened. I'd put fear in her, fear I would bring her absence to her superior and let consequence rain down on her. I was a cad if I threatened her job to get what I wanted. "I didn't think there would be any harm. The morgue was empty."

"That's what I came to talk to you about," I said. "I was going to do a death examination on one of the bodies gone to the crematorium yesterday. How did it happen that all the bodies were transported?"

"Dr. Matheson came down yesterday, asking about the last full sanitation procedure done," Mrs. Riggins said.

My mouth dried up. Why would she care? She was General Medicine. Enforcing the cleanliness of the morgue wasn't her job. "She told you to send the bodies out?"

"No. She told me to do the sanitation and have the bodies rearranged so they were all in clean drawers." She clasped her trembling hands in front of her. "Only I couldn't find the sanitation manual, so I went to Materials for a copy, and—"

I waited.

She gulped and confessed. "I left the hospital."

"Ah."

"I went to a pasty cart—" She wrung her fingers and looked up, her eyes shiny with mounting tears. "I had to clean the morgue to sanitation standard. I'd skipped breakfast to get my children to school. I knew I'd need something to tide me over. And when I came back—"

"You found the orders already filled out."

She hung her head. "The sign-in clipboard was sitting on my desk. I know I'm supposed to keep the morgue supervised. I didn't mean any harm—"

"I'd have done the same, if it were me. But Dr. Matheson didn't sign the bodies out?"

"She must have changed her mind. I came back and found the order to have them removed."

"Did anyone else come into the morgue during your shift?"

"No. I was alone until I—"

"Until you left early to get your children."

"Please, Doctor." Mrs. Riggins's voice broke. "There were no bodies."

I gave her my handkerchief. "It's not your fault," I said. "You did as you were told, and there didn't seem to be any harm in leaving an empty morgue. You had to tend your children. Your husband's shift overlaps?"

She sobbed. "It's only—one day a week—"

"And it leaves you in an awful spot," I said. I would do my end-of-shift paperwork down here next week. It didn't matter where I did my charting. No one needed to know. "But you didn't see Dr. Matheson fill out the orders."

"She'd come down at ten thirty, and left again right after."

"When did you leave to get a pasty?"

"Eleven o'clock. I was gone for twenty minutes at the most."

"Do you remember what she was wearing?"

"Her doctor's coat." She dabbed tears from her eyes. "A surgeon's bonnet, but she had curl rods in underneath. One of her suits, you know, with the . . . trousers."

So she hadn't been dressed for lunch. "Thank you, Mrs.

Riggins. You've been a great help. If you remember anything else about yesterday, will you ring my office?"

She thanked me when I wrote *"Please Disregard, Matter Settled"* on the page where I'd written my note in the duty log.

I passed the warm, tested potsherd from one hand to the other as I climbed the stairs, pausing on the third floor to knock on Dr. Matheson's door.

"It's open," she called.

I opened the door on a space big enough to fit four of my office. I dropped the bit of warm teapot into my pocket and crossed wide pine planks to set the inspection forms on her desk.

She picked them up, stripping off her glasses to focus on the form's tiny print. "Why do you need to do an environmental inspection?"

"One of my patients—"

"Are you investigating a patient discharge condition?" She tucked the glasses into the breast pocket of her white coat and stood. "Come along, I was about to check on the nurses. Which patient's home do you need to check?"

I opened the door for her, and stood by while she locked it. "Nick Elliot. He died in Urgent Care, night before last."

"What did the death examination show?" She took brisk strides to the stairwell, heels clicking on the floorboards.

I hurried to catch up. "The body was ordered cremated yesterday. He was gone by the time I arrived to examine him."

She glanced at me, her eyes narrowed. "So. You're chasing clouds."

She took the inside, her left hand on the banister, descending in quick echoing steps.

"Nick Elliot told me he'd been poisoned," I said. "His symptoms put me in mind of arsenic."

"He must have vomited. Test the clothes?"

"Incinerated by the morgue staff."

"So you have nothing but his declaration." She handed me the forms. "I can't approve this."

What? "Dr. Matheson?"

"You care too much, Miles. I don't mean you're soft. You're thorough, conscientious, and compassionate. It makes you my best in psychiatry. But you haven't chosen who to discharge, and I need those beds free for next week."

"That's why you—"

"I need sixteen empty beds in two days. I don't need you chasing a penny-book mystery. Rule the death a suspected homicide and move on."

Suspected homicide with no report from the doctor who examined the body? The police wouldn't lift a finger. I could do something. I was the only one who could do so officially.

Did it matter that I didn't have an official reason? I had to know what had been done to him, and why. There was no one but me and Mr. Hunter to fight for him. Damn it, why wouldn't she sign?

Unless Tristan was right and I was wrong.

"Dr. Matheson, the order to have the bodies removed for cremation was initialed E.M.," I said. "Was it you?"

Her eyes widened. "Dr. Singer. Did you just—"

"Miles! Oh, what luck."

Grace stood in the midst of the lobby crowd, carrying a straw lunch basket. The lid was ajar, the necks of a pair of wine bottles poking out one side.

"Grace, what are you doing here?"

"I thought we'd have lunch," she said. A basket lunch, like she always wanted as a child, with a cloth spread out even if we only ate in the playroom. Did she remember those times too? She offered her hand to Mathy. "Dr. Matheson, how do you do?"

Dr. Matheson stood up straight. "How do you do. Thank you for your impressive donation to Beauregard Veterans'."

"It's a worthy cause," my sister said. "I'm afraid you caught me, Doctor. I was coming to entice my oldest friend into sharing lunch with me. We didn't have nearly enough time to catch up yesterday."

First she showed up to my house, and now she was here with a picnic basket. "I have afternoon rounds, Grace, I can't while away the day over a bottle of wine."

Dr. Matheson patted my arm. "I'll reassign your rounds, Miles, not to worry. Enjoy lunch with your friend, and then work on choosing your sixteen. If you need a tiebreaker, just knock."

She swept off toward the nurses' changing rooms, her disapproval of my tardy work no longer an issue. Grace lifted the basket again, a trace of the girl in her contrite smile.

"It's not skiving off work if you have permission."

Her donation might as well have been a bill of sale. The whole hospital would bow to their most generous benefactor. But I knew my responsibility. "I have a mountain of paperwork to do. I shouldn't miss my rounds."

"Just for today, Miles. Show me your office."

"It's minuscule."

"It's a good view," I grumbled. "Why doesn't anyone notice the view?"

"Because they're trying not to bark their knees on— everything." Grace sidled through the narrow space between my filing cabinet and the corner of my desk.

"I don't see patients in my office." I cleared my desk of pens, inkwells, and wipers, and dropped the stack of reports I needed to file on the windowsill. "I don't usually have visitors, either."

She looked down. "I needed to see you."

"You saw me yesterday. Twice." I'd gone to the wash-house this morning, stepping over the fragments of her ill-fated tea-cup. Something was coming for Grace. Something bad. "Why do you need to see me?"

She touched my face. I tensed, but didn't flinch away. "You almost don't feel real, Miles. I thought you were dead, your bones rotting in the bloody earth of Laneer."

"I should have died there," I said. "So many did, but not me."

"So don't you see? I needed to see you. Alive. Safe, and living as you deserve."

Which wasn't living in a single room and working as Beauregard Veterans' most insignificant doctor. "I'm content where I am."

She rolled her eyes. "Let's not fight, Miles. I'm sorry I disrupted your day. Next time we'll go to a dining room."

And be seen together in public? "We can't go to a dining room."

"A tavern, then. The one you liked. The Roebuck."

I choked. "Grace, the Roebuck's a . . . a men's establishment."

"I know, Miles. I'm not a child." Grace opened the first wine bottle. She unstrapped porcelain soup bowls and silverware from the basket's lid, and dished out crab chowder from a heated steel pot.

"Crab chowder."

"You don't like it?"

"I had better like it," I said. "It's on the menu at home three times a week. I'm surprised you do."

"I have eaten in a tavern before. I'm not completely sheltered."

"Why are you doing this?" I asked. "Someone will notice."

Grace smirked. "Everyone thinks you're a schooldays flame. I didn't disabuse anyone."

"But you're getting married."

Grace broke open a bun. Steam escaped as she buttered it; then she handed it to me. "And your absence at the wedding will only make people more certain you're a dear friend. Everything's fine, Miles. Eat your soup."

The chowder was delicate with wine in the broth, more finely herbed than I was used to. "So you donated a hill of money to the hospital."

"I should have offered more. You really don't have a lift?"

"We really don't."

"The least I could do for them. A parting gift."

I put my spoon down. "A what?"

"I know what to do." Grace leaned over her bowl, elbows firmly on the desk. "Your own practice."

"No."

"Hear me out. You can have privileges at every hospital in the city—"

"I wouldn't need privileges unless I was doing surgery—"

"You can," she said. "You'd never have to worry about being discovered."

Oh, of course. I leaned back. "Because my patients would be from the Hundred Families. An exclusive clientele, getting their maladies treated with magic."

"Exactly."

"No, Grace."

"But isn't that why you left?" she asked. "You wanted to be a healer when everyone said Secondaries only did stupid tricks. You've proven them all wrong. You come home—"

"And consent to be bound to you."

"You'll get to practice medicine! You'll show the other Secondaries how they can use their own abilities in useful ways too. You can inspire them!"

"Why? So they can be even more useful to the people they belong to?"

Grace scowled. "Nobody thinks like that."

"Father thinks like that."

"Our generation doesn't," she said. "We could change the culture, Miles. We could make it better. You must know I wouldn't compel you, or make you defer to me, or all the awful things Storm-Singers expect of Secondaries."

"So we would be leading by example."

"Yes! Exactly. We would lead the new way."

"I'd have to give up my life here. My work."

Grace looked all around my office. "There's so much here to hold you, I see."

"They need me, Grace."

She turned her attention on me, the cords of her throat straining to hold back the full gale of her emotion. "I need you, Miles. I mourned you. I couldn't stop dreaming you were a ghost, and you were alive this whole time. When I needed you."

"Me, or my obedience?"

"My brother. Our family. I know you never saw eye to eye with Father, but you have leverage now."

I dragged my face back into a neutral expression, smoothing the surprised furrow of my brow. "I'm a department doctor in a veterans' hospital with humble wages. Not leverage worth even mentioning."

"You raised at least five thousand in donations yesterday," she pointed out.

I let my eyes narrow. She cast a red herring in my path to keep me arguing about whether I had leverage or not. "Grace. What are you hiding from me?"

She sipped her wine. "I was going to wait to tell you."

"After I'd accepted your renovation of my life? After I'd been properly buttered up? After I had another taste of the good life I left behind? Leverage, Grace. Against our father. That means power."

Grace turned her face toward the window.

Nobody had power over my father. He was the head mage of the Queen's Invisibles. He was the royal Chancellor. He answered to Queen Constantina and Crown Prince Severin, and even that was debatable.

"I don't have power over my father, unless I have something he needs." I looked at my hands. "He's sick, isn't he."

She kept her face turned away. "I'm sorry. Maybe I should have told you right away."

A ribbon of pain unfurled in my chest. Foolish. I knew better. "So he doesn't need me; he needs my talent. And you were going to buy it for him."

"He needs you, Miles. He misses you. When he received the cable reporting you missing, he was a force of nature."

"He's still on the Security Council, is he? Or has his illness made him slow down?" Fury burned in my chest, and pain too. This was the price for regaining my sister: looking away from the cage she held in her hand.

"Some days, he has to work from bed," Grace said. "Other days, he can bear a carriage ride. He can't Call, and we have a major Work at Frostnight."

"How long has he been sick?"

"A year." She dropped her shoulders. "It grew worse three weeks ago."

"You need to sing in winter?" I asked.

"It's a storm year, Miles. We have to manage it carefully. I've never sung winter in, and it's a storm year, and Father is so sick."

A storm year. It made my stomach clench.

Aeland's weather was calm. Not too warm in summer. Cold but bearable in winter. Rain fell, but gently, and snow stayed long enough to be pretty before it melted in mild weather. But the common Aelander didn't know their ideal climate was a continuous act of magic.

Whirling cyclonic winds would devastate all but the sturdiest buildings. Incredible tantrums of rain and lightning would flood Aeland's densely populated coasts and fertile river valleys if not for the Invisibles, who kept the weather pacified. Every year was hard work. But storm years were vicious, and demanded everything the Queen's secret mages had.

"He did it last year?"

"Yes."

"What are the symptoms?" I wished I could take it back.

"Chest pain, weakness, trouble breathing," Grace said. "Sometimes rest eases it. On bad days, nothing does."

Could be anything, but it was nothing good. "And you're not married, and you haven't bonded anyone."

Grace closed her eyes. I knew what she saw, then.

"If he dies too soon, will you become the Voice of the Invisibles?"

The breath hissed out of her. She slumped in my folding guest chair. "I won't have enough support."

"Who does?"

"Sir Percy Stanley."

The delicate chowder turned to cement in my stomach. The antiwar polemicists had called the Laneeri War Sir Percy's War, and as the Minister of Defense that accusation wasn't far off. If Stanley hadn't wanted the war, it wouldn't have happened.

I couldn't see Grace with a poison vial, but I could see Sir Percy giving an order to be carried out.

I reached across the desk. Grace seized my hand, twining her fingers through mine, and we sat beside cooling bowls of chowder. Shattered bits of teacup preyed on my mind. If I knew, could I prevent it? Did her fate in the tea leaves mean she'd lose her place?

If Sir Percy became the Voice, none of the reforms my sister believed in would come to pass. Stanley used his firstborn son as a slave, a battery to enhance his storm-singing power. I had no doubt the marriage he had arranged for his son was an attempt to breed the proper talents back into the Stanley line.

I liked Darcy. Friends I'd left behind depended on Grace's rule. I wouldn't leash myself to her cause, even if it was noble. But once Father died, she was out of time.

I could give her time.

"I'll examine Father, but I have conditions," I said.

"Tell me what you need, and I'll arrange it."

"It's rather a list of demands."

"I'll arrange it," Grace said.

Once she heard them she argued, but in the end I had my way.

"Keep the other bottle." Grace closed the lid of the picnic basket on our dirty dishes. "I'll see to everything you need."

I helped her into her coat and walked her down all the stairs to the lobby, mindful of the courtesy one was privileged to give a lady. Patients gazed at her, but her silver fox coat and the height of her fashion kept them from calling to her or trying to catch her eye. Everyone except Bill Pike, who'd left his bed to say goodbye to his wife and child. He stared at Grace with a burning anger lighting his face, his fists clenched, his lips moving as he muttered something under his breath.

As we neared the doors, they opened. Mr. Hunter stepped inside and smiled as he caught sight of me. "Miles."

He held the door open for Mrs. Pike and her daughter, smiling a greeting. Bill stared at Tristan with fear-bright eyes, his mouth agape. He stumbled in his haste to get away.

"What—?" I should go to him. Talk to him. But Bill fled in scuffling haste, and Grace would take my abandonment of her amiss. I settled back into my place between my sister and Tristan, who regarded each other with narrow-eyed dislike.

"Miles, who is this?"

I winced. "Grace, this is my . . . friend, Mr. Tristan Hunter." Her hand tightened on the crook of my elbow and I blundered on. "Mr. Hunter, this is Dame Grace Hensley, Her Majesty's Royal Knight."

Tristan swept off his hat and bowed. "How do you do?" The gesture was perfectly correct, but it was no gesture of courtesy.

Grace stood with her feet and shoulders squared up to face him. She bristled with hostility. What on Earth—?

Of course. She could see Tristan's veiling magic.

"Grace," I said, gently. "Mr. Hunter is my friend."

She continued staring at him. "Indeed."

"Grace." I flexed my bicep under her grip. "People are noticing."

She turned her chin away, remembering herself. "Excuse me. I should go."

She kissed my cheek, marking me with her pool-of-blood lipstick. She gave Tristan one more searching, hostile look and marched out of the hospital.

Tristan watched her leave, staring at the door as it closed.

I cleared my throat. "What are you doing here? I wasn't expecting you until later."

He looked back at me, his attention riveted to the lip print on my cheek. "I have interrupted you with your—"

I moved in close and kept my voice low. "My sister. It's a secret."

"Your . . . oh." Tristan fiddled with the brim of his hat. "I was going to tell you my coachman Michael had an emergency, so we won't have the carriage."

"Do you have a bicycle?"

He nodded. "I bought it on the way here. But I have an appointment, so I'll be late."

"Conveniently, I will also be late. Please collect me when you're ready."

"I will." He stood up straight, back to the tall and easy posture he had lost when Grace kissed me. A little flame leapt in my chest at the notion that Tristan had twinged at it.

That made me a fool. "Do you have a lead on Nick?"

"I've found a woman claiming to be a medium. She doesn't receive clients until three."

I cocked my head. "Something to do with your quest?"

He smiled at the old-fashioned word. "Yes."

"I hope you meet with success."

"Thank you." He paused a moment, searching for something to say. "I look forward to dinner."

He inclined his head, blue eyes locked on me, then turned and left the hospital.

I did my rounds an hour late, and at the end of my shift I had the haunting task of choosing sixteen men to send home. Young and Old Gerald would go, so I wrote their names on a list titled Discharge. Bill went on the list marked Retain. The list of names on the Retain list grew faster than the Discharge lists.

I added a fifth name to the Discharge list, spreading ink along my knuckle. I wasn't going to get this finished today. Grace wasn't going to arrange my trip to heal Father without him knowing in a single day, either. The letter I'd retrieved from Nick Elliot's mail sat unopened on my desk, waiting for Tristan to arrive. I was more nervous about his arrival than I should have been, than I should have allowed myself to be. I knew what he was, and he wasn't safe.

A knock sounded at my door, and Robin's silhouette stood framed in my door's frosted glass.

"Come in, Robin."

"Miles, I heard your boyhood friend donated five thousand dollars to the hospital." She shut the door and leaned on it. "Enough money to refit two more operating rooms and all the staff to use them."

"Funny, I heard it was enough money to replace every bed in General Medicine with new, and pay five more nurses for three years."

The gap between her teeth showed. "Your sources are biased."

I set my pen down. "I want to ask you something."

She sat on the corner of my desk and took out her pouch to roll a gasper. "Go ahead."

I eyed the tobacco with longing. "Have you heard anything about the morgue needing to be sanitized or an emergency that meant we had to transport all the bodies for cremation?"

Robin cocked her head. "I haven't heard anything about an emergency."

I leaned back in my chair and bit my knuckle. "Let me have one of those."

"Forget it," Robin said. "Only on bad days."

Robin was a tyrant, but I hated to think of wasting all her effort to help me quit. "I think someone deliberately destroyed Nick Elliot's body so I couldn't examine it. Bad enough?"

"No." She licked the glue on her paper and sealed a perfectly rolled cylinder. I couldn't do better, even with my surgeon's hands. "Why would anyone do that?"

"To keep me from determining his cause of death as murder."

"Murder. He was poisoned?"

"I don't know. I never did the examination."

"He said he'd been murdered." Robin looked up at the ceiling. "But his declaration's the only reason to suspect anything."

And what I'd seen when I touched him, but I couldn't tell Robin about that. "But then his body's gone before I can find out what killed him."

"Tell the police?"

"No body, no murder."

Robin's mouth pinched up. "Miles. Leave it alone."

"Why should I?"

"Because if you're right, and it was murder, and someone disposed of his body . . . why wouldn't they dispose of you, too?"

Another shadow fell on my office door. Robin left her tobacco on the desk to open it.

"Mr. Hunter." She bowed.

"Miss Thorpe." Tristan bowed in return. "How are you?"

"I'm well, thank you. Have you come to inquire about Nick Elliot?"

"I am curious, I admit, but I've come on another matter."

I cleared my throat. "Mr. Hunter has . . . he's asked me to dinner."

Robin's eyebrows rose. "Really." She turned back to Tristan and stared him down.

"I promise to have him home by ten."

She smirked. "See that you do, Mr. Hunter."

She retrieved her tobacco pouch and stood expectantly before Tristan, who backed out of the doorway to let her through.

He shut the door behind him. "She'll gut me if I hurt you," he said with a grin. "She didn't even need to say it. You inspire a true friendship, Miles."

"She's never met anyone who claims to call on me."

"I question the taste of every man and woman in this city."

My face grew hot. "How fares your investigation?"

Tristan made a face. "The medium was a fraud, I regret to say."

"I'm sorry."

He leaned against my desk and sighed. "At the rate I'm going, I'll unmask every mountebank in Kingston trying to find out why you're all still alive."

I blinked. "What?"

"What's this?" He picked up the letter to Nick Elliot. "You haven't opened it."

"I was waiting for you. What do you mean, why we're all still alive?"

"I can't believe you didn't open it. You probably never went looking for New Year presents."

Not without Grace to lead the way. "I have willpower."

He laughed, softly. "I know." Tristan turned the envelope over in his hands. "Good quality paper. Popular publisher?"

I gestured at the penny novels on my shelves. "Those are all Gold and Key editions."

"And this is . . ." He took up my letter opener and slit the envelope. "Oh. Expensive envelope, cheap paper."

I sniffed the air. "Barrel printed." But handwritten too; ink bled through the thin paper on bold strokes and dots.

"Curious." Tristan unfolded the letter. His eyebrows went up as he read the letter aloud:

"*Dear Sir: Thank you for your recent submission to Gold & Key, but your manuscript does not fulfill a need of this publisher. Good luck placing it elsewhere.*"

"Ouch. A form letter."

He moved the paper, inviting me to look. I leaned over his shoulder. Underneath the violet-black ink, in tidy blue script:

Nick: If your editor doesn't want this, I don't want it either.

The note was signed L.R.

"Too personal a postscript for a stranger," Tristan noted.

"Doesn't want what?" I asked. "Not a novel, if L.R. is talking about Nick's editor at the newspaper not wanting it."

"Whatever it was, I think we had better go to the paper and ask." Tristan tucked the letter back into the envelope. "Are you ready?"

"Mr. Hunter."

He turned to face me, even though we barely had a handsbreadth of space between us. "Someday you'll call me Tristan."

I swallowed. So close I could feel the energy radiating from him, the tension as he waited for my word. "I want you to teach me how to disguise my power."

"I shall. What else do you want to learn?"

"I can't see the power on anyone else unless I'm touching their skin."

"An excellent first lesson. Hold still." He reached toward my face. "You have an eyelash. . . ."

I stilled. Smooth fingers brushed my cheek, and a short, curved hair rested on the ridges of his index finger. "Did you wish on these, as children?"

My skin held the feeling of his finger, and its gentle ghost lingered, touching me again. I found my voice, but it was hoarse. "We did."

He held his hand closer to my mouth. "Don't tell me what it is."

"What if I don't know what to wish for?"

He smiled. "A problem we never had as children. Be selfish with your wish, Miles. Blow."

He had once been a child. I tucked the thought away, and blew. My wish had no words, but it smelled of fennel. The eyelash puffed away and fell out of sight.

"Well done." Tristan made a loop of my scarf and draped it around my neck. I stood still for his attentions, because I was foolish. Reckless.

I stepped back and buttoned my coat. "For making a wish?"

"For being selfish with it."

Heat prickled my skin.

He pulled out his gloves, adjusted his hat. "We'll begin training after supper."

TEN

W. 1703 Halston Street

We passed through the hospital lobby and I had a feeling of being watched—the one that used to make me duck behind cover when I emerged from the surgery tent to have a smoke. Coming from . . . there.

Tristan touched my shoulder. "Miles?"

"That man, with the paper." I took in every detail of his appearance, starting with his brand-new hat, his tidily waxed mustache, and ending at the cuffed legs of his trousers. Every stitch and crease said *money*. Too much money to be loitering in a veterans' hospital.

"What about him?"

"Nothing," I said. "Let's go."

The stranger walked out of the hospital with the paper tucked under his arm as I unchained my bicycle. He turned a corner and disappeared from sight as I pulled the chain loose.

"That was the man?"

"Yes," I said. "It's nothing."

"Maybe," Tristan moved a little way up the fence and unchained a bicycle that had all the little touches that made it a rich man's ride—handpainted scrollwork on the tubes and fenders, a fully enclosed chain case, a handsome double-sprung leather saddle and wheel locks—and waited for me to lead us into the street.

Afternoon bicycle traffic in Kingston was hair-raising to anyone who wasn't used to it. You join a draft of cyclists, and move up in the draft line until you're the leader. There are subtle signs, etiquette, and customs to joining a draft we never think about until someone comes along to mess it up. Tristan fell in behind me, calling, "Halston and West Seventeenth."

A fine neighborhood—lined with tall, narrow townhouses and their tiny gardens—with an apple tree at its center. I rang twice, called out "New fish" to the draft I joined, and some of the riders ahead waved to acknowledge the recent two-wheeled convert.

We'd fallen into a clump of men in sack suits and shiny shoes, probably clerks or managers. Tristan pedaled beside me, grinning. "Completely refreshing," he said. "What an advantage, the bicycle."

"Going to sack Michael, are you?"

"It's only a few more days." He glanced behind him, and glanced again. "Don't look."

I fought the urge to echo his gesture. "What?"

"The man from the hospital is behind us."

I glanced at my handlebar mirrors, but there were women riding just behind us. "He could be minding his business. Let's take the next right."

We broke out of our draft and turned southward, and this time my mirror captured him—at a casual distance, but he'd turned our way.

"Left on that alley," I said, and we had to veer sharply to make it. The cobblestones rattled my bones as we pedaled through the stink of restaurant refuse and grease barrels, dodging parked wagons and horse droppings.

Tristan sped ahead and turned left, spilling us back onto smooth blacktop. The man with the mustache pedaled harder, pursuing us.

Adrenaline surged through my limbs. I pedaled harder. "Left," I called, but where Tristan darted through a gap between drafts and made the turn back onto Wakefield Street, I dodged right, nearly cutting off a slow-moving draft.

They shouted at me. "Scofflaw! Freerider!" One even identified me as an organ of elimination, but I watched my mirror. Left or right? Which one of us did he want?

He turned right. Me, then. In spite of it all, I grinned. If he wanted me, he'd have to catch me.

I cut across drafts and drove into the intersection before twisting my bike in a hard turn, straight up a short, steep hill. Climb that, blackguard. Let's see how you do. I stood on my pedals and muscled it out, but he was in better shape than I supposed and soon I was speeding along a street heavy with foot traffic crisscrossing from shop to shop in pursuit of the day's errands. I rang my bell, shouted warnings, and dodged alarmed customers who shook their fists at me, then squawked in outrage when my pursuer came flying after.

I raised one hand in a universal sign of insult and startled a carriage horse when I ducked into another cobbled alley. He'd tire. His blood was up, chasing me like this. A cooler head would have let me go on my way.

Everything was sharp and clear. I rode under clothing drying on a line strung between the alley's buildings, trouser legs bannering gently in the wind at my back. A cat saw me coming and dashed for safety. I popped out onto the street, legs churning, and my pursuer came barreling after, his mustache a dark curl in his exercise-reddened face.

I turned a corner and Tristan rode toward me, past me, intent on my pursuer. My blood sang as I leaned into a looping turn to join Tristan's pursuit. There were two of us against him, and we became the hunters as he fled Tristan's grim face, racing along the smooth black road to get away from us.

But he didn't ride five miles uphill from work, or climb up and down stairs every day. We gained on him. He tried to lose us with sudden turns and tricky maneuvers until we came to the King's Way, the train-crossing bars lowering across the street.

A train was coming. We had him, and I was going to ask him more than a few questions.

But he pedaled harder, straight for the tracks. We were close enough that the exposed copper cable strung above the tracks whined against my ears, and the train's warning horn sounded with an awful howl as the rider drove over the tracks, directly into the train's path.

The rails screamed as the engine man tried to brake, but a passenger train needs four times its length to come to an emergency stop. Cyclists waiting at the lowered barrier shouted, some of them averting their eyes—

And our quarry scooted across the tracks, shot out like a bar of soap from a wet fist.

The train rolled to a stop as the man with the mustache got away.

Tristan leaned over his handlebars, breathing hard, but he caught my eye and grinned. "That was fun."

Tristan was a madman. But so was I, for the bubbling feeling in my chest made me want to laugh. Our pursuer had escaped, but we'd turned the tables on him, and damned well.

"Did you get a good look at him?" I dropped my voice to a hush. "Was he a witch?"

"I did, and yes. He's a witch." Tristan appraised me. "Follow me home. Eat until you're ready to burst. We're going to work hard."

Tristan's townhouse was a house of mirrors. Instead of art and photographs, mirrors hung on the walls, framed in gilt and rosewood and pale, hand-rubbed birch. The mirror next to Tristan's umbrella stand stood inches above my own six feet, the frame carved in a garland of ribbon and woodland creatures peeking from behind lobed oak leaves. Identical silver-framed mirrors flanked a narrow corridor leading to the kitchen where Tristan prepared a meal with his own hands.

I was still energized from our adventure, but excitement was turning into jittery nerves. That man had been waiting for me. Had followed us, and while we'd turned the hunter into prey, the meaning sank under my skin and shivered: Nick's murderer knew I was involved.

I turned my sherry glass with fidgety fingers and watched Tristan work in shirtsleeves. He could cook, handling knife and pot with speed and grace.

"You seem surprised."

"I thought that Amaranthines didn't—"

He laughed. "Didn't eat?"

"Didn't cook."

"What, that we conjured ambrosia from magic?"

I shrugged, embarrassed.

He sliced, sautéed, and served us slabs of beefsteak and a motley of greenhouse-grown vegetables with browned mushrooms.

"More where that came from." He urged me to have more. "It's fuel; you'll need it."

I ate until black spots swam in front of my eyes, and then he led me to the parlor. I stood in the doorway to take it all in. None of the furniture pieces matched, but they were all tufted, stuffed, and dripping with pillows in bright fabrics and bold embroidery. It was a cross between a jumble shop, a lady's boudoir, and a gentleman's retiring room. All it needed was a cat.

"You haven't said anything."

"I'm speechless."

"Oh, do try." Tristan sprawled over a deerskin-covered chaise.

"It looks comfortable." It did. This was a room to relax in, to smoke and talk long into the night. It was a room for close friends and intimates, not company. Comfortable.

"My home isn't what you expected."

"You're not what I expected. I mean. The Amaranthines are figures of awe and terror, and you're . . ."

"Do you have any idea how much work it is to be majestic? The high court is exhausting. I escape it whenever I can."

"What's the high court like?"

He covered his eyes. "Polite. Mannerly. Dangerous and beautiful. Everyone has a ladder on their back."

"Sounds like Lucus's court, before the Hundred Families stood against him and raised Queen Agnes." I took two strides to a deep armchair and sank inside it. My elbow bumped a mouth-blown glass water pipe, and I leaned over to sniff it.

"Hashish," Tristan said.

"If it had been opium it would have meant a lecture."

"I'm a good boy, Doctor. Amusement, not ruin." He sat up and patted the place next to him. "Come sit. I want to know something."

I sat next to him, keeping space between our thighs. "What do you want to know?"

"Why do you persecute poor witches? Why do you say they'll go mad?"

I blinked. "They do. They all do."

"But your people, the aristocrats—they don't?"

"No. Well. They're just as prone to melancholy or over-excitement as anyone else, but witches are different."

"They're not," Tristan said. "The difference is wealth and power. You have it; they don't."

I shook my head. "Witches aren't like mages."

"Such snobbery, Miles. Where's your evidence?"

"But they do go mad. There're cases. Loads of them."

"Have you ever met a witch?"

"I saw one, once. She'd been confirmed at trial. She was at Kingston Asylum awaiting transport." She'd been bound so she couldn't hurt herself, but she was beyond protest, beyond tears, sunk deep into herself to escape what was happening to her.

When she saw me she screamed, her face ugly with rage. She'd known. She could see it on me. She hated me, for being free where she was bound.

I didn't blame her.

"Only one." Tristan broke my reverie. "And one mad witch is proof?"

The question stung. "But if they don't go mad, why do we commit them?"

"Why, indeed."

What he was implying couldn't be true. There had to be a difference. Why else would they be sent away? "Are you saying it's a lie? That they're . . . put out of the way?"

"Have you ever researched the hearings?"

I shrugged. "Seen articles in the paper."

"I've attended hearings and read transcripts. Do you know the most common proof of a witch's madness?"

"Delusions."

"Specifically, a delusion that moves them to accuse others of being witches. They usually name people from the highest levels of society: Royal Knights."

My dinner was a lump in my belly. "But that's . . ."

"True," Tristan finished. "I'm sorry, Miles. I thought you knew this, as a psychiatrist."

"We have specialties." How many witches went to asylums? How many had gone to the gallows before the enlightenment convinced the people witches were not evil, but simply mad? How many had been plowed under so we of the Hundred Families could stride about, free and rich and powerful? It made a lump in my throat. It made bile sneak up and taint the back of my tongue. A bolt of hatred lanced through me. I hated them; I hated myself.

"Miles. Your people, the mages. Why do you enslave each other?"

"There's only one kind of mage that matters: Storm-Singers."

"And you're not a Storm-Singer, so you don't matter?"

"Those who can't control the weather are bound so Storm-Singers can draw on their Secondary's power as if they were walking batteries."

"Why?"

"Power," I said. "The group rituals take every last shred of power from every mage involved. If someone figured out how to bind two Secondaries at once and draw on both without killing one first, they'd do it. Storm-singing is that important."

"So your people would see you as denying your power to their purpose?"

"Yes. I'd be put under extreme control because I deserted."

Tristan put out his hand, but drew it back before touching me. "Do you want to go home?"

"No." I didn't want to be alone with this. I didn't want to have to lie in my lumpy bed and feel this sick anger. I needed to put it away, think about it later. "Teach me something."

"First you must learn to see without touching. It's a block in the psyche, but it isn't hard to fix."

The matter was dropped. A rush of gratitude warmed me up. "What do I do?"

"Pick a mirror," he said. "One where you can see yourself and me. Watch the reflection; let your mind wander. You need a certain state of consciousness for this to work."

"Which?"

"Look in the mirror," Tristan said.

I settled in and chose the mirror with the simplest frame. "Now what?"

"Keep looking until you're ready to cry with boredom."

"And then what?"

"Keep looking."

I looked for hours. Tristan read a book. I fidgeted, fought to stay still, dragged my wandering mind on track, and finally sighed. "This isn't working."

"Are you thinking too much?"

"Probably."

"What do you think about?"

I'd spent the past minute mooning after his straight nose and the studious way he read. It would be satisfying, to lounge in this room over books and brandy, talking or reading, or . . .

I couldn't say any of that. "I have to learn how to do this. It'll help my patients; it'll keep me safe. So much depends on it."

"Thinking too much." Tristan reached out. "Touch my hand."

I kept my gaze on his reflection. It shimmered, and I sat up. When Tristan let go of my hand the distortion disappeared. I sank back into the cushions. "I'll never get this."

Tristan took my hand. Calluses across his palm rubbed against my skin. I stared hard at the shimmering effect of his mortal guise, willing it to remain when Tristan let go.

It didn't.

"Let's do something else," I said. "Distract me with talk."

"What should I talk about?"

"Tell me why you're here. How long have you been here?"

"Nearly a year. I'm here to solve a mystery," Tristan said.

"You don't mean Nick Elliot."

"No. I was sent here to find out why you'd all died."

I turned my head. "What do you mean?"

Tristan stroked little circles on the back of my hand. "Keep looking in the mirror. What do you see?"

"I see you, but there's a wavering look to it. What do you mean? We're alive."

"You are. There are millions of you Aelanders. But your souls don't come to the Solace. You haven't for years."

"Why? Where do they go instead?"

Tristan shrugged. "If I knew, I'd be on my way home. What do you see when you heal?"

"I see anatomy," I said. "I watch your heart beating, your lungs swelling with air, the pulse of blood. If you have a bullet in your chest, I can see the bullet, and the disrupted flesh of the bullet's path."

"I didn't know how it worked." Tristan's reflection wavered, as if I saw him though water falling down a window.

"Why did you come here now?"

"Hm?" Tristan cocked his head. "To Kingston?"

"You said you thought we were all dead for years. Why now?"

"Magic started to flicker out elsewhere in the realm. We sent someone there to see why. Sending me to a dead land was . . . an afterthought."

"So they sent you on a useless quest?"

Tristan's reflection looked away. "Any quest would have sufficed, so long as it meant I wasn't at court. What do you do with the bullet?"

I blinked. "What?"

"I was asking you about your technique. Do you take the bullet out with surgery?"

He'd changed the subject. "Yes."

"I thought you willed the body to heal. I didn't know it was so detailed."

"Maybe that's how you Amaranthines do it. Once the bullet's out, I can make the flesh knit back together again. Or I should say I can give it a push. Then I'm dizzy and the world is turning black on the edges."

"Because you reach the limit of your power," Tristan said. "Did you take out bullets?"

"Bullet wounds were the least of it. Grenades, mines—those were my downfall."

"You couldn't heal them?"

My laugh was bitter. "Oh no, I could. I caught the worst injuries. Those closest to dying, the lost causes. I saved them. A lot of them."

I'd worked miracles.

"You're powerful. And you found a way to teach yourself." Tristan said. "Can you see old wounds on me?"

I sat up again.

"There. You had a wound. The right side of your chest. It pierced your lung, hit the scapula—what happened?"

"I got in the way of an arrow."

The scarring took a straight path. A bullet could have tumbled inside to tear through more flesh after bouncing off his shoulder blade. "Amazing. How did it happen?"

"It was an assassination attempt."

I blinked. "Someone tried to assassinate you?"

Tristan laughed. "Not me. I'm—I was one of the heir's personal guard. I stepped between her and an arrow when she was a child."

"That's brave."

He shrugged. "Simply my duty."

"So if you're the heir's bodyguard, what are you doing here?"

"Did you notice we're not touching anymore?"

We weren't. He sat with his hands on his thighs. I gazed at his reflection, at his beating heart and the story of his life, told on skin and bones.

"You broke your wrist."

"Took a bad fall learning the sword."

"I can see it."

Tristan took my hand again. "You did it."

He was his true self, and my breath caught. He radiated power, stronger than I'd ever felt from a single person, Storm-Singer or Secondary. The edges of it fuzzed over my skin, and I leaned toward him, iron drawn to a lodestone.

He put his other hand between us. "Wait."

I let go of his hand and covered my eyes.

"You can look." He was back to human, with a human's imperfection and regret in his eyes. "I'm sorry. I wasn't thinking."

"It's all right." I stood up. "I should get home. It's probably close to . . . damn."

My watch ticked a quarter to ten.

"Too late?"

"It's fine. I can go back to the hospital. I've slept there before."

"Or you could stay here," he said. "There's an extra bedroom."

"I can steal a cot in one of the recovery rooms."

"It's softer than a cot. Plenty of blankets, plump pillows, hot breakfast in the morning. We're near enough to the same size. You can borrow one of my shirts, and the guest bath is fully stocked."

"I keep early hours." Five thirty in the morning wasn't a gentleman's hour. He likely didn't rise until nine.

"I'll survive." He led me up the stairs.

The deep shearling carpet in Tristan's guest bedroom was new. The scent of wallpaper glue still lingered in the long chamber. It shared the same mismatched, magpie style as the room below: the wardrobes flanking the wide bed didn't match; the overstuffed chairs paired around a tiny tea-table were brothers, not twins. An open door revealed a private bath, the cold stone tiles patched by thick cotton mats.

"Will it suit?"

Tristan stood in the doorway, a neatly folded shirt in his hands. I blinked at the distortion over his features. I could see it now, touching him or not.

"I like it." I did. It defied taste, embracing comfort instead. This room invited you to burrow under the down-filled quilt and rest a little longer, to stay up and read a few more pages before sleeping between smooth cotton sheets.

"No one has ever used it," Tristan said. "You're my first guest."

"Thank you for letting me stay."

He held the shirt out. "You could stay here, you know. Until I have to leave."

"As your guest?"

"I can't ask you to give up your work for learning magic and catching murderers. You're a healer. You'd never do it."

"You're right."

He stepped closer. "We need every minute you can spare, Miles. It's a good solution."

I took the folded shirt from his hands. "It's sensible."

"Practical."

He lived closer to the hospital. The room was comfortable. We'd spend our evenings in each other's company in privacy. For the sake of learning, for the investigation.

Tristan stepped closer. "Say you will."

"I keep early hours. I should be in bed right now." I grimaced. "Asleep."

He didn't stop his amused smile. "Very well, Miles. Mrs. Sparrow will wake you. I'll see you in the morning."

"I need to be at the hospital by six thirty."

"I'll leave a note for Mrs. Sparrow," Tristan said. "Sleep on my offer. Have pleasant dreams."

The mattress cradled me. The blankets were warm and heavy. But the front door opening roused me minutes before my own door opened and a plump woman entered, bowing her head as she saw I was awake.

"Good morning. Mrs. Sparrow, I presume." I rubbed at my eyes, but the inflammation around her knuckles showed plainly, refusing to go away.

"And you're Mr. Hunter's guest. Do you drink coffee, tea, or chocolate?"

Chocolate? I hadn't had any since I was a boy. Grace drank chocolate, served to cheer her up or as a treat for academic achievements. "Coffee, please. I'm Miles Singer."

"I'll put the burper on, Dr. Singer."

"How did you know I'm a doctor?"

She gestured toward the tiny writing desk. "A doctor's bag, isn't it, embossed with balm leaves?"

"It is. Most observant."

She shrugged. "I don't mean to pry in your business, Doctor. I can't help what I notice. I'll put on breakfast."

She closed the door. I made use of the bathing chamber, unwrapping a new razor from its paper. Joint pain. She suffered from joint pain, and I could see it whether I willed it or not. Perhaps it would subside, the way the feeling of carrying Nick's power had faded. I was in for an interesting day.

The water from the taps was hot, the cake of shaving soap undented, and I was downstairs in Tristan's fine cotton shirt and yesterday's tie in a few minutes. Mrs. Sparrow stood by the sink, washing a chocolate pot.

"Good morning, Mrs. Sparrow."

She wiped her hands. "Mr. Hunter left instructions for me to find out what you liked to eat, as you'll be his guest for a few days." Mrs. Sparrow brought me a mug full of coffee and a plate of buttered toast. "It's no trouble. I'm doing the shopping today."

"Anything's fine; I'm not picky."

"None of that. What's your favorite food?"

"Oranges."

"It's the end of the season," Mrs. Sparrow said, "but I can manage. Oh! Mr. Hunter's chocolate. He asked me to wake him to see you off."

"I'm here, Mrs. Sparrow." Tristan dragged out one of the chairs and sat down beside me. "Good morning, Miles. Did you sleep well?"

His hair hung free of its usual plait, spread over the shoulders of his quilted dressing gown. Even half-asleep he caught at my heart, even with the wavering distortion I could now see without touching him. He laid an elbow on the table and propped his head up with one hand, covering his mouth as he yawned. "Excuse me. It's earlier than I'm used to."

"I slept well, thank you." I said. "Your guest room is comfortable."

"And will you be my guest? We'll have to fend for ourselves at week's end, I warn. Mrs. Sparrow has the time off."

The weekend, alone with Tristan. I had a sip of coffee to buy a moment to think. I shouldn't. I wanted to.

"He likes oranges, but insists he's not choosy," Mrs. Sparrow said.

"So you'll stay."

I set my cup down. "It's practical."

Tristan drained his mug of chocolate. "Did your boss sign your inspection forms?"

"She didn't."

He set his cup down. "Did she give a reason?"

I took a bite of toast, chewed, swallowed. "She said I was chasing clouds. She told me to rule the death as suspicious, but she didn't want me distracted from my other duties."

Tristan narrowed his eyes and leaned in. "It might not mean anything, but—"

"How could she have anything to do with Nick's death?"

"I don't know," Tristan said. "But it's a possibility we shouldn't ignore."

"Right. I should leave a bit early. Quarterlies are coming in. If we can get ahold of Nick's, it might tell us something."

"Quarterlies?"

"Bank statements. Every single transaction Nick Elliot made in the last quarter year. Every check he wrote, every deposit, every withdrawal." I drained my cup and rose from the table. "Hope for a full mailbox."

ELEVEN

Quarterlies

I suppressed a triumphant hiss as I pried an envelope almost too big for Nick's mail compartment free. It bore the seal of East Kingston Savings Union and was as thick as the width of my thumb, three times the sum of the paper used on my own statement. This was luck! Nick had to be one of those people who wrote checks instead of dealing in cash, making the story of his movements even more detailed. I couldn't wait to show Tristan.

I tucked the envelope inside my medical bag. It rested atop my instrument case, and I had to use the last holes in the tongue strap to buckle the top closed. I stepped out into the street, humming a dance tune. A wind caught my scarf, plastering it across my face. I pulled it away in time to catch a glimpse of brown serge and brass buttons, the nameplate almost colliding with my nose.

I'd walked into a policeman.

Fisher, the nameplate read. Disquiet puddled in my middle.

"Sorry!" I wove around him, the bag a lead weight. "I should look where I'm going."

"No harm done." The policeman reached out to steady me. "All right?"

"Yes, thank you." Constable Fisher had the beginnings of a headache pulsing in his temples. I dropped my bag in my bicycle's front basket. The sight wasn't fading away. I didn't know how to turn it off.

Fisher gestured at the black painted door marked 1455. "Do you live here?"

I fought for a calm breath and a regretful look. "No, sorry."

"Were you visiting someone?"

"No . . ." *Lie, Miles. Lie your head off.* "I'm looking for a flat. I wanted to have a peek inside, see how well the place is maintained. I shouldn't have."

He nodded. "How long have you been searching?"

"I just started."

"You've got a hard job ahead of you," Fisher said. "I wish you luck."

The blood in my veins thawed. "Thank you."

I unlocked my bicycle with shaking fingers and waited for a draft of cyclists to pass before I let the wind carry me to the end of the block. I waited at the tail of the draft for crossing traffic to clear, seeking the source of the aroma of roasting coffee. The sense of being watched writhed along my spine, and I broke away from the draft to turn right, borrowing a trick from yesterday.

A pair of women followed, but no one else. I breathed in the sea-tinged air and kept looking behind me all the way to the hospital.

The nursing station was a concert of sniffles and coughs. Dr. Crosby handed me finished night logs with bleary eyes. "Finished your discharges, Dr. Singer?"

"Still reviewing. You?"

"There wasn't much to agonize over. They'll start leaving today." He gave me a smug look. "Do you want some help?"

Back at the field hospital, I could have told him where to shove that. Here, I settled for a frosty smile. "Thank you. I have it in hand."

Everyone had yellow-green mucus clogging up their faces and coating their throats. No one blamed me for shutting myself in the tiny office four shift physicians were supposed to share.

The bottom half of this morning's *Star* read, *Minister Stanley says No to Recuperation Act.* My spirits sank. The act included additional operating funds for veterans' services, like the job corps and this hospital. We needed that act, and honestly, after they were done looting Laneer for its timber and gold, couldn't they spare some for the men who did the killing and faced the horror to make it possible?

But something had bumped this story below the fold. I flipped it, dreading what I'd find there. A murder took over the top half. Pvt. Jack Bunting, wife, child. Neighbors reported he had been withdrawn since coming home. I shoved the paper aside and tried not to wonder what Jack Bunting dreamed about while I went about my rounds.

My patients had to be gone by tomorrow, and investigating Nick hadn't brought me any closer. The quarterlies wouldn't tell me who was safe to send home. I discharged patients whose minds were not surrounded by the cloud, but how many more were there? How many wives dreaded the return of their husbands? How many men outside these walls feared something lurking inside them? The questions flogged me. I had to find the answer.

And I had to discharge two more men. Perhaps another look at my patients would help me decide.

Gerald Grimes the elder and Gerald Martin the younger or-
ganized their belongings and arranged their affairs. I noted the
men who looked at them with envy. Cooper. Wilson. Both of
their minds unclouded by the mass that would have disquali-
fied them. My list was done.

I dodged housekeepers stripping beds and stuffing sheets
into a laundry cart to sit at Bill's side. He'd had another nightmare of the killer inside him rising up to murder everyone,
dragging him through a horrific return to his family on puppet
strings. The cloud in Bill's head had grown, the murkiness
spreading down his spinal column.

Bill watched the others get out of bed. James Austen moved
from the narrow cubby to his bed with an armful of clothes,
beginning the careful process of packing his bags. Bill plucked
at the patchwork blanket covering his legs and sighed.

"I'm not going home, am I."

"I'd rather you stayed here, Bill." I sat next to him, took his
pulse, and watched that dried blood cloud spread down his
spine. "I saw you in the lobby yesterday. Did something happen?"

"The mesmerism didn't work," he said. "I thought I felt better, and then I saw the lady and *He* wanted to—"

Bill clamped his lips shut. I fished a stethoscope from my
pocket and set the chestpiece over his ribs. "Deep breath."

I didn't need to listen to his lungs. I needed him to center
himself, and telling a panicked patient to breathe can get patron-
izing. He calmed as I set the diaphragm on various places on
his chest, listened to his breath, and then asked, "What happened with *Him?*"

Bill's heart thumped harder. "*He* got real angry, Doc. *He*
wanted to kill her. *He* hated her, and I held on to the chair so *He*
couldn't . . . strangle her. *He* wanted to. And then the other one
came, Doc, the one in the high hat, and *He* was scared of him,
deathly scared."

I put the stethoscope away, using the motion to buy a few seconds of thinking. He hated Grace and feared Tristan on sight. Was that a coincidence? "What about me?"

"What?"

"Does *He* hate me too?"

Bill nodded. "But *He*'s scared of you. Why doesn't the mesmerism work, Doc?" His fingers washed and wrung over each other. "I sleep, but then I wake up and *He*'s back. *He*'s always there. Why did it work for Old Gerald and not me?"

"I'm not sure." It was nearly true. "But if you'll let me, I want to do some tests."

"You want to show me the pictures and I tell you the story of them again?"

Good idea. "That, and some other tests. I want to look at your blood, and maybe some other things."

"All right. Today?"

"Could be," I said. "What do you think of going out into the garden?"

Bill looked away. "It's cold."

"Do you need another book?"

"Do you have *The Virtue of Persistence*?"

"I'll bring it to you at lunchtime. Do you want to have a shave before the parade tomorrow?"

"I should," Bill said, but he stared up at the ceiling, listless. I let him rest.

My lunch was crab salad on a bun. I ate it twisted around in my desk as I paged through the record of Nick's banking, tracing the history of his journeys through Aeland by train. I couldn't figure out why he'd gone to such tiny, insignificant towns. At the beginning of the report, he had a charge for a train ticket to Norton. They grew peaches there. Maybe it was for a festival?

I found a trip to Mary's Wish, a town I'd never even heard of. The middle of his quarterlies detailed another journey to the north. Red Hawk was on the edge of sheep country, a center for meat and wool, not gardening. What was Nick Elliot doing there?

A shadow passed in front of my door, short and crowned by many braids.

"Come in."

Robin slipped inside, weaving around my desk to stand by my bookshelves. She frowned at the quarterlies and cocked her head, plainly reading upside down. "Those aren't yours."

"Robin." Robin wasn't sick. But there was something oddly static about her aura. Usually they shimmered and flared, like the green lights one could see in the sky during a clear winter night.

Her head popped up. "Right. Crosby pulled your patient files and stomped off to phlebotomy, demanding an explanation of some tests you ordered."

"He did what? Why?"

Robin's shoulders sank in exasperation. "Miles, he spies on you. Didn't you know? He's desperate to report you for something so you'll get in trouble."

"How do you know this?"

"He hates me too, so I keep an eye on him. Plus, I have more than one friend at the hospital, unlike some doctors I could mention—"

Leather-soled shoes clomped up the stairwell. Robin watched as another shadow darkened my door, her eyes widening as my door swung open without the courtesy of waiting for permission, let alone a knock to ask for it. Dr. Crosby stood on the other side of the hall, scowling as he caught sight of Robin. A headache flared across his forehead. Stomach acid crawled up his esophagus. His heart beat hard and fast. I nearly asked if he was all right.

"Singer," he said. "Might I have a word."

His tone didn't make it a request. He stared hard at Robin, his knitted brows spelling *get out* across his forehead.

Robin came around the desk, waiting.

Crosby stared at her for a moment before he realized he had to step back, give way to let her pass. His dark gaze followed her departure. If he uttered even one wrong word . . .

He swung his grizzled gray head back to glare at me through dark eyes and a dissatisfied set to his mouth. "Do you believe your patients have syphilis?"

What the deuce was this? "No."

He planted his hand on the frame and leaned into my space. "Then why are you ordering them tested for syphilis?"

"Dr. Crosby, I don't interrogate you when you monitor your patients' health, do I?"

His chin tilted upward a few more degrees. "I don't think you even notice what the other doctors in Mental Recovery do, Dr. Singer. But I do. I know Gerald Grimes is fully recovered from the condition plaguing our unit. A cure he credits to you."

I had to shut this down. "If you have a *specific* question about anything in Mr. Grimes's chart," I said, "feel free to bring it up with me."

He smiled, the light in his eyes satisfied. "I do, actually."

Fantastic.

"You wrote you mesmerized Mr. Grimes on Seconday morning. I was on the night shift when he was extremely distressed. Do you expect me to believe you swung your watch in front of his eyes and he recovered?"

That's all I would admit to. "It's possible Mr. Grimes was suggestible enough—"

"Don't try to claim you mesmerized away his delusion, Doctor!"

"I'm not claiming anything. I don't know what I did, or even if I did anything."

"You just looked over my shoulder."

"What?"

"You're lying, Dr. Singer. I know it, and you know it."

It didn't matter. It was my word against his. "What exactly are you suggesting, Dr. Crosby? What could I possibly have done? How could I have cured Mr. Grimes's madness?"

"You're letting him go," Dr. Crosby said. "You're keeping all your patients with the delusion, except him. Now you're ordering expensive blood tests on patients with the same delusion Mr. Grimes had. You're up to something."

"Dr. Crosby—"

"No." Dr. Crosby shook a pointed finger at me. "Dr. Matheson might be fooled by you, but I'm not. You think I haven't noticed how you charm patients? How the nurses can't do enough for you? I know, Dr. Singer. And I will prove it. To everyone."

I swallowed bile. My miracle hadn't gone unnoticed after all.

"Do you hear yourself, Crosby? I think you ought to go home. Get some rest. Read a pleasant book, maybe in a nice bath."

Blood suffused Crosby's face. "Suggest that again, outside."

My own blood was up, and I didn't care. I'd had enough of this gadfly buzzing around my cases. "Gladly."

"What's going on here?" Dr. Matheson's voice dashed cold water on my fighting mood.

I stood up, feeling like a boy who had just been caught misbehaving. Dr. Crosby stepped back from the doorway, straightening his tie.

Dr. Matheson stood with her hands on her hips and stared both of us down. "Dr. Crosby, Dr. Singer, is there an issue I can help you with?"

"No, Dr. Matheson," Dr. Crosby said. "I was just leaving."

He marched away with his head high. Dr. Matheson came closer, brows bunching up her forehead.

"Miles?"

"He doesn't like me," I said. "Sorry. I didn't mean to be dismissive. Dr. Crosby noticed I had ordered some tests on some of my patients and he wanted to know why."

"And he came up here to accuse you of . . . what?"

"I don't know." Someone had put a new notice up on the hallway's pin board promoting a games club. I looked back at Dr. Matheson, hastily.

"Why did you order these tests?" Dr. Matheson asked.

My ear itched. I kept my hand by my side. "Honestly? I'm chasing clouds."

"Miles."

"There are diseases that make people exhibit signs of madness, like syphilis," I said. "What if that's why some of our patients have this delusion? What if there's a physical cause?"

Dr. Matheson crossed her arms. "Miles . . ."

"They all think the same thing, Mathy. Have you run across a case of anyone with the hidden killer effect who wasn't a soldier? Who hadn't gone overseas to fight? What if it's physical?"

"You're chasing clouds."

"Fifty thousand men are coming home right now." I scrubbed my hands through my hair. "How many have battle neurosis? How many of them have the hidden killer effect? I should have been chasing this cloud a month ago. Two months ago."

She studied me for a moment, the corner of her lip folded under her teeth. "Do you have any of this written down?"

"Notes," I said. "Do you want a report?"

"Yesterday. You should have come to me before you started this pursuit."

"I'll get you a report," I promised. "And a study proposal. One of them should be Gerald Grimes."

"I agree," Dr. Matheson said. "Finish your accounting, Miles, and try to mend fences with Dr. Crosby?"

I gave her a rueful look. "We almost came to blows. I don't think he wants to mend fences with me."

"I will mediate if you don't find a way to get along. He's on the midday shift over week's end, but he's trying to get on your schedule."

"My schedule? What about Dr. Finch?"

"She's pregnant. Resolve this dispute with Dr. Crosby."

"Peaceably?"

"Yes." Dr. Matheson turned back to the stairwell, and I rejoined my sandwich and Nick's quarterlies. I'd just settled into the rhythm of reading the statements when the phone rang.

I stared at the damned thing, then sighed and picked it up. "Ahoy."

"Miles," Grace said. "Everything's set. The morning after the parade."

"So soon?"

"He doesn't have much time."

"You're right." I'd have to sacrifice most of the day to rest. I slept round the clock after a long day in surgery, and ate enough to feed a regiment. "I'll be there at six."

"I'm sending the carriage. You won't be able to ride back."

"You're right." I wouldn't be up to a twelve-mile bike ride, and it wasn't like Grace didn't know where I lived.

"Thank you so much for doing this, Miles. Father won't be able to thank you, but I do. If there's anything you want—shall I donate to Beauregard again?"

"You've already given five thousand," I said.

"Something you want, then. Anything."

"All I want is freedom, Grace. That's the best thing you can give me."

Silence, for a moment. Then: "I understand. I'll see you on Sixthday, Miles."

———————

I packed the wine bottle from Grace's lunch when I gathered everything together at the end of my day. Tristan and I could drink it with supper, and then we could work on figuring out how to turn my sight off. I'd have to be careful around Dr. Crosby. He was already convinced I was uncanny, and being able to diagnose everything ailing a patient wouldn't ease his suspicion of me.

There were no well-dressed strangers in the hospital lobby this afternoon. I unlocked my bike and wheeled onto the street, joining a draft of five women in bell-shaped hats. They seemed to know each other, for they called out to each other in conversation and laughter. I did my best not to listen in as they spoke of Dot's prospects with a fellow named Harry, but they were having a ball teasing their leader. A bit of movement on my left made me raise my hand in greeting, ready to comment on last night's rain, before I realized the rider was coming in too fast, too sharp.

"Watch out!" I cried, but we crashed. I collided into the lady next to me, landing hard on my right hand. She knocked over her draft-mate with a sharp cry, and then the cyclists behind us crashed into the whole mess.

Pain flared bright and hot in my wrist, fierce enough to send my stomach roiling. I drew it in close to my body, gritting my teeth at the fresh waves of pain from moving it.

Shocked exclamations sounded behind we unfortunate ones. People edged around us, stopped in front of our mishap, and helped untangle people from the scrum. The lady I'd collided with favored her ankle, but she stoutly turned down my assistance and my apologies.

"Are you all right?" a man said. "I saw everything. He drove into you on purpose and stole your bag."

My bag?

I scanned the mass of people righting themselves. The wine bottle lay smashed on the street, the elliptical splash of red liquid spread across the lane. People were already cleaning up the glass so no tires could be punctured. The metal basket mounted over my front wheel was empty, and my bag wasn't on the pavement.

"Which way did he go?"

He pointed down the street. "Turned the corner, I think. He's long gone. Was your bag important?"

My heart sank. "I'm a doctor. That was my medical bag."

The cyclist scowled, setting his curled mustache on an irritated tilt. "He was after your drugs, Doctor. It's a disgrace." He watched me try to walk my bike off one-armed. "Are you hurt?"

"Landed wrong." I joined the ranks of people trying to sort themselves out on the sidewalk. My bag was stolen. My scalpels, gone. My stethoscope and years of tools, gone. Was it stolen for a few dollars' worth of medicine?

I'd have to be a fool to believe it, with Nick Elliot's quarterlies sitting inside.

I locked my bicycle and limped up the street. I wasn't far from Tristan's. I tried to remember the names of the towns Nick had visited. *Norton, Mary's Wish, Red Hawk.* I repeated it with the rhythm of my steps. I had to remember.

TWELVE

Healing

The brass lion knocker on Tristan's door was old but lovingly polished. I grasped the ring with my left hand and rapped on the door. I was weary with the effort of enduring the pain. I wanted to lie down with my wrist cradled to my chest and try to sleep, if only to escape it.

I wanted to go back in time so I could have braked, or somehow evaded without causing a pileup. I wanted to have leapt to my feet and grabbed the villain by the scruff of the neck. I wanted to have noticed him lurking about so my excellent instincts could have alerted me and I could have cleverly had him detained so we could find out who had sent him to steal evidence.

My regretful, wishing fantasies popped as Tristan's front door opened and his housekeeper stared at me in horror. "Why, Doctor Singer! Have you had an accident?"

"I was attacked." I stepped inside as she opened the door wider. "They knocked me off my bicycle."

"In this traffic? What a disaster," Mrs. Sparrow said. "Can you take the stairs? Oh, your poor coat."

I unbent my arm cautiously and felt ill when a jolt of pain ran up my forearm. Reluctantly, I upgraded the seriousness from *sprained* to *fractured.* I didn't have time for a cast and one-handed awkwardness. I didn't have time for stolen bank records, either.

Mrs. Sparrow helped me get my topcoat and sack jacket off, fussing out "you poor dear" whenever I winced or, in one shameful instance, yelped. Soon I was protectively curled around my wrist and hobbling into Tristan's parlor, where Mrs. Sparrow guided me to the deerskin fainting couch.

"You've a tear in your trousers," Mrs. Sparrow said. "It's just a seam ripped out, mostly, nothing I can't mend."

"I can't take them off," I said.

"You'll need a blanket to cover yourself," Mrs. Sparrow said, "but it's nothing I haven't seen before. I've had three husbands."

"I mean I can't undo the buttons," I said. "My wrist."

"Well, I'd better do it, then," Mrs. Sparrow said.

"Perhaps you'd better," I agreed. It was an awkward business, being undressed by someone who wasn't my valet. Mrs. Sparrow was neutral as a nurse, but my cheeks burned as I drew a violet-fringed blanket over my lap as I sat down, half undressed.

"There's a wine stain on your shirt," she said. "Did you spill at lunch?"

"I had a bottle with me. It broke."

She helped me sit up. "Best to treat it quickly."

She was careful as she could be. I had to take the shirt off, regardless. But when she said, "I'll find you a dressing gown, dear," I didn't want to move for anything, until I heard the jingle of carriage harness and the gait of Tristan's horses pull up to the front door.

"Mrs. Sparrow?" I tried to draw the blanket up to my chin.

"Miles? Are you here? I've uncovered yet another fraud claiming to speak to the dead—"

"Don't come in, Mr. Hunter!" Mrs. Sparrow announced, bearing a scarlet brocade dressing gown in her arms. "Dr. Singer is undressed."

Rather more than merely undressed. I was in my drawers and socks. I should have been in a bedchamber. I groped for the dressing gown, and Mrs. Sparrow tried to help me put it on.

"What?" Tristan stopped inside the pocket doors. "Why?"

"There was an accident. Turn your back," Mrs. Sparrow said.

Tristan grumbled but he turned around, shielding his eyes in a theatrical fashion. Heat flooded my cheeks, but I caught my finger on a seam in the sleeve and the noise I made had him three strides into the room.

"You're hurt," Tristan said, trying to look around Mrs. Sparrow. "Where are you hurt?"

"My wrist," I tried to say, but Mrs. Sparrow shooed at him with flapping hands.

"Turn your back, Mr. Hunter!"

Tristan looked up at the cloud-painted ceiling and sighed, but he turned around.

Mrs. Sparrow fastened every button on the gown. "There. Enough jostling about, I expect. Time for Mr. Hunter to learn what happened."

She took my clothes away and left us in the parlor. "I'll check the hen in the oven, Mr. Hunter. Doctor, I'll have this tear sewn up in a blink."

"You're very kind, Mrs. Sparrow," we called out, and my embarrassment eased when he grinned at me. He pulled his chair close and leaned in. "You'll have to wait until I dismiss Mrs. Sparrow before you can heal it."

"I can't use it on myself."

"Damn," he swore. "I think I can show you. For now, would you like some morphine?"

"You shouldn't play with that," I said. "Cannabis is harmless enough, but morphine is addictive."

"So I've heard." Tristan moved into the room he used as an office instead of its proper function as a dining room, and opened a cabinet. "If you've broken your wrist, I'm your bone-setter. I'd feel better about it if I wasn't hurting you much."

"They stole my bag," I said. "They knocked me off my bicycle and stole my bag."

"Who? The man who followed us?"

"It might have been." The idea that more than one man was following me put a chill down my neck. Whatever Nick knew about the war had killed him, and now I was on the same trail. . . .

Next time, it might not be a simple shove off a bicycle. And it gets easier to kill after you've done it once.

"Nick Elliot's banking records were in my bag," I said. "I think that's why."

He returned to my side with a brown bottle in his hands. "Annihilation. Did you wait to open it, again?"

"I looked at them. Write this down," I said. "Norton. Mary's Wish. Red Hawk. They're places—places he went in the last year."

"I'll remember." Tristan pushed a medicine spoon to my lips. I swallowed and gasped at the bitterness. "L.R. stands for Lorelei Ross, but Gold and Key's secretary wouldn't let me see her."

"Drat." My tongue tingled. Morphine tangled me in its strands already.

"I have an appointment with the leisure editor of the *Star.*"

"When?"

"Tomorrow." He peered into my eyes and nodded. "Is the pain subsiding?"

"A little. Do you know how to set bones?"

"Not really."

I sighed. "I better tell you now, before I'm completely taken by your tonic."

I think it was harder on him than on me, even though he didn't hesitate or flinch when I hissed in pain, whimpered, and gave a shout so loud Mrs. Sparrow came in to find out what had happened. But he set it and improvised a splint-board with an incense tray, the bandage one of his silk neckties. He handled my wrist as if it would break again, but the tonic had dulled the pain.

"My uniform. I'll need it for tomorrow," I said.

"I haven't dismissed Michael yet. If you'll trust him with your key, he can bring it here."

Her glance darted between the two of us. "Mr. Hunter, perhaps I should stay to attend Dr. Singer tonight."

"I can manage, Mrs. Sparrow, but it's very kind of you," Tristan said. "Would you arrange Dr. Singer's things, when they get here?"

"Of course." She bustled out of the room, and Tristan helped me rise. The pain had subsided to a dull throb I needn't concern myself about. My relationship to gravity had changed, and if I didn't set my feet just so, I would float. And wouldn't I look absurd?

One place setting had a plate with the chicken already cut into small bites. I fed myself with careful dignity. The thump of the door knocker sounded, and Mrs. Sparrow went out to answer it.

Tristan jerked his chin to indicate my plate. "Have some more chicken, even though you don't want it."

"Food feels funny. Are you going to show me how—"

"I am," he promised, and went quiet as Mrs. Sparrow came back.

"Are you certain you don't need me, Doctor? It's no trouble to stay," she asked me, but she glanced at Tristan.

"It's just a sprain, Mrs. Sparrow." I smiled at her. "I look forward to cutting my own meat at breakfast tomorrow."

Mrs. Sparrow gave Tristan a long look, but he had turned his attention back to his plate. Finally, she curtsied and went out. Tristan sighed in relief.

I laughed. "She wouldn't let you in while I was undressed."

"You were blushing." He sipped his tea.

"Because she'd made such a fuss about it!"

"I'm glad you came to me when you needed help," he said. "What do you say to a tart?"

"Love some." My wrist was far away. Tristan cut narrow slices, and I enjoyed the sweetness mixed with the scent of oranges. I washed it down with my tea and waited for him to guide me back to the fainting couch in the parlor.

"The mirror trick should work." He chose a square mirror from the wall. "Look in the mirror at your wrist, while you can see your own."

"All right."

"Focus on the one in the mirror." From the angle, it looked like his arm. "Now see it, the way you see what needs to be healed."

I looked at the reflection, and let my eyes drift out of focus, but there was nothing to see.

"I've never been good at these lessons," I said. Grace had been. I could do what I stumbled on by myself, and instruction did me no good. That's why I never made Father happy.

"Don't think of that," Tristan said softly. "Imagine this room floating in the middle of the sky. Imagine the clouds all around us, the city far below. Don't think of painful things."

Floating. High in the sky with the stars all around, only we two and our secrets. I knew what my wrist would look like if I could see it—a scarlet glow tinged with tiny stars rushing to the broken place low on my ulna. Each little star would pile on the broken ends and knit back together, regrowing the bone back to a whole. It wanted to be whole, the machine of my body. All I did was draw more spark-stars to the break, faster than nature could do it.

But then I felt weak. I was so close to filling the whole gap.

It hurt now, as if all the dull ache of the process over the weeks had been crammed into these few seconds, and I nearly lost my grip on the sparks.

A surge of power steadied me, and knitting up went faster. More solid, until all the small lights massed together and held.

"Splendid," Tristan said. "Lie back now. You're—"

Oh. I fell against the embroidered cushions, dizzy as the room tilted.

"I've never felt that before. I hit the end of my strength, but then there was more. Was that Nick's power?"

"You didn't draw on your soul-stars first?"

"My what?"

He tilted the mirror up, showing me my own face. And something more; two points of light hovered over my head. One was a soft pink, the other green like spring leaves, nestled in the blue-green light outlining my body. My witchmarks, as Grace called them. Blemishes on my aura.

"What are those?"

"The reason why your kind are called Starred Ones. You didn't know? I watched Nick bind his power to you when he died."

"The green."

It wasn't just his power. He'd given me his soul. He'd bound it to me instead of floating off to rest and rejuvenation in the Solace. I would have staggered if I'd been standing. Why give me such a sacrifice? I was a stranger. Whatever Nick had been investigating, he'd given up everything on the chance that I would help.

"Yes. You already had the first. Who does it belong to?"

I wanted to disappear. "I don't know."

I lied. I knew whose soul had bonded with mine.

"You do," he said. "They died. You were there. You were touching; they poured their being into binding to you, and then died."

I closed my eyes. I squeezed them tight, but I couldn't close my ears, unhear what he said. Tristan caught my hand. I should have pushed him away.

"Miles," he said. "You remember. Who bound their soul to you?"

My chest ached. My throat closed on the spiny lump blooming there, robbing my voice. I licked dry lips and told him.

"My mother."

Memory showed me the fine red spray she had coughed on my father's suit before she fell, and the bleeding inside her body when I tried to save her. She had squeezed my hand, smiling at me with bloody teeth. The rosy light around her body slid off the shell of her skin and rushed over mine, wrapping me up as tight as one of her hugs. Then the light left her, and I was alone.

Had she seen what I had done with my life? Did she forgive me?

I didn't see how she could, when I hadn't.

"Doctor?"

We'd been sitting together in silence while I gazed at the rose-gold globe of light hovering near my ear. My witchmark. I had been trying to hear her, or sense her presence, but all I had was the light, shining in the mirror.

Tristan shook my knee. "Miles."

"Hmm?"

He peered at me. "Maybe you don't need any more morphine. Do you want to go to bed?"

I blinked. "What time is it?"

He levered himself off the fainting couch and hauled me upright. "Come on. It's time for bed."

We made it upstairs with my left arm slung over his shoulder, and I hardly stumbled, for my part. He guided me into the cheerful mismatched guest room and stood back. "Can you manage?"

"Hmm?"

"The buttons."

"Oh." I reached for the top one and winced as I tried to twist it free. Tristan brushed my hands away, fingers on the covered button, and he unfastened it.

Cool air snuck under my collar, turning my skin to gooseflesh. "Mr. Hunter."

"Four more," he said, his voice quiet in the dark.

I stood still. "Go on."

His fingertips never touched my skin, but I burned for it. Dizzy and gone with morphine, with my wrist grumbling complaint, I stood still while he sought each button by touch, sliding each silk-covered disk through its hole until my dressing gown fell open and I was undressed before him.

But that was all right. I was in a bedchamber.

He stayed in reach of my good left hand and held me with the intent gaze of a man who has exactly what he wants in his sights. For ten heartbeats, he stood right where I could lay my hand on his shoulder and waited.

I lifted my hand and his mouth opened, just a little, as I drifted my fingers over his cheek.

"Tristan," I said. His eyes flared wide. I would never tire of saying it, not when it put such a light in his eyes. "I should go to sleep."

His throat moved as he swallowed. "Sensible Miles." He turned his head and dropped a kiss on my palm. "Pleasant dreams."

He gave me one last intent look before leaving me to privacy. Sensible, responsible, *stupid* Miles. I let the dressing gown pool on the floor when he left.

THIRTEEN

A White-Handled Knife

I woke up in the dark. My splinted arm ached; my head pounded. I could only see vague shapes, darker shadows among gray: My hatbox perched on the tea table, and my uniform hung on a hook on the back of the door. It was parade day. Sixteen patients sent home, and those beds would be full by the time I returned to work on Firstday.

I tried flexing the fingers of my right hand. A little stiff, but it could have been worse. It had been worse, and I needed to watch my back. But I couldn't stay in bed, or hide, or abandon my responsibilities. Hunted or not, I had to keep going. At least I could sleep in tomorrow.

I groaned. Not tomorrow. I had to go back home. I couldn't stay here tonight. I didn't want Grace to know anything more about Tristan, let alone where he lived—

"Blast."

I'd staggered straight to Tristan's house from the accident. Idiot! What if I'd been followed? What if they knew where I was right now?

I had to warn Tristan. What if they came after him, if they targeted Mrs. Sparrow?

I flung the coverlet off and planted my feet on the floor.

The scarlet gown was just where I'd left it, and I rose from my bed and scooped it off the carpet. I belted the sash over the unbuttoned front and found my way downstairs. Tristan lounged in the parlor, still dressed in waistcoat and shirtsleeves. He read with his peculiar speed until he noticed me. He looked up and set the book away.

"Good morning," he said. "How is your wrist?"

"It was fractured. Now it's stiff," I said. "Listen. After the accident, I came straight here."

"You're worried you were followed."

"Yes. I should have known better. I should have thought of it."

"I'll be careful. And I'll tell Michael. He'll look out for Mrs. Sparrow."

I'd put them in danger. Tristan and Michael wouldn't let anything happen to her. But if I'd stopped to think, this wouldn't have happened.

"Miles." Tristan interrupted my thoughts. "Don't borrow trouble. Are you hungry?"

"Yes." I could eat a house. "Er. I need to eat. Quite a lot—"

"You used your own reserves before you tapped into your souls, Starred One," Tristan said. "Do you always do it that way? Draw on your personal energy until there's nothing left to give?"

"I guess I do," I said.

"We'll have to fix your technique," Tristan said. "But another day. Come into the kitchen before you fall down."

I sat in what was becoming my chair. He set a thick slice of apple tart in front of me and kept the food coming: eggs, leftover chicken, all the coffee I could guzzle.

He joined me once he'd dished up a small mountain, a cup of chocolate next to his plate. "Do you suppose our man with the mustache is our poisoner?"

"Yes. But I don't think he's our murderer."

Tristan gave me a quizzical look. I held up a hand while I swallowed some eggs.

"I mean I think he's our murderer's man."

"Ah. Someone too influential to get his—her?—hands dirty."

"Exactly."

He tilted his head and nodded for me to go on.

I gulped down sweet black coffee. "The Minister of Defense. Sir Percy Stanley. He's one of us. A mage, I mean."

"A powerful man."

"I don't know how we could bring him down, honestly."

"Oh. Leave that to me." Tristan's smile bared his teeth. The light in his eyes made me shiver. "Toppling him will be a pleasure."

Part of me exulted at the idea, but the rest rushed to speak. "You can't. Not until we have proof. Not that I like the man, I don't, but—"

"For you, I will wait until you're convinced."

For me. He'd hold back on meting out justice until I gave the word. He entrusted his vengeance to me, and it made my palms tingle with warmth that spread to my chest. "Thank you." I laid my fork down and rubbed my chin. "Damn it. I need a shave."

"You do," Tristan agreed. "Leave it to me. I'll be ready when you're done with bathing."

It took longer to brush my teeth, and bathing without my right hand went slowly. I went downstairs in a new dressing gown left for me outside the door.

Tristan didn't have a barber's chair, but he had a seat with a reclining back and a basin behind it. A small table held the tools of shaving as neatly as any of my surgical trays, and he stood beside it, rolling his sleeves to the elbow.

Tristan gestured to the chair. "Sit."

He helped me rest my head with one hand at the back of my neck. The top of the chair was high enough so my head hung slightly back.

"I can manage."

"Indeed you can. Let me do it."

"There's so much to do."

"Not right now. Close your eyes."

The scent of shaving oil came close, and Tristan's fingers massaged my cheeks, lightly covering my beard before he wrapped a hot towel over my face. His fingers were in my hair before I could say anything, firm fingers massaging my scalp. "Forget about everything. Just relax."

I kept my eyes closed against the heat of the towels. It felt glorious—every last trace of my headache erased by his firm hands. "You're good at this."

"I could open a shop."

I kept my eyes closed, but I smiled. "You'd make a good valet."

He scoffed. "More money in owning the shop. How did you wind up a veteran?"

Tristan scrubbed his fingers through my hair. I barely bit down a moan, covered it up with an explanation. "I ran away and joined the army. It seemed like a good idea. I could do what I was born to do: heal people, fight death."

The teeth of a comb scraped gently against my scalp. "But then the war broke out?"

"Aeland invaded Laneer just as I was finishing a surgery fellowship."

The towel came away, and he rubbed lather into my beard. "And so you went over."

"It's what I signed up for."

Water splashed behind me as he washed his hands in the basin. "You're brave."

"You stepped in front of an arrow."

"Well, I'm brave too," Tristan said. "I'm one of the Queen's Hunters."

"What does that mean?"

"We're bodyguards. But more than that. We're truth seekers and justice bringers."

"That's why you're here, right?"

The tiniest pause elapsed before he said, "Essentially. Are you ready?"

"Do your worst. If you cut my throat, I can heal it now."

He quirked up one corner of his mouth. "Good."

He planted his thumb high on my cheekbone to stretch the skin. Tristan's razor was a single naked blade, honed to a breath. The edge never skipped or bit into my skin, and the blade floated over the pulse of my throat. Could he see how fast it beat? He had to.

He tilted my chin up, stropped the blade, and my beard scraped against the edge as he shaved. I fought a shiver that would cut my throat, and he lifted the razor away.

"All right?"

"Yes. I . . ."

"Relax. Breathe, slow."

My hair stood on end. Just his voice near one ear made my skin tingle. I breathed. He touched every inch of the space where my beard grew, going over it with the razor if it wasn't smooth enough for his liking. The razor cut through my beard with a crackly scraping sound, and I breathed. Slow. Even. And when he carefully daubed away the last traces of soap from my cheeks, the corner of my mouth, I nearly moaned again.

He ran his fingers across my cheek, circled my chin with his fingertips, and nodded once.

"A handsome shave."

I could reach up and pull him closer, bring his head down

to where I could taste his fennel-scented mouth for myself. My fingers twitched.

"I appreciate it," I said, surprised at the hoarseness of my voice. "It was very kind of you."

"I can be kind," he said. "I am often kind."

He kept the veiling spell on, but I couldn't look away.

"You should dress," Tristan said. "Can you manage?"

I knew what would happen if I said I couldn't. A vivid guess bloomed in my mind's eye, down to the morning sunlight shining off his hair.

My heart pounded. I licked my lips. "Tristan—"

The front door opened and Tristan stepped back, cleaning the soap off his razor.

"Good morning, Mrs. Sparrow," Tristan called. "I'm afraid I've demolished the kitchen."

I retreated upstairs, leaving Tristan to assure Mrs. Sparrow we would manage the week's end alone. I leaned against the door of my room to clear my whirling thoughts. The week's end, alone, after we had come so close to—

I couldn't pretend I was imagining it. I knew enough about how a man carried himself around someone he wanted. If I reached out my hand, Tristan would take it. And he'd stay in reach, putting the burden of resistance on me.

I shrugged into the band-collared shirt that went under my uniform's dress tunic. There were stories of what happened to mortals ensnared by an Amaranthine's enchantment, what happened when the Amaranthine grew bored and left them. He hadn't enchanted me, but Tristan was leaving. That was enough reason to refuse anyone.

The buttons were a trial, but I could twist my right hand

around to push them through the holes. When I discovered I'd buttoned my shirt askew, I cursed and undid them.

"Doctor," Mrs. Sparrow called. "Do you need any help with your uniform?"

"There are too many buttons, Mrs. Sparrow." I opened the door to admit her. "If you could help?"

Mrs. Sparrow came right in. "Barrel cuffs were too much for you, Doctor?"

"Yes. Tristan already made me breakfast," I said. "I think he stayed up all night."

Her eyes came swift up to mine. "How did you sleep?"

"Like a log, shortly after supper."

She did up the doubled row of buttons, clasped the standing gold collar at my throat, and stood back to admire the effect. She eyed the embroidered circles on the tunic's left breast and said, "You'll need help with your medals."

I would have pinned them on the jacket first, but too late now. "Yes, if you'd please help."

"Of course."

I had two racks of medals. Each one held three. I never looked at them. "The one with the olive green ribbons first."

"A Beauregard Star," Mrs. Sparrow said. "You were first to fight."

"First and most foolish, Mrs. Sparrow." I gave her a smile and pulled the collar away from my throat. "The others are the Kingston medal and the Order of Healers. I got those for showing up."

She knew what the other rack meant. A silver coin with the Queen's face in profile was my medal for serving at the front. The golden cross and crown was my reward for crawling through muck and dismembered parts to fetch a boy who was still alive after they'd dumped him on a hill of corpses. His medal had been awarded posthumously.

The last medal, an oval copper coin, bore an engraving of

shackles broken; the motto ENDURANCE curved along the left half of the coin, and COURAGE along the right. Mrs. Sparrow stared at it, her eyes glittering with tears.

"I'm here now, Mrs. Sparrow." I'd put a handkerchief in my left pocket, and I dabbed at the trails spilling down her cheeks. "You only get to walk around in that medal if you survive it."

She wouldn't ask me what they had done. Most of us never speak of it. She reached up and patted my cheek, a brave and watery smile on her face.

I squeezed her hand. "I appreciate your help with my uniform."

I followed her downstairs with my peaked cap tucked under my left arm, kid gloves held in my right. The uniform tugged me to stand taller.

Tristan stood up when I entered and smoothed his hands over his waistcoat. "You look dashing, Doctor."

"Thank you."

"Michael will take you to the hospital, and we'll arrive at about four."

"And then we're off to the *Star*?"

"Yes. The appointment is at four thirty. It'll be close."

"I'll be ready."

Beauregard Veterans' woke up early to get dressed. Oiled canvas bags rested on the feet of made beds, their patients lined up in the bathrooms to shave cheeks and comb mustaches into tidy curls. The corridors filled with the gray uniforms of soldiers and the scarlet tunics of officers, and I wished I could go to my office and do paperwork until it was all over.

But they saw. They all saw.

We could construct the story of someone's tour by the medals on their chest. I did my best to go about my business, but

Kate Small saw my copper coin and brought me coffee. Young
Gerald's face wound up, and he bit his lip to keep it from trembling. People patted my shoulder, squeezed my hand, and told
me they were glad I'd made it.

But Bill asked flat out. "How did you do it, Doc? Why aren't
you in one of these beds? How?"

"You all need me," I said.

"Minerva needs me." Bill looked up at the ceiling. "But here
I am."

I rubbed my tingling hand on my trousers. I couldn't help
him. I didn't dare. The cloud spread deeper down Bill's spine.
Drawing spinal fluid was painful. I didn't have a clear reason to
run this test, and Dr. Crosby had his nose in my files.

"We'll get you out of bed, Bill. Don't give up."

But Bill was already staring at the white-painted ceiling.

I went back to the nurse's station and did my best to fill out
charts. Kate brought me a Lost or Stolen Equipment and Medi-
cation form, and filled it out for me while I dictated the answers.

"What a shame your bag is gone," she said. "All your tools."

I agreed it was and took the form up to the Materials office,
where the clerk looked over my papers and asked, "Engraved
with M.H.S. on the plate, embossed with balm leaves, tobacco
brown leather?"

"Yes. How did you—"

She shoved her chair back, opened a storage closet, and
brought my medical bag to the desk.

"I had to fill out these forms when you already had my bag?"

"The tyranny of paperwork," she said. "Check each item on
the list as received, and it's all yours."

I scanned the list. My fine syringes were gone, as were all
the drugs. But so were Nick Elliot's quarterlies.

I checked off the inventory and stopped at one line: *pendant
chain with weighted pointer of polished agate.*

I skipped over it and kept going. I found another:
White-handled knife with curved blade.

She wasn't looking. I checked the items off, and took my filthy property upstairs with me.

I turned the lock behind me and emptied everything from my bag. My scalpels were there, still wrapped in paper. I'd have them sterilized again. I'd hone them, wrap them, and tuck them away. The bandages were a filthy mess. They went into the wastebasket. Each item was either set aside or thrown away until I came to the last items.

Why did I keep these? I had no doubt my bag had been carefully searched, and those items left behind. To point the finger at me and call me witch. Suspicion was enough to make an accusation. I'd never withstand examination, and I wouldn't escape the asylum. They call it a hospital, but it's a prison all the same.

I pulled out the boline first, careful of the sharp blade. It wasn't engraved, thank the gods. A plain knife with a whitewood handle, a knife of hedge-spells and physicality. This one was mine, given to me when I was eleven. Grace had cut her oath to me with the little blade she kept on her person. Mages used them in rituals. So did witches, according to the stories.

Next was the pendulum. Hold a pendulum in your hand, and the pattern of the swing told you what you couldn't know—truth from lies, the sex of a child, the presence of the dead. Mages didn't use these, but witches did.

I had held onto these items the way I'd held onto my scalpels, as pieces of the past. The knife is a letter-opener. The pendulum a prop I use for mesmerism. Easily explained, readily dismissed. I put the pendulum in my pocket and the knife on my desk.

I left my emptied bag on my desk and went downstairs for the parade.

FOURTEEN

Parade Day

Sixteen beds wouldn't be enough.

People waved scarlet handkerchiefs and cheered loud enough to drown out the music in the streets, music to set your feet itching to move to the beat, to shuffle and stamp your heels. Citizens dashed into the street to give a soldier an apple and sometimes a kiss, darting back to pluck another fruit from the baskets lining the raised walks. They cheered; they laughed; they danced with arms raised.

I stood still in my uniform and counted the uninfected men. Each square was sixty-four soldiers, marching, waving, kissing girls, eating apples. That square had fifteen. The next, twelve. That one, eighteen. The rest were crowned with writhing clouds of dried blood, and I fancied their smiles strained, their joviality the mask they knew they should wear.

Discipline kept me standing even as my insides roiled. This was a disaster. I had to do something, spread the news among the staff—but what could they do? Why would they do anything? I had no proof, and a success story I didn't want prodded.

That one had nine. The job in front of me mounted higher, threatening to spill. I had to find the cause. I had to find the cure.

I'd have to take my mask off and shout it from the rooftops. A mouse couldn't make the medical community listen.

I turned my face away and paid attention to the crowd— those who had waited for family and loved ones to return. Only soldiers had the miasma. The civilians had head colds, indigestion, ailments I could ease with a touch. The crowd glanced disapprovingly at a young parent with a crying infant. The baby had an ear infection, and her face streaked with tears and snot as she screamed her inconsolable pain.

I shuffled closer, made eye contact with the child's mother. She gave me an apologetic smile. I stroked the child's curls, cupped her ear, and she quieted.

"What did you do?" her mother asked.

"She's overtired. The noise," I shouted. "Keep her ears covered, or better, take her home and let her sleep."

"We're looking for her uncle. He's in the parade." She picked up her baby's hand and waved it at the marching soldiers. The baby endured this with a wide-eyed look at me.

"I hope you see him soon. I'd better go back inside."

"Say bye-bye, Mary." She shook her daughter's paw at me.

I caught a hug from a pretty girl who gave me a kiss on the cheek and an apple.

"You look a little pale, Captain." She gave me a grin and sashayed into the street. I bit into the apple with gratitude. It was barely a healing, but the fruit was juicy, sweet with a drop of acid tartness. It crunched, firm and the perfect thing to chase away the tremors.

A chill ran down my neck, the hairs rising to shout alarm. I checked sight lines. Too many in the trees. The crowd cheered the soldiers home, but one face turned pale and pinch-lipped toward me.

Dr. Crosby glared hot enough to set my cap on fire, the downward twist of his mouth suppressing revulsion. His gloved hand curled around his throat. He turned toward the hospital, dodging the crowd to get back inside.

He'd seen me. What had he seen?

I had approached a woman with a crying baby. I'd touched the baby, and the crying had stopped.

But what had he believed?

A bewitchment. A spell. Whatever believers thought witches could do. It was my word against his. But if someone believed him, if I warned anyone about the avalanche of soldiers coming to crowd too many beds . . .

Blast it, I had to be a mouse.

I followed Dr. Crosby's path to the doors.

The lobby teemed with discharged patients bearing heavy sling sacks—the same gray canvas bags each soldier packed their life into before sailing to Laneer. Some wore their uniforms, and if crutches and canes weren't regulation, no one seemed to mind. My scarlet and gold braid stood out, and the way to the stairs parted before my officer's uniform with nods of respect.

"There you are." Robin hurried over to stand in front of me, her hands resting in the pockets of her skirt. "I missed you before the parade. The nurses are giving me a farewell party on the first of Frostmonth, and I know how much you love cake."

I stretched my face into a hopeful look. "Chocolate cake?"

"If you're lucky," she said. "I have to go. We're going to cut a man open and look for the shrapnel that's been tearing his intestines to shreds."

"Lovely thing to talk of, after tempting me with cake."

"You'll come to the party?"

She was leaving me the same day Tristan was. "I wouldn't miss that. Not if there's cake."

She left laughter to trail behind her as she rushed off to the Surgery Wing.

"Dr. Singer!" Young Gerald thumped over to me, his sack strapped across his back. His smile could light a room brighter than aether. "Old Gerald didn't want to go without saying goodbye. He's in the unit."

"I have a moment." The crowd parted for us again, down the corridor to Ward 12. Old Gerald stood next to his stripped bed, loading the last of his clothing into his sack. He turned with a smile already on his face, and my heart kicked in my chest.

The infection clouded the inside of his mind, one tendril dripping slowly down his neck.

"We're on our way," Old Gerald said. "Thank you, Doctor."

I had to do something. "I'd like you to follow up, Old Gerald. Come see me if you need anything, or if you have trouble sleeping."

He flinched, but smiled wider. "I've got a script for your tonic. I expect I won't have trouble sleeping."

Would he take it? Would Gerald trust the tonic more than the fear *He* would rise up?

Old Gerald shrugged the sack into place. "Maybe if I came back for a mesmerism."

"They make you fall asleep," Young Gerald objected.

"I could make a house call. Say in four days' time?"

"I'll ask Marie to make tea, Doc."

Away from the hospital, I could keep him treated without suspicion falling on me. "Then expect me."

"Marie will be pleased to see you. We'd better get on, Doctor. Thank you for all you've done."

They filed out of the ward.

Once the patients had cleared out, I put Bill through agony with my large-bore needle, drawing fluid from his spine. I had expected it to be murky or rusted to the color of dried blood, but it was clear even though I chose my draw site from within the clouded, furious boundaries of the infection.

An hour in the lab produced nothing. I wouldn't get full results on all my tests, but I ordered them. I needed the paperwork for my research, even if I knew there would be nothing to find.

I hadn't captured any of the muck in my needle, and I should have. Bacteria, virus, parasites—I should have evidence of something, because something was there. I had to find it by mundane means. How could I develop a test to prove the existence of what I saw with my gift?

I tried to put it out of my mind with simple work. Prescient clerks had put together new patient files, their blanks ready to be filled by countless hands. I had forms of my own to include, but sorting papers didn't ease my frustration. Nothing in the blood. Nothing in the urine. Nothing in the spinal fluid.

Maybe I needed a biopsy of the spine, but I'd never get permission. If I could examine someone with the infection who had died, perhaps. Jack Bunting's body was in the police morgue, far from where I could reach it anyway.

The weight of my task pressed on me. Doctors believed the delusion to be a product of the imagination, a defense against the atrocity of murder and the outrage of violence. A rejection of our base and brutish nature. Who wouldn't flee from such memories?

But I knew. I saw. These delusions accompanied the dried blood cloud in the heads of the hundreds—no, thousands—of soldiers who'd gone over.

I shoved the new patient files aside. I laid out Bill's chart to the left of my blotter and unlocked my desk drawer to retrieve my treatment journal.

I had written, *Mass persists in Bill Pike's skull and extends along the spine, appearing to follow the brain and nerves,* when my telephone rang. Because what I needed was an interruption, of course. I picked up the receiver and rubbed ink on my temples. "Ahoy."

"Miles."

I fought a sigh. "Grace."

"I'm glad I caught you in your office. How's your day? Did you see the parade?"

"It went right by the hospital. What can I do for you?"

"I found a flat," she said. "Halston Park. Eight rooms."

"Too big. Too far west."

"Miles. You can't live in Birdland. Anyway, I had an idea. You could spend the night in my suite in the Edenhill before the carriage comes to fetch you in the morning."

"I have an engagement tonight."

The silence on the line chilled my ear. I capped my pen and waited.

"With your . . . friend?"

"Yes."

"You shouldn't associate with him. It's dangerous."

"How?"

"I know you can't see what I saw." Her voice spilled sympathy through the line. It clashed with the skin-crawling feeling of aether pressed to my ear. "But he's a witch, Miles."

I clenched my teeth, remembering the conclusions about the true difference between witches and mages I had come to last night. I quivered, too, because Tristan was in danger. If Grace wanted to, all she'd have to do was report him, and they'd scoop him up. I didn't know if they could manage to keep a half-divine guardian of the dead, but I didn't want to know.

"You didn't know. I'm sorry."

"I knew."

"What? How could you? They're dangerous! You can't trust him—"

"That's not what this is about."

"I don't care. Stop seeing him. Meet somebody else. How you could pair off with a jumped-up witch fixing to run mad any moment—have you lost your mind?"

"You cannot tell me what to do, I am not going to dinner with you, I am not spending the night at the Edenhill, and the conversation about my acquaintance with Mr. Hunter is over." I shoved my secret journal in a drawer, and it closed just a little too loudly. "I have to go, Grace."

I hung up. Counted to ten, deep breaths, all of it. She had grown up ordering me around; the moment it became clear that I wasn't a Storm-Singer she'd taken charge. She had to learn that I wasn't hers to command—that I was my own person, with my own career and my own problems.

Like my patients. I set my mind to the task of puzzling over the results. Something was there. I had to figure out how to test for it. But then what? Diagnosis wasn't a cure. What if I couldn't find a way to cure it?

I had to. Thousands of soldiers were infected.

A shadow filled the door to my office.

"Come in."

Tristan wore a scarlet silk scarf that matched my tunic. He reached for my coat. "Michael is parked a few streets away."

My cap waited in his hand as I donned my Service coat. "Couldn't get any closer?"

"Traffic is a mess. People are dancing in the street."

"I wish I could change." I clamped my lips together. *Shut up, Miles.*

"Most people will look at the uniform and see little else. Come on. We can't be late."

FIFTEEN

The *Star*

The *Star of Kingston* lived and chattered in a twelve-story building east of the King's Way, its limestone pediment marked with the legend *Accurate, Interesting, Timely*. The *Star* tended to lean past interesting and into lurid, but I read it every morning as my neighbors did.

Tristan followed the progress of a woman with two cameras around her neck dragging a trolley bag behind her. She raced for the lift in high-heeled shoes, and when it closed in her face she let out a string of words I'd never heard a woman utter until I'd gone to war.

I slowed my pace as Tristan sped up. She was the woman who'd come to Nick Elliot's apartment, the woman with the high cheekbones and elegant carriage. Nick's lover.

"Bad luck," Tristan said. "Would you like help with your luggage?"

"I have to beat this pox-riddled deadline or Cully will have my head." She tugged her gloves off finger by finger, revealing nails painted glossy black. When she finally looked up at Tristan, she smiled. "Lovely to have a gentleman's assistance."

"Tristan Hunter," Tristan said. "This is Dr. Miles Singer."

She pushed my coat lapel aside to read my medals. I stood still as she drifted a fingertip over my Queen's Cross of Valor. "Well hello there, hero. I'm Avia Jessup."

The look she shot me was so heated I felt it bloom on my face. "Pleasure to meet you."

"Oh, I do hope so." Her hand was warm in mine as I bowed over it. She was the tiniest bit drunk, but in otherwise excellent health. "What brings you to the *Star?*"

"We have an appointment with the editor of the Leisure Desk."

"What a happy coincidence. I can take you right to her." She took my arm and I led her inside the lift. As the brass cage rose to the fourth floor, Avia leaned into me. "Tell a girl what this is all about?"

"We're here to ask for information about Nick Elliot," Tristan said, and I closed my mouth.

Avia's eyes widened and she drew in an openmouthed breath. "He's dead, isn't he."

"I'm afraid so, Miss Jessup."

She sighed and turned her face up to the ceiling. "I was afraid of this."

Oh, really?

"Did you know him well?" Tristan asked.

"We were good friends," she replied. "How did he do—? How did it happen?"

"I believe it was arsenic," I said.

"Oh, Nick." Avia closed her eyes, but she opened them again, intent on my face. "What do you mean, you believe?"

"The circumstances around Nick's death are suspicious. Did Nick have any enemies?"

"No. Everyone liked him, no matter what he thought of himself." Avia stared at me. "He was murdered?"

I opened my mouth, closed it. She suspected suicide. What if we were wrong? What if Nick had gone mad? He might have been mad when he begged for my help, but he was certainly murdered.

"We have reason to believe he was," Tristan said. "If you can help us—"

Avia spun on one foot and straight-armed the double doors to the leisure desk open. "I can't believe anyone would do that to Nick. Everybody loved him."

A woman pushed past us with a cup of black coffee in her hand. "What's this about Nick?"

She looked us up and down, her survey halting at my medals. I should have changed.

"He's dead," Avia said. "Murdered."

"Nick Elliot was murdered?" the woman exclaimed, and the newsroom's dull roar fell all at once.

They stared. Pens and pads were snatched up and reporters closed in, prey spotted.

"You're not police," the woman went on. "Why are you here and not them?"

I hesitated. Tristan stepped in. "Dr. Singer is collecting evidence to present to the police."

"Didn't you have enough reason for their interest with the death examination?"

"How did Nick Elliot die?" someone else asked.

"We believe it was poison," Tristan said.

The crowd leaned closer. "You believe?"

"That's enough."

Twenty heads turned toward a petite woman in a rose walking suit, her long hair arranged in an intricate crown braid, a popular style from my boyhood. She used a cane to steady herself. "You may go back to your work. Gentlemen, if you'd join me in my office?"

Avia made to follow us. The woman stopped her with a narrow-eyed look. "Have you developed the plates from the ladies' red-ribbon luncheon, Miss Jessup?"

"I need to select a print."

"You have work to do, then."

Avia huffed out a breath and marched across the room, the wheels on her trolley bag squeaking.

"I'm Caroline Miller," the little woman said. "You must be Tristan Hunter."

Tristan bent over her hand. "My companion is Dr. Miles Singer. He's the official investigator of the case."

She gave me another look. "An army surgeon?"

"I practice at Beauregard Veterans', Mrs. Miller. Mr. Hunter brought Nick to my hospital."

"I see."

She let us into her office, a long, narrow space with a glass wall looking down at the staff desks. Her guest chairs were handsome, hand-carved wood with perfectly curved backs. I breathed a contented sigh before she pierced me with a look. "You squirmed like a worm on a hook out there. Why do you pursue this when the police claim there's no evidence?"

"The body was destroyed before I could examine it," I said.

"Mr. Elliot went on a number of journeys earlier in the year," Tristan said. "Were they for his work here?"

Mrs. Miller looked up at the ceiling and huffed. "Those blasted trips. I never should have agreed to them. He'd done his work in advance to take the time off and still make deadline. Now everyone on the leisure desk thinks they can dash off some drivel and go have a holiday."

"They were personal?" I asked. "Did he say what he was doing?"

"He said he was doing some research for a new book."

Tristan broke in. "So he never offered you a story based on his research?"

Mrs. Miller stared at Tristan. "What was he really doing on those trips?"

"We're not sure," Tristan admitted. "Do you know where he went?"

"You should ask Alice Farmer," Mrs. Miller said. "She's a typist, but if she had any hand at writing at all I'd give her a press card in an instant."

Tristan cocked his head. "That's an interesting lament."

"She never forgets anything," Mrs. Miller said, "but she can't write. Too literal. She's the one in the green blouse, at the corner."

Alice Farmer's forearms rippled with strength and dexterity as she typed a transcript. Her posture was perfect, upright and poised. She watched us approach—

Well, me. She stared at me, her fingers never losing their tempo, reaching up to bat the platen back into place to conquer the next line. She didn't even glance at the notes she transcribed. Her forehead furrowed with the permanent surprise of her eyebrows, her large eyes wide and brown. Staring. Only when we came close enough to offer our hands did she look away, shoulders rising in defense.

I put my hand down, and so did Tristan.

"Miss Farmer? I'm Tristan Hunter, and this is—"

"I know who he is." Her voice was soft, almost watery. "Everyone thinks you're dead, Sir Christopher."

The room rocked.

Tristan grabbed my elbow and held me steady. "How do you know him?"

"The Kingston *Royal Herald,* Leafshed nineteen, in the fourth year of Queen Constantina's rule. You appeared in a photograph with your father," she said. "You cut the ribbon on the children's garden in Hensley Park." She tilted her head and squeezed her fingers together.

I *had* cut the ribbon that day. I'd been six, and not yet a disappointment.

"Dr. Miles Singer, at your service," I said.

"Nick had a picture of you," she said. "It's nice to meet you, Dr. Singer."

"He what?"

Alice shifted out of her seat and walked with her head bowed to Nick's desk. She slid open a drawer and handed me a photograph. I stood on the sidewalk next to the wrought iron fence of Beauregard, waiting on Robin to unchain her bicycle. The composition was slapdash, as if someone had simply pointed the camera at us and shot.

"Leafshed sixteen," Alice said. "It's not a very good picture, but I knew you as soon as Nick showed it to me. He seemed surprised when I told him who you were. He even asked me if I was sure."

It explained how Nick had learned my name. Why the photo? It made sense if I assumed that Nick could see auras. He could have been at the hospital investigating the men and seen me there, taking the photograph as part of his quest for the truth.

"Excuse me," Alice said.

We followed her back to her typewriter. Tristan held her chair for her and said, "Mrs. Miller told us you could answer some questions about Nick Elliot's trips this year."

Her gaze slid off to the side. "He traveled. Hedleigh, New Year three to seven, for personal reasons. Kirford, Snowglaze fourteen to nineteen, to write an article about southern glasshouse farming. Red Hawk, Firstgreen twenty to twenty-five, for personal reasons. Norton, Merrymonth four to nine, for the Peach Blossom Festival. Mary's Wish, Summerstide eleven to sixteen. Personal reasons." Her hands sprang free of each other, and she twisted her skirt in grasping fingers. "I should be working."

He'd gone somewhere recently. "Was that all?"

"Bywell, Leafshed five to nine," Alice gulped. "To see—to see his mother, Ann."

Tristan and I exchanged looks. "His mother."

Alice dropped her gaze to her hands, twisted together in knots. "He had all his work done. I typed all of his columns. He predicted the lovely gardens of the week perfectly, even when he wrote them three weeks early."

Tristan stirred beside me. "What was he like, Alice?"

"He was kind." Alice's smile made her pretty. "If he wanted to look something up from a previous column, he'd ask me instead. I liked him."

"Did he change? Did he seem unhappy?"

"He tried to hide it," Alice said. "Maybe no one could tell."

"How long ago did he start hiding it?"

"After he came back from Norton. He was quieter. He stopped smiling."

A few months. It could have been longer, but I trusted Miss Farmer's memory.

"If you remember anything else, Miss Farmer, will you inform me?" Tristan handed her a calling card on stiff cream paper with embossed borders.

"Thank you for the card, Mr. Hunter. I will keep it. Goodbye, Dr. Singer."

Alice returned to her transcription, typing without referring to the original page.

———

We nodded to Mrs. Miller and left, unspeaking until we were alone in the elevator.

"She didn't call me Sir Tristan."

"She probably has the names of the peerage memorized," I said. "Hunter's not on it."

"There's a connection between those towns," Tristan said. "Find the connection, we find the reason for the visits."

"He kept what he was working on a secret," I said. "Gold and Key rejected it, but someone stole it. Dead obvious he found something somebody didn't want getting out."

"Someone with power and resources?"

I thought of Sir Percy. I didn't have proof. But if any of the Invisibles wanted an antiwar agitator with a press license dead, he was the most likely. How could I find evidence on him? I couldn't get anywhere near him.

But Tristan might. If we found enough to point toward Sir Percy, or more accurately, his underlings. "Have to be, wouldn't it? I was robbed by a henchman; Nick's flat was burgled, his body cleverly destroyed. . . . We have to find out what he was writing."

We emerged onto the street. No celebration here, but the block south of us was filled with people who sang and danced. Michael sat atop the carriage with a penny-book in hand, but he jumped down to open the coach door to us.

"Thirty-nine twenty-one Magpie Road East, Michael."

"Sure, Doctor. I remember."

"If you want help packing your clothes, I can get in the way while trying to be helpful." Tristan sprawled on the sprung and padded bench at the back of the coach. "Now, what do you say to a bite? Mrs. Sparrow put a shoulder on the stove, and it should be ready to fall apart by now."

"I should stay home. I have . . . I have to do a healing to-morrow."

Tristan tilted his head. "You hide your gift, but you're doing a healing."

I didn't want to talk about this. A hot, sour lump swelled in my stomach, reached an acid hand up my throat as the carriage lurched into traffic. "My family."

"Ah."

It was a short ride home. Tristan put out a hand to stop me, reaching for his breast pocket.

"I want to give you something."

I stared at the long iron key in his palm. "Your key?"

"In case you need a refuge."

"I couldn't—"

"I expect it back on Firstday," Tristan said. "For now, take it."

I took the key. It bore nicks and scrapes from years of use, heavy in my hand. I was welcome, any time of the day or night. Friends didn't give over the keys to their homes.

Lovers did. "I can't—"

Tristan met my eyes, caught my hand in his. "Miles. Use it. We have work to do. Frostnight is coming. It's easier this way."

Frostnight would be here too soon. "I'll take it."

Tension melted from his shoulders. "And use it."

"I will. As soon as I'm done."

"People will wonder after the coach," Tristan said. "I'll see you tomorrow."

SIXTEEN

Binding

I took the key from my pocket and laid it on my bedside table to rest next to my windup clock set for five am. It caught a sliver of the light from the street as I closed my eyes and slept, and it was still there come morning, free of illusion or trickery. It weighted my trouser pocket as I toasted bread, the first to rise on Sixthday, awake even before Mrs. Bass came down to open the boardinghouse doors.

"Dr. Singer." She stood in the threshold of the kitchen, head cocked, but she came forward to accept a freshly burped cup of coffee. She sipped, and nodded at the quality of my brew.

"Do you have an extra shift at the hospital?"

"Just an early day," I said, my fingertips pressing into the whiteware mug, gathering up its warmth.

"Will your friend's fine carriage be picking you up?" She raised her coffee mug. "I never had a gentleman living under my roof before you."

"I'm not a gentleman any longer, Mrs. Bass."

"Some things you can't shed like an old coat, Doctor." Mrs. Bass smiled at me. "If you need to move suddenly, I understand."

She finished her cup and headed for the hall, and I followed after. Mrs. Bass unlocked the front door, and beyond the weekend edition of the *Star*, a heavy, steel-sprung landau bearing the Hensley seal waited at the end of the walk. Four blindered and crested black carriage horses stood quietly, matched as peas in a pod.

Mrs. Bass looked back at me. "I believe that's for you."

"Thank you, Mrs. Bass." I bent and retrieved the *Star* for her before I stepped over the threshold and down the walk.

"Dr. Singer."

I stopped. "Mrs. Bass?"

She held the paper with white knuckles, gazing at the carriage. "Be careful. You and Dame Grace."

"Mrs. Bass?"

She gave me a tense smile and swung the door shut.

"Do you require assistance?"

The footman had snuck up on me. I gave him my bag and led the way to the landau. This was the old family carriage, refurbished to look as it had a dozen years ago. Grace blinked at me, and took her feet off the opposite bench to let me sit. "What in the name of the gods are you wearing?"

She regarded my tweed jacket and flat cap with astonishment.

"Working clothes." Some imp of rebellion had guided my hand in dressing—instead of my good gray flannel suit, I wore a tweed check made on a machine to average measurements. The shoulders fit, the body billowed, and the check on the trousers didn't quite match.

It wasn't that bad.

Grace wrinkled her nose. "You live in a single room and dress yourself in rags. I thought the suit you wore to the luncheon was a bit dated, but you look a laborer in that thing."

Unfair. I wasn't wearing a neckerchief, and the suit had a waistcoat. "I think we should talk about something else."

"I brought you breakfast." Grace gestured to the basket on the opposite seat, and I sat beside it, lifting the lid.

Grace rapped the roof of the coach and it shuddered into motion. I regarded my breakfast with pinched lips. Forced strawberries from a glasshouse, suspended in cultured double cream. Knots of egg-bread stuffed with eggs, bits of mushroom, sausage, and cheese. My mouth watered. A stack of pink bacon, drizzled with sweet mustard sauce.

This was a disaster.

"This was my favorite breakfast."

She smiled, proud and fond. "I remember."

"Grace . . ." She'd only meant to make me happy. "You shouldn't have done this."

"Oh Miles, please. No more of your ridiculous self-denial. Eat your breakfast."

"You banished the servants from the house," I explained. "And then you had Cook make young Master Christopher's favorite breakfast, to take with you before the crack of dawn."

"Oh." Grace's mouth turned down. She worried at her lip. "Do you think she figured it out?"

"She'd try to cheer me up with my favorites." I used to hide in her kitchen on bad days. On the worst days, I wouldn't want to leave at all.

"I'll tell her to keep quiet."

"Then she'll know she was right."

"I didn't mean to—" Grace sighed. "I'm sorry."

"You didn't mean any harm." I took up a silver spoon and ate my breakfast. The strawberries, all three of the stuffed egg-buns, every scrap of bacon. Grace was slack-jawed by the time I was finished.

"Healing drains me, like storm-singing drains you," I said. "Magic's magic. Even second-rate tricks."

"I know," she said. "Secondary powers have their own value.

But yours is— They should have treated you better, Miles. They should treat all the Secondaries better."

"Oh come on, Grace. We're housed. We're clothed. We live in luxury, don't we? Shouldn't we be grateful?"

"Don't snap at me, Miles. I understand what it's like."

"You don't. You imagine. You sympathize. But you can't understand."

Grace looked out the windows at Kingston, growing sleeker and wealthier with every turn of the coach's wheels. We were past Wellston Triangle and into Halston Park. Tristan's front door was somewhere behind us.

"We're nearly home," Grace said.

My breakfast weighed down my stomach.

The Western Point is a park with houses scattered inside it. The roads curved around trees so enormous that you needed ten men to circle a trunk with clasped hands. Between them, long rolling lawns and formal gardens carpeted the grounds around massive homes built well back from the roads. The satisfied neighborhoods west of 15th couldn't hope to match the grandeur and privacy of the Western Point, claimed entirely by the Hundred Families. The apples planted here were a deep wine red, their flesh acid and perfect for pie and cider. Did Grace still love apples, or had she outgrown them?

I looked back at the woman who sprawled comfortably in her seat. I didn't know my sister. She'd still been so young when I left, about to come out to society and take on some of Father's responsibilities with government.

The coach slowed and turned, wiping my thoughts away. Hensley House dozed in the sunrise, rose and amber light falling on the stables behind us. I craned my neck. Small windows lined this side of the house, bunched together so each narrow servant's room would have their own. We exited the carriage, and Grace opened the servants' door herself. I lingered to touch the hand-hewn gray stone, surprised when I felt nothing. I had once lived here, but this wasn't my home.

The servants had been given the morning off. Most weren't here. The rest were enjoying luxurious sleep. I set my feet carefully on these steps, quiet as a mouse until we walked on hand-knotted carpets woven with interlocking squares. I passed my old bedroom without turning my head and walked between small tables supporting clear glass statuettes of my forebears—Great-grandmother Fiona and Grandpa Miles centered on pedestals a little higher than the rest, to mark how they had ascended to the highest position among the Invisibles. Father's statuette stood high as well. There wasn't one for my sister, as she wasn't yet thirty. My mother had never had one made.

Grace stopped, and we occupied ourselves with listening to the quiet. She pressed light fingers on the door lever, and we crept inside.

I should have expected it.

The man who lay sleeping on the left side of the wide, heavy bed dominating the master chamber was . . . old. His hair was frosted by age, the bristle of his beard snowy white. He loomed so huge in my memory. This man was thin, wasted, the lines on his face deepened with a year of painful dying.

I studied his mind, the sparks of thought and response slow with the deep relaxation of sleep, with none of the animation that indicated dreaming. I had to sit beside him, touch him, keep him asleep while I worked, but I stared instead. So old. How could it be, that my father was dying? For even after I worked on his lungs, the machine of his body was running down. I could give him a year. Perhaps two. I would leave here and never speak to him, never let him know I lived. This was what had become of the giant who overshadowed my life? He looked so . . . small. So frail. But the growths inside his lungs were strong. They grew. They thrived, some large as the end of my thumb, others merely specks, but too many and too strong. I couldn't save him, but I could buy Grace some time.

I needed to get on with it and didn't want to be in the same room with this man any longer than necessary. I let my fingertips rest on the exposed part of his breastbone and worked off breakfast. It was too much. I was too late. If I'd seen this a year ago . . .

Growths shrank under my will. I attacked the largest, making them smaller. The smaller growths I killed outright. I worked until my vision went dark at the edges and my head felt swollen and hot.

Father would rise from this bed. It would be a miracle, if not a complete one. I couldn't cure him. But he had more than his fair share.

Grace watched, her lips pressed to white. She squinted as if she tried to see what I was doing, and her eyebrows rose in worry. I wished I had better news for her and tried to smile.

Grace's look went from worry to horror. "Miles."

She focused on the frail figure behind me.

The bed shifted.

Father snatched my hand quick as a snakebite. Power threatened to crush me small as it pressed on my skin, dug and burrowed its way into me.

I fought, but I was drained from pouring everything I had into the healing. His papery grip squeezed my fingers as tight as his power.

"Stop struggling."

"Let me go!"

"Oh, don't be ridiculous, Christopher."

I yanked on his grip, tried to tear the net of power away.

I didn't give up even as the room spun and the blackness swam in front of my eyes.

I came to in a padded chair. My skin felt too tight. Something foul sullied the air under my nose—smelling salts.

"Miles."

Grace's voice, Grace's hands on me. This was too much. I waved the foul smell away and struggled to stand up.

A wave of power held me down. How—

And then I knew. Father had me wound up in his power, and I was held as surely as he used rope. My heart beat against the cage of my ribs as his power squeezed my chest, forcing me to take shallow, rapid breaths. I fought to raise my arm, and the power squeezed the bones in my wrist. I struggled, nauseous, beating my wings against the bars of a cage.

I looked over my sister's shoulder. "Release me."

"No," my father said. "It's time for this nonsense to end. You've nearly destroyed this family with your selfishness, and you will do your duty."

I couldn't fight. I was so drained I'd fainted. "I won't be your slave."

"You're for Grace, not me."

"Shut up." I gripped the arms of the chair tight. My wrist hurt, hot and throbbing. Father's power encased me. If I could pierce it, I could tear it, I could break free.

Father confirmed what I suspected. "You're not bound. Merely held. But I will bind you, if you won't do what's right."

I lifted my weary head. Grace knelt in front of me, hands on my knees.

"Miles, he'll do it," she whispered. "Please. It's the only way."

"Did you plan this?"

"Idiots. You two were always indulgent. Grace told me what

she did when I tried to give control to her. I should hold onto you just to make sure you fall into line."

"I never meant for this to happen, Miles."

"Consent," my father said. "Consent to be bound to Grace, or I'll take you."

There was a weak spot. A wavering at the small of my back. I felt it, touched it, made my touch a knife—

Father flexed his hand. My throat squeezed shut. I struggled, the suffocation dragging me into a panic. I lost my hold on the power. Stupid. Stupid. I scrabbled for it again, feeling my prison for a weak spot while everything grew dark and my body cried out for air.

"Stop fighting."

"Miles," Grace begged. "He'll bind you."

I was looking through a tunnel and fading fast.

Father flexed his strength again. He wasn't drained from a healing. He was on his feet, full of my power. I needed to touch him. I couldn't fight him power to power.

I pushed out of the chair, but my knees wouldn't hold me up. I dragged myself across the floor, but he stepped out of reach. I crawled a little farther, and all he had to do was move out of my grasp. I lifted my head, stretched out my hand, and everything went dark. I let go of my power, and Father granted me breath. My head swam, but I could breathe.

I dragged in two breaths, greedily took another and coughed. "I consent."

"Say it outright."

"I consent to you binding me, Grace."

"Ask her to do it."

"Father—"

The power crushed me again. "Ask."

My life as a mouse was over, my freedom gone, and I still wasn't brave enough to die.

I offered my hands to my sister, palms up, wrists together. "Please bind me, Grace."

Grace wept, but she did it.

I was too weak to walk on my own, but I was only dimly aware of Grace carrying me along the corridor. I was far away, in a place where nothing mattered enough to fuss over.

"Not like this, never like this. Miles, I'm sorry. I never wanted this."

The grip of Grace's power crawled over my skin, but it happened to someone else. Someone else's wrist throbbed, warm and bruised. Someone else felt sickness and pain. Someone else struggled and beat paper-thin wings trying to escape the pin that impaled him.

I simply watched, calm and separate.

Depersonalization was a trick of the psyche, a separating of the sense of self-in-body to cushion against horror. I knew perfectly well what it was, and knowing didn't change it. I was an observer. So I observed as Grace carried me down the geometric carpet, past the glass figures. I swept out one arm, and Grandpa Miles smashed on the boards.

"So, so sorry, Miles. It wasn't supposed to be this way."

She pushed a door open with a toe.

My bedroom didn't have a speck of dust. The bedding smelled of verbena, the linens fresh and laundered. Everything I'd left behind was exactly where I had left it, even the phonograph horn pointed to the bed. I sank into the featherbed, and Grace drew a brocaded spread over me. She sat on the side of the bed, smoothed one hand over my forehead.

"Say something, Miles. Anything. Hate me. I deserve it."

I closed my eyes. And my voice, my own cool, unruffled voice whispered to the sick hollow feeling inside me: *I don't know this woman.* I knew the girl, the loyal and talented girl who couldn't bear the burden of a secret. Could the woman? Did she plan this, or had she simply been unable to keep a secret from Father?

"Say something."

I kept my eyes closed. "Go away, Grace. Leave me alone."

"Do you want anything?"

"My freedom. Release me."

"It won't be so bad, Miles."

That didn't deserve an answer.

She put her hand on my shoulder. "I want you to practice medicine. I want you to be independent. It's vital people see what a Secondary makes of himself, given free rein."

"Free rein, but not free, Grace."

"I need you, Miles. If I'm to become the Voice, I need you. I wanted to convince you. I didn't want this."

"But you won't release me."

Silence.

I rolled away from her hand, turned my back to her. "Go away."

The bed shifted. The floor still creaked just by the door. It shut, and the scrape of a key turning made the calm, distant part of me nod once.

I'd given all this away, thrown it all aside to be who I wanted to be. A doctor. A healer, not some subservient battery bound to a real person. Thirteen years, I'd been free.

No. Thirteen years I'd been in hiding, folding myself up small in fear of this moment—when they would find me and stick me back in my place.

Here I was. Everything exactly as I left it, every book and record in place. Those years didn't matter here. They didn't even exist.

My life was over. My career gone to dust. All the skill I'd

worked for would go to waste. I was returned to the family cage, nothing more than Grace's Secondary, expected to defer to her, obey her, my only worth the power she could take from me whenever she wished.

I had come so far, even if I had had to hide my power behind the practice of medicine. I'd cure Grace's colds, now. Shrink the cancer in my father's body. Tend to people who already had the best of everything.

I wanted to sleep. I wanted to forget. Many Secondaries never went a day without drinking, trailing behind their Storm-Singer in an alcoholic haze. Some of them smelled of the flowery-sweet perfume of the opium pipe, their gazes unfocused, barely able to walk.

Some of them took enough to make them dream until they never woke up.

So many things can kill you. I knew a hundred without pausing for breath. For the first time since Camp Paradise, I listed the means within reach. I was mentally measuring the cords that tied the silver-gray silk curtains back—strangling to death wasn't pleasant, but it would work.

Another thought poured ice water into my veins—if I died, my soul wouldn't travel to the Solace. Tristan still hadn't found where they were really going.

We had to find out the truth. I couldn't die. I had to fight.

The teeth of Tristan's key pressed into my thigh. I shifted and drew it out of my pocket, turning it in my fingers, touching the scratches and dents. Tristan would wonder what had happened to me. He would look for me. He might know how to undo the binding, and if he didn't, he'd help me fight back.

I slipped it back into my pocket.

I sat up, throwing the spread off my legs. Grace had locked the door. I moved through the narrow corridor connecting bedchamber, dressing room, and bathroom to the sitting room. It was precisely as I'd left it, even the desk sitting before the window with an elm tree a few feet away from the sill.

I hadn't climbed out this window since I was a boy. I was sick. There wasn't anywhere I could run where Grace couldn't eventually find me.

I opened the window, crawled over my old desk and ignored my wrist as I shinnied my way along the rough-barked branch. It dipped under my weight, and brilliant golden leaves shivered and fell at my disturbance. I climbed down, hanging by my hands off the lowest branch to make the drop to the lawn.

It wasn't the best landing. I favored my left ankle as I hobbled to the carriage house, darting inside. The landau was parked, and I stared dumbstruck at the vehicle beside it, long-nosed, sleek, and gleaming.

An automobile. There weren't more than a handful of Sadie Lancer's inventions in the city, being worth more than what a common man could make in a dozen years. They were fabulous objects of spectacle, capable of racing at speeds beyond the fastest horses or the strongest riders.

Grace could catch me in a minute, driving this.

I turned my back on it and found what I wanted. The black painted bicycle I was stealing might have belonged to a servant. I shoved the guilt in the same corner where I ignored my shaking limbs and pedaled over the picturesque, teeth-clattering driveway to the smooth black street.

How long would I have before Grace realized I was gone? She might know already. My spine crawled, but I kept pedaling. I turned the bicycle into Halston Park, riding along its hypotenuse to the opposite side and out of the still-drowsing district.

Wellston Triangle was awake and open for business. I passed bookshops, milliners, tailors, and tea shops, riding into a headwind. A wave of dizziness and darkening vision convinced me to dismount and walk. I had no lock, but Tristan's home wasn't far.

I would have vomited in the street if I'd had anything left to expel. A light sheen of sweat chilled me. But I pushed on to Tristan's front door.

The key fit in the lock. I turned it and let myself in, dragging the bicycle along with me. My reflections were pale, hollow-eyed with shadows. The stairs loomed, steep and narrow. The kitchen seemed a mile away.

But I'd already bicycled for three.

I walked with heavy steps, ignoring the twinge in my ankle, the throb of my wrist. I stumbled along the short corridor to the kitchen.

Tristan sat there in a yellow silk dressing gown, nursing a cup of coffee. "Miles." He stood and helped me to a seat. "You're three-quarters dead, from the look of you. What happened?"

I put my good hand against the table and fought my heaving, empty stomach. "They bound me, Tristan."

"Your family?"

"Yes. I escaped."

"Good for you. Are you well?"

"I'm starving. And it's dark—"

It stayed dark for a while.

SEVENTEEN

The Greater Good

The acid and sugar tang of an orange wet my tongue, and I bit. Juice burst bright as sunshine, grains of sugar melting in my mouth. Deerskin stretched smooth and warm under my skin.

I opened my eyes.

Tristan sat on the edge of the fainting couch, another sugar-sprinkled wedge of orange in his hand. He lifted it to my mouth, and I bit again.

Piece by patient piece, he fed me wedges of orange while the scent of burping coffee and simmering oats carried into the parlor. I tried to sit up, but he pushed my shoulder.

"Relax. You literally fell swooning into my arms. You're not getting up for a while."

"I do not swoon."

"You passed out, drained to your limit. I'm amazed you made it here on your own."

"I had to."

"I suppose your family lives on the Western Point."

"We have a view of the Ayers Inlet, next to the park."

"I tried to explore the point, once. I was politely escorted out of the neighborhood. Your family is powerful."

"Yes. We're all mages, you know. Every one of the Royal Knights."

"And you're bound. To . . ."

"My sister."

"Ah." Tristan gathered up the rinds in one hand. "She'll be looking for you. I'll be back in a minute."

He left the room, and I let my head fall back on the cushions. I felt a little better, but I had starved. I couldn't eat a mountain of food and be ready to fight again. I had to refuel slowly. I would be sitting still for Grace to find. She would find me before I recovered.

The air grew heavier, fuzzy with power. It pulsed, passing over my skin, seeping into the walls with each beat. When Tristan returned, I couldn't hear the noise from the street.

"What did you do?"

"I veiled the house. She can't sense you."

I was safe. "Perfect."

"That depends." Tristan returned with a tray and two bowls—a hearty helping of oats for him, and a smaller portion for me. He handed it over. "I don't have to tell you to eat slowly, but eat slowly."

"I will. What does it depend on?"

"How smart is your sister?"

"Smart. Patient. She will find me eventually." I peered up at him. "You can't . . . Is there a way to sever it? The bond?"

"I can't," Tristan said. "You might, when you've recovered. You're stronger than your sister."

I swallowed warm cereal and nearly choked. "How do you know?"

"You've two soul-stars. She'd have to be a massive talent to match you."

I was stronger than her. All this time, all these years, I'd been second to Grace, less important, less valuable . . . and I had possessed the strength to resist the whole time. I didn't know whether I should feel angry, or foolish.

No. I had no part in the subtle mutilation of my sense of self-worth. And now it didn't matter. I was stronger than Grace. I had Tristan's word on that.

I had the power my mother hadn't. She had made sure that I was strong enough to do this, and I would.

"How do I free myself?"

"If she won't let you go? Drain her until she can't hold the bond anymore."

I set my spoon down. "What happens if I try and I'm not strong enough?"

"You might die, as your mother did." Tristan said it straight out, no hedging or murmuring. "It's not up to me, but I'd rather you didn't."

"But I'm more powerful than her, you think."

"With two souls bound to you? Yes. But you'll hurt her before she gives up and lets go."

"She'll hate me for it."

"Do you wish to remain her thrall so she'll still like you?"

"I'll hate her for it." I ate my oats. They were rich with aromatic spices, studded with chunks of baked apple. "So I stay here until I'm ready to face her."

Tristan drank coffee. "You can stay here as long as you need to. I'll keep renewing the veil. Whom did you heal?"

"I didn't heal him," I said. "I bought him some time, but he's going to die."

"Who?"

"My father."

"Chancellor Hensley?"

"More than that. He's the Voice of the Invisibles," I said.

"He's . . . My father is a spider in an enormous web, and he's dying. My sister would be the one to take over, but there's been a shift in power."

I scraped the bottom of my bowl by the time I finished explaining, the last bite of my oats gluey and cold. Tristan listened, nodding thoughtfully.

"Your return would help improve your sister's chance of taking over. And if she fails, life for the . . . Secondaries wouldn't improve. But your sister wants reform. Do I have it right?"

"Yes," I said. "She wants me to be the example of what a properly valued Secondary can do. She wants them to be more useful."

Tristan tilted his head. "Why do you value Storm-Singers above all?"

I blinked. "The Invisibles control Aeland's weather."

Tristan stared at me. "They control the weather across the country? How?"

"They link," I said. "Hundreds of them work together. Without it, this whole area's natural weather is ruled by terrible storms. It's something to do with water currents, the cold air coming down from the north. . . . The Storm-Singers came to Aeland and turned back the worst of it; then they tamed it; then they calmed seasonal changes to make an ideal growing season. Aeland feeds millions on its measure of land."

Tristan looked astounded. "They link. More than two of them together."

"Amaranthines don't link?"

"Not to such a scale. We link up to three, but it gets hard to control after that. Hundreds?"

"They gather here to sing in the seasons and stay in Kingston over the winter to turn back storms until they sing in the springtime. The country Circles hold local patterns."

The implications clicked together in Tristan's mind. I

watched him think it over. "Brilliant. But if the organization falls apart . . ."

"All of Aeland will suffer. Kingston would be crushed inside a year. The interior would flood, or suffer drought, over and over. Crops will fail. People will starve." I looked away. "I know running away was selfish."

Tristan caught my hand. "They make slaves of you for the sake of their prosperity."

"The greater good of the country. We need Storm-Singers. The fact that they use their powers to make life better for all, beyond simple survival . . . Wouldn't you want the best for your family? For your community?"

Tristan waved it away. "It's not right. It's one thing to serve others. Quite another to be forced into it, however noble the cause. Would you have left, if they didn't bind you?"

"No," I said. "I didn't mind not being important. I can't will the winds. I wanted to heal the sick. I wanted to save lives, not be a battery and a breeder."

Tristan's eyebrows went up. I glanced away.

"Secondaries are . . . matched."

"I'm glad you ran away," Tristan said. "I hope you inspired others to do the same."

"I think I must have," I said. "I don't think my disappearance would be enough to bring my family low."

"Stay here until you're ready to face your sister," Tristan said. "Hopefully you'll have enough time to regain your strength."

"I'm already feeling better."

"Good. I have to get dressed. I'm expecting a caller."

"Who?" I set my bowl on Tristan's tray, and sat up.

"Alice. At least, I suspect she'll come today."

"I should probably hide when she comes. I'm not dressed properly."

"I wasn't going to say anything."

My cheeks grew hot, but I laughed. "I wanted to look like a servant out of livery."

His lips twitched. "Congratulations on your success."

"I suppose I could say I was in disguise."

"You left clothes here," Tristan said. "Mrs. Sparrow cleaned the wine out of the shirt you borrowed the day of the accident, and she mended the tear in your trousers."

I tested my ankle. Not bad at all. "Bless Mrs. Sparrow. My jacket?"

"Still out for treatment. You'll have to settle for shirtsleeves."

"Better than this." I followed Tristan upstairs.

Breakfast wasn't enough. I felt dizzy enough to worry Tristan, and he tucked me onto the chaise, where I dozed under his watchful eye. I dreamed vividly of a house whose rooms changed if you closed a door and then opened it, where I'd been looking for the tall black horse I'd left in the library. I woke with a feeling of dread, for dreams of black horses were a death-omen.

A knock sounded on the door. Tristan set his book aside, but I had to move and clear the last tendrils of the dream from my mind.

"I'll get it." I pushed the stolen bicycle farther down the hall before swinging the door open for Miss Farmer.

The figure standing on the step was taller, more elegant, and less welcome. Grace's long black car rested next to the curb, and Grace herself sighed in relief.

"I haven't come to drag you back," she said. "I want to talk to you."

I pushed the door closed, but Grace blocked it. "Miles, please."

I jerked it open again. "Are you going to release me?"

Grace folded her arms. "So we're going to argue in the street?"

"Go away, Grace."

She lowered her voice. "Miles, we can make this work for both of us."

"How?"

"Will you let me in?"

"This isn't my house."

"It's fine, Miles." Tristan stood behind me, his hand warm on my back. "She doesn't want a spectacle, but she'll make one if you give her no choice."

I sighed and opened the door wider.

"Right," Tristan said. "I'll make some tea."

He deserted me, while Grace took off her coat and came in. She stared at the mirror-covered walls and the mismatched wallpaper. She gave a gusty sigh. "You shouldn't be here, Miles. He's a witch."

"So are we." I opened the door to the parlor.

"We are rather more than common—"

Grace blinked at the bright colors, the profusion of plants, the mirrors on the walls. She inspected the seat of the wingback chair before settling herself, and went fish-eyed at the three-foot-tall water pipe next to the chaise.

"Miles, you can't be serious."

"I find it comfortable."

"It's vulgar."

"Probably why it's comfortable."

"We should go somewhere else to talk. Somewhere private."

I put my feet up on the table. "I'm not leaving. How did you find me?"

"We're linked now."

"I was shielded."

"I was already following you when you vanished. I knew vaguely where you were, so I went looking for wards."

Tristan returned bearing a tea tray. "Pity. I was hoping you weren't that clever."

He sat beside me and poured, stirring in a cube of sugar before giving me a cup. He rested his hand on my thigh as he sipped his own. Grace's nostrils flared as she watched Tristan lean against me as if we were lovers.

I let him.

Tristan spoke into the silence. "What you've done is atrocious."

"This isn't your business."

"Why don't we speak of the weather?" Tristan sipped from his cup. "How do you plan on managing the winter? Do you ever let a snowstorm through, or do you simply shove them away from your borders?"

Grace turned a shocked look on me. "Miles! What have you done?"

"He hasn't done anything. Do you know what you've done?"

Grace ignored him. "Miles. I understand you were lonely and he offered you what you wanted, but a commoner can't be allowed to know our secrets."

Tristan went still next to me. "What will you do, then? Accuse me of witchcraft, put me through one of those farcical trials? Lock me up in an asylum for insanity?"

"You *will* go insane," Grace said. "They all do."

"But you and yours do not," Tristan tilted his head. "Don't you find it strange?"

"They're not equipped to handle power."

"Grace," I interrupted. "There's probably no difference between witches and mages."

Tristan snorted. "The only difference between them and you is that they were born poor, and you weren't. You don't want them around."

Grace squinted. "Them? Not us? Do you think you're some-how different from the other witches?"

"I am no witch." Tristan stood up, taller, more imposing, and shredded the veiling spell hiding his true appearance. Grace gasped and twisted her hands in a protective sign, one Tristan erased with an annoyed swipe of his hand. "Miles is my friend. If he says the word, I will unleash my irritation with you, Dame Grace Hensley. You have the promise of my revenge if you hurt him."

Grace's eyes screwed shut. "You stay away from my brother. Let him go."

"I do not hold him. You do."

Grace was on her knees now, fighting the effect of Tristan's full power. "Let him go. Please. He means nothing to you. He's my brother, my only brother. Please let him go."

My sister begged for me, thinking I was under Tristan's spell. Because she loved me, or because she needed me?

"Tristan, don't." I touched his arm, and he subsided. "Grace. I know you didn't want this to happen this way. So let's set it aside. Release me."

"I can't." Grace picked herself up off the floor. "Miles. You should hate me. You should. I can't let you go. Too much depends on you. Ten Secondaries ran away after you did."

I had suspected as much. "Did they get away?"

"Only two weren't found. The others are under severe con-trol. One killed herself. We can make things better, but if I don't succeed Father, Sir Percy will take over."

Tristan sniffed. "And why should Miles care?"

"You can't understand, Amaranthine. But Miles does."

It was sickening. I did care. I couldn't help it. Sir Percy in charge was terrible for Secondaries. He'd be the Chancellor, with even more power than he had as the Minister of Defense. If he kept his Cabinet post, like Father had . . .

I had to make him answer for what he'd done with this war, and if he were responsible for the soldiers' condition, too—I wished my conscience would let me turn Tristan loose on him, just for the imaginative and terrible vengeance he would visit on Sir Percy. I couldn't. An Amaranthine's revenge could have consequences that rippled beyond the person who paid.

Grace looked at me. "Miles. I swear. You know I'll never mistreat you. I need you to help *them*. And when I'm the Voice, you'll be able to do exactly as you please."

"But you still won't release me."

"It will only matter on the days we sing in the seasons and the half dates. Eight nights a year, Miles. That's all."

"It's not freedom," Tristan said.

"It's not," Grace said. "But it's what I can give."

"I'm sorry, Grace. I can't accept."

"I'm sorry too, Miles. But you don't have a choice."

"I do."

The tie between me and my sister wasn't a string, exactly, but I could see the connection reflected in one of Tristan's mirrors. Through it, she could take my power and use it as if it were her own, as if—

As if my soul were bound to her, the way Mother and Nick were bound to me. But with one difference: souls were just power. I had a will.

I grabbed her wrist.

She startled. "Miles, what are you—Miles!"

Her aura was golden and strong. I had to be stronger. I tried pulling on the bond between us, but it was as solid as the cables holding the Ayers Bridge.

She tried to yank her hand away. "Miles, stop."

"Will you let me go?"

"I can't!"

"You won't." I pulled, testing the bond again. I could do this. I would be free.

"Please."

"He forced both of us, Grace."

"It's the only way!"

"Find another."

The edges of her aura diminished. It lay closer to her skin, thinner, paler. The bond was supple, if you could call steel cable supple. I'd have to pull until it became a strand, and I was already dizzy.

Grace hauled backwards, and we fell into a heap on the floor. She balled up a fist and punched me in the eye, but I didn't let go—not of her arm and not of the power.

"You're hurting me."

"You can make it stop. Let me go."

She kicked out and hit me again, a solid blow to the delicates.

"Miles!" Tristan moved as I drew my knees up and gasped.

The tie was a hemp rope now. I was winning. Blood seeped from Grace's nose. I hadn't hit her, but red ran down her chin, dripping onto her oyster silk blouse and stormy mauve tie, scarlet and bright with oxygen.

"Miles," Tristan gripped my shoulder. "She's dying."

Grace coughed, and red flew from her mouth. She bled inside, her heart and lungs weakening under the assault. For an instant I saw Mother, and remembered how she had fought Father's grip on her wrist as she had coughed up blood and rasped, "Let go."

Father had held fast and said, "I can't."

This was how Mother had died—she had pitted her lesser strength against Father's, trying to sever the bond between them, and Father had let her die rather than unbind her. I was stronger than my sister. She had to see that.

"Let go," I said. "Please, Grace."

"I can't."

Grace tried to pull the power away from me. The effort was so feeble a child could do better. She went limp, blood bubbling on her lips, but she wouldn't let go.

I would be free, but she would be dead.

I let go of the power and yanked on her bloody tie, my fingers on the pulse of her throat.

"Grace. I'm sorry. Come back."

She coughed again, but her nose stopped bleeding. I fought to put the life back in her, to undo what I'd done. Tristan kept his hands on my shoulders and gave me a steady stream of power tinged with sadness and guilt, mixing with mine.

"Grace!"

I wouldn't let her die. Her breaths evened as I repaired the little tears in her lungs, soothed her overworked heart, massaged liver and kidneys back into function. The room tilted crazily, but I didn't dare stop.

"I'm sorry, Grace. I didn't know. I would have never—"

She lifted one hand to my face. Mother had done that, before she had poured her power into me. "Miles."

I held onto it and looked at Tristan. "I can't."

"You can't," he said. "She'd rather die than free you."

"He's right." Grace's voice was hoarse. "I'm a coward."

"Stop. It will be all right, Grace. We'll work it out."

"Now you'll hate me."

"Never," I said. "I could never hate you."

Her smile slid across bloody teeth. "Maybe not today. But you will. I can't let you go, Miles. I have to lead the Invisibles. I have to."

"Shh. Tristan, help me."

He knelt and picked up my sister, carrying her up to the room I slept in. He brought me a basin of warm water and a sponge, soaked her blouse in a sink full of cold while I cleaned the blood from her skin. He took the sponge and basin away, and steered me back downstairs to rest on the chaise.

"You look like I ought to tuck you in by her side," Tristan said.

"I'm fine."

"You're not." His hand was warm on my shoulder. "But I'll let it be. She'll be hungry when she wakes up."

My own stomach growled. "Is there still some sausage?"

"Mrs. Sparrow will return to a bare larder."

I shivered. I'd almost killed my sister. "What do I do now?"

Tristan caught my hand and squeezed. "You find a way to live with it."

EIGHTEEN

Compromises

Grace slept through the knocking at the front door that interrupted my early supper. I expected Alice Farmer, but Avia Jessup sauntered into the parlor dressed in wide-legged trousers paired with a black and white knitted vest, a burgundy tie snugged under her collar matching the paint on her lips. She paused on the edge of Tristan's hand-knotted wool carpet, one foot forward, the other back, and one hip thrust in a smooth curve. She raised two fingers to her mouth, planting an unlit cigarette between them. I ached for a smoke of my own.

"You look like a starving man, hero." She took the chair Grace had occupied with a lazy grace, leaning forward for my light. "For food or a smoke?"

"If you have another of those, I'd be obliged."

She snapped her handbag open, and a silver case rested in her hand. "My treat. Mr. Hunter? A smoke?"

He grimaced. "No, thank you."

Avia blew violet-tinged smoke to the ceiling. "I took Alice's card. She didn't need it. Never forgets a thing, poor girl."

"It's an extraordinary gift," I said.

She shook her head. "Good things and bad, hero. Your bad times have faded. Hers never will." She ignored the tea service. "You're sure Nick was murdered?"

"We are."

"When he hadn't come to work, I thought—" Her little finger tapped at the corner of her mouth as she thought, decided. "I thought he'd killed himself."

"What were your reasons for believing that?" Tristan asked. "Was he unhappy?"

"It wasn't quite unhappiness. Look, I know it's still an hour for coffee, but do you have anything a girl could brace herself with?"

"Whiskey?" Tristan asked.

"All the gods bless you." Avia waited for the cut-crystal tumbler and drank it down. "When did he die?"

"Firstday."

She swallowed another mouthful. Tristan had poured a deep one. "I was there the day he died, then. He'd come home from one of his journeys. I watered his plants while he was gone."

"So you were at his home on Wellston Street?"

She nodded. "He was . . . he stared at the wall. He wouldn't talk. I was used to him keeping secrets, but he was a wreck. I should have stayed with him, but I'm not the one you call when you're sick or sad. I didn't know what to do for him."

"What did you try?"

"There wasn't so much as a stick of butter in the place. I called Swanson's for him, so he'd have something to eat."

Tristan leaned in a little closer. "What did you order?"

"Nick wasn't much of a cook. He liked pocket pies. I ordered a half dozen. Frozen crab chowders. Grapes and cookies, apple pockets. He was hopeless in the kitchen."

"Did you eat with him?"

"I was on the city beat," Avia said. "I ducked in to say hello, but I was supposed to be 'capturing the spirit of Kingston in the days anticipating the return of our soldiers.' I only stayed long enough to answer the door when the groceries came."

"Had you done this before?"

"It's why Nick and I were never serious. He'd shut himself up writing, forget to eat, and he grew quieter and stranger. I'd gone there to—" She drew on her cigarette. "I'm a good person."

"You were going to break off your tender friendship," Tristan said.

"I like a man who can take care of himself. And Nick was getting worse. Every trip he'd come back with more secrets, working on his damned book."

"Do you know what the book was about?" I asked.

She shook her head. "He said he had to keep it a secret until it was published. So it wasn't about gardening. Nick should have stuck to flowerbeds. He was killed for that book, wasn't he?"

"What makes you think so?"

"I went back to check on him when he didn't show for work," Avia explained. "I already feared the worst. I went looking for a note. There wasn't a scrap of paper in his office. Not even the list I'd written for the grocery order."

My heart pounded. Tristan and I shared a look. "What were you looking for?"

Her shoulders slumped. "A note, maybe. But then I looked for his manuscript, any papers at all. It was all gone."

"Including the grocery list. You said you'd ordered groceries for him before," I said. "Was there anything different about this order? Anything at all?"

"It wasn't Cedric."

"Cedric's the delivery boy?"

Avia nodded. "It was a man. Recently fallen on hard times, I thought."

"Why?"

"His clothes. Oh he was in tweed, but it wasn't scrap woven. It was fine stuff. And he had a beaver hat. Much too good for such a humble job."

I wondered if he rode a brand-new bicycle.

"Thank you." Tristan rested his elbows on his knees, leaning as close as he could get. "What you've told us is very helpful. Would you recognize the man, if you saw him again?"

"Unless he shaved off his mustache."

"It was memorable?"

"It was the pride of his face. The ends curled up, like a soldier's." She eyed me. "Did you wear one? You probably looked quite dashing in yours, hero."

"I had to, Miss Jessup. Regulations." I smiled back. "They're a bother to groom."

"He had watery blue eyes. Not like yours, Mr. Hunter. They were pale. If I saw him again, the mustache is how I'd know him."

"Would you give a witness statement?"

She sat back. "You think he's the murderer."

"Don't go looking for him," Tristan warned. "All you newspaper people would follow curiosity to your death. If he is, he's dangerous. Promise you won't."

She put one hand up as if swearing an oath. "By my heart's own blood, I'll be a good girl."

"Thank you, Miss Jessup."

"One more thing," I said.

Avia smiled. "Whatever you like, hero."

I hoped the heat in my cheeks wasn't a blush. "What was Nick's opinion of the war?"

"He hated it," Avia said. "He read *The Peaceful Press* and *The People's Voice*, you know. Kept his mouth shut at work, of course—nobody at the *Star* would listen to an antiwar argument for a second. . . . He'd never disrespect you for going over, Dr. Singer. He wasn't angry at the soldiers."

"Who was he angry at?"

"The War Committee, of course. Sir Percy Stanley chief among them. Did you know that Sir Percy's on the board for half a dozen companies with particular commercial interest in Laneeri exports? I'm no slogan shouter, but this victory is lining his pockets with gold, and I mean that literally."

"I didn't know."

"Oh, sure. Crown Lumber, Royal Mining, Queen's Textile and Export, Aeland Aether and Lights, National Rail and Shipping . . . I can't remember the last. It adds up to a mountain of gold though, doesn't it? I can see why Nick was cynical."

"I see," I said. "It does put a rather personal cast on Minister Stanley's motives, doesn't it?" My hands shook for another cigarette. If I were to follow this to the end . . .

Well. I no longer needed to worry about getting caught by my family. Perhaps a mouse could hunt a fox after all. I wasn't foolish enough to believe that Percy would ever answer for Nick's murder, but we could keep him from taking the Invisibles, and perhaps I could find a different way to make Sir Percy pay for Nick's life.

Miss Jessup rose to accept Tristan's bow over her hand, handing me another cigarette before she left. I stashed it in my breast pocket while Tristan escorted her out. He opened the parlor windows on his return.

"I prefer the scent of burning hashish," he said. "But Miss Jessup saw Nick's murderer. Do you want to bet it's not the man we chased through the street?"

"I wouldn't even bet a button against it."

"Cedric, hmm? Mrs. Sparrow buys our groceries from Swanson's. We have a quest," Tristan said. "Swanson's isn't far. We'll go tomorrow. They're closed by now."

"I should check on Grace."

She lay on her side with the blankets pulled up to her ears, but she wasn't asleep. I waited by the door. "Do you want me to bring you something to eat?"

She didn't move. "How can you be nice to me?"

"You're my sister."

"I made your worst nightmare come true." She rolled over and lifted her head. She looked near bloodless, she was so pale.

Guilt and shame touched me from our link. She knew what I had fled as a boy, and here it was, done to me.

It had been the worst thing I could imagine, at seventeen and brought up in the palm of privilege. But I had suffered worse. I had the medal to prove it.

I laid my hand on her forehead, reading her health. "What's your worst nightmare, Grace?"

"Losing the Voice."

She would be fine. She needed a good night's rest, plenty to eat, and no magic for a day, but she would be well. But . . . "Have you ever wondered what it would have been like if you didn't have to be the Voice?"

"I have to. Father—"

"Has a couple more months."

"That's all?" Distress cracked her voice. "Will he live until the wedding?"

"At New Year? He might."

"It's not enough time."

"It has to be. Why do you care so much about Secondaries?"

"You're a Secondary. Edwin . . ." Here she faltered, and her lips and eyelids clamped shut as she remembered her girlhood love. "He's bound to Regina Howard."

"Regina Howard isn't an Invisible, is she? What does she need a Secondary for?"

She gave me a pointed look. "Regina Howard isn't married, but she's pregnant with her second child."

It took a minute to sink in. "That's monstrous."

"It has to stop. As the Voice, I can stop it."

"And Sir Percy won't."

Grace's laugh was bitter. "Children are a blessing, Miles. There are Invisibles who effectively have two wives . . . only one doesn't have the legal rights of a spouse."

"Why didn't you tell me before?"

"Before you climbed out the window and came here?"

I shrugged. "Fair enough."

"I mean it, Miles. I don't want to control you. But I need you. I need *you*."

She did, blast it. And she needed me to be the Secondary everyone expected, so my return to the family would be a triumph.

"I want my independence. I will live my own life. I will continue to be a doctor at Beauregard. I will have my own home."

She took my hand. "Miles. I promise you. You will be as free as I can let you be."

"You'll negotiate cause for unbinding for Secondaries," I went on. "So one who is mistreated or ill-used can petition to be freed."

She sat up, face alight. "Yes. And training of gifts. Calling them gifts, not tricks—oh, there's so much to do, Miles. So much."

"Perhaps we should discuss it over supper, downstairs."

The fire in her eyes faded. "You know what he is, don't you?"

"His name is Tristan."

She narrowed her eyes at my familiar address. "Miles, you can't stay with him."

"He hasn't hurt me, Grace."

"You know what happens after Amaranthines tire of their mortal toys. You can stay at the Edenhill. As long as you like."

"I'm not his toy. Tristan is my friend."

"His kind don't have friends."

"He has one."

"I can't lose you to madness."

"Grace, you know the stories as well as I do. Tristan's a vain, restless creature. He's arrogant. He's kind because he chooses to be." The criticisms flowed from my mouth, unfettered. "Am I bewitched?"

She bit her lip at my frank recitation of Tristan's faults. "No. But he could—"

"I trust him."

"You shouldn't."

I folded my arms. "I pick my friends."

She let her head drop back to the pillow. "Why's he even here?"

I turned to the slim collection of shirts in my wardrobe. Tristan had loaned me a few, and I picked out one of those, linen soft from laundering. "That's his story to tell."

"He won't tell me." Grace sat up and stuck her arms in the sleeves, flopping back against the pillows when dizziness made her pale. There was a spot of blood browning on the lace border of her chemise.

"Maybe you shouldn't be a prat to my friends." I lifted her hands and buttoned the cuffs, closed the buttons on her borrowed shirt. "I'll fetch you something. Stay right where you are."

Tristan met me in the hall in front of the kitchen. "How is your sister?"

"She can't get out of bed yet," I said. "But plenty to eat and some rest, and she'll be perfectly well."

"What about you?"

"I'm practically recovered."

Tristan folded his arms.

"But I wouldn't mind another orange."

"Feed yourself before you tend your patient." Tristan led the way into the kitchen. "And tell me what you're going to do."

"The situation is more serious than when I left." I picked out an orange from a painted blue bowl. I tried not to defend the Invisibles as I explained what Grace had told me. Tristan's face was stone before I finished.

"Come with me. Hang all of this."

"I have to help them."

"Why?"

"Because they matter," I said. "I can't leave them to suffer if I can do something to help."

Tristan twisted up one side of his mouth, folding his arms. "And your sister cares about this. The way you do."

"No. But she does care. She sees it's wrong."

"And the best way to help them happens to be her holding one of the most powerful positions in Kingston." Tristan scooped up my orange rinds and took them to the trash. "That seems suspicious, but very well. Will she be well enough to leave in the morning? We have to find this Cedric before I have to go back."

We didn't have much time. Only today, and Restday—I had to work on Firstday—and then Tristan would go. The delivery boy was our latest lead, one more piece of a picture jumble, and I didn't know where to find the rest.

NINETEEN

Carnage

The chaise lounge wasn't too bad to sleep on, and after a late breakfast Grace was well enough to take her automobile west while Tristan and I walked east, impatient to be on our errand. Swanson's Groceries boasted a bright yellow awning shading the stands of fruit and vegetables displayed half in the sidewalk, with a stand of local apples free for anyone to take. Tristan picked one up and bit into it.

"I've never bought groceries," he said. "Mrs. Sparrow does the shopping."

I'd only done it a few times myself, but I knew enough. Workers wore yellow aprons over their clothes, so I found a boy putting up tins of preserves.

"Help you find something, sir?"

"I'm looking for a delivery boy named Cedric. Is he here?"

"If he is, he'd be in back." He stopped stocking shelves long enough to point to a door next to sacks of porridge oats and dried vegetables.

The back area held more food in storage on stacked wooden platforms. A gingery-haired man set a wooden crate full of produce on a shelf made of horizontal cylinders, and a shove sent the box on its way to the end of the line, where boys read the order slips and packed the crates on three-wheeled bicycles to take away.

The man glanced at me and Tristan. "Help you, gentlemen?"

"I'm looking for Cedric."

He put his fists on his hips and squinted at me. "What's he done?"

"Nothing bad," I said. "I want to ask him about a delivery he made last week."

"Something wrong with it? You can't take it out on him; he's just the one who brings it." The man scowled.

"There's been no trouble," I said, soothing. "I'd just like to speak to Cedric."

"He's a valuable part of your service." Tristan offered a bank note. The man blinked. It was a generous, even outrageous tip, but it disappeared into the man's pocket.

"Cedric!" he bellowed, and a boy startled like he expected a blow. "These men want to talk to you."

He trotted over, eyebrows aslant with worry. "Did I do something wrong?"

"Not at all. We wanted to ask you a question about your delivery route. Do you share your territory with anyone?"

"Janey Cooper. She does my route when I'm not working."

"But you were working in the afternoon last Firstday?"

He nodded. "Busy day. I was loading three orders at once."

"Do you remember delivering to Nick Elliot at 301, 1455 Wellston Street West?"

He nodded. "Sure. That one was easy, since the man waited for me downstairs."

"Nick waited for you downstairs?"

He shook his head. "No, sir. It was his friend. Said he'd take it up for me, since he was going to see Mr. Elliot. He gave me three dimes for a tip."

Three dimes could buy enough candy to make him the best fellow of his peers for a week. "Do you remember what the man looked like?"

"Rich. Not like him—" He pointed at Tristan's cashmere coat and kid leather gloves. "But almost. He had a mustache like a Serviceman, but he wasn't wearing a coat like yours."

"Was he tall?"

"Not like you," Cedric said. "What's the matter? Did he steal the food after all?"

Tristan and I shared a glance. "What do you mean?"

"He went in the hall downstairs," Cedric said. "Mr. Elliot's on three, and the building's got no elevator."

Where the utility rooms were. He could have hidden down there, doctored Nick's food, and then delivered it. I remembered what Nick had said: "in the tea." He meant the meal meant to tide one over to supper, not the drink.

"Thank you, Cedric. If you saw the man again, would you recognize him?"

Cedric scrunched up his brow. "He was kind of ordinary. Nothing special about him."

"But the mustache."

"Right." Cedric touched his own upper lip, tracing the down there with his fingers. "Did you want to know anything else? I have to work."

"For your time," Tristan said, and silver coins dropped into Cedric's palm. "You're a sharp-eyed lad."

"Thank you, sir." The coins went into a pocket, and Cedric trotted off.

I led the way back into the public part of the store, stopping at an ice-cooled case for bottles of apple soda. Tristan browsed down the aisle, waiting for me to get through the lineup to pay.

He touched the covers of magazines with photos of cinema stars. I sorted past the *Herald* to see the *Star,* and bile rose in my throat.

Carnage! the headline read, and a picture of a uniformed policeman barring the way to a brick rowhouse dominated the page.

"The paper too, sir?" The cash-girl asked me.

I paid and stuffed it under my arm, headline hidden in the folds.

"You take the weekend paper? I didn't think you a devotee of the leisure section," Tristan commented.

"There's been another murder."

"Another? What do you mean?"

We were out on the street now, shoulder to shoulder with the wind at our backs. "You remember the first night, when the police wouldn't come because they were at another murder?"

Tristan gave me a rueful look. "Vaguely."

"Veterans have been killing their families. Wives, children, and then themselves," I said. "It's happened again."

We shared the paper between us, back in the parlor at Tristan's house. I read about Cpl. Terrence Pigeon, a Serviceman recently returned from Laneer who'd slit the throats of everyone in his home, then attacked people in the street until police subdued him. Tristan leaned on me, reading over my shoulder.

"This is awful. And this happened last week?"

"Yes. All ex-soldiers, recently home from the war."

Tristan cocked his head. "You treat soldiers at your work."

I nodded. "They captured this one. The other two killed themselves."

"And you wonder why."

"The soldiers I work with are . . . War is terrible. I can't even describe to you what it was like over there. What happened to us, what we did to them. It hurts the psyche in profound ways."

"Does it make them murder their families?"

It was speculation. I didn't have any evidence. I didn't want to believe it—not with the number of men I'd seen at the homecoming parade with the same infection as Old Gerald, the same as Bill and the twenty-one other patients I'd kept off the discharge list. But I told Tristan the truth.

"I fear that it does."

Tristan rubbed my shoulder while I stared down at the policeman on the cover of the *Star*. "Go on."

Outside, someone shouted a merry invitation to share a drink. Sunshine slanted across mirrors, the bright light of afternoon. I leaned into Tristan's hand and went on. "Some of the men have a delusion in common. They believe there's a killer inside their bodies, who wants to lash out at everyone. I think there's a physical cause, but I can't find it."

"Is this something you can see with your power?"

I sighed. "Yes. I've been keeping it a secret while I try to discover the problem with a mundane test."

"Because it would betray your talent," Tristan said. "However, you were a surgeon when you were in Laneer. I know enough to know people revere surgeons and think psychiatrists shouldn't even be called doctors. Why did you switch?"

I closed my eyes. "The Laneeri raided a field hospital to take me. And if all they wanted was a good doctor saving their lives, that wouldn't have been so bad."

Tristan's hand slid over my shoulders, the material of my shirt slipping under his hand as he stroked my spine. I touched my patients like this, to see them through the darkest parts of their stories.

"They made me save them," I said. "My own men. They'd been tortured. Mutilated. They knew how I could work miracles.

They put a gun to my head and held it there until I passed out from healing. Then they'd feed me until I recovered, and make me do it again. One man, I healed him four times, so they could question him again. He didn't know what they wanted. It didn't stop them."

"You were coerced."

"I should have let them kill me."

"No one wants to die, Miles."

"They did," I said. "They begged me. I should have—"

Tristan put his finger over my lips. "You were rescued. You think you didn't deserve it. You were kidnapped, imprisoned. It's not your fault."

How many times had I said that to my patients?

He pulled me into his side and I leaned on him, unashamed that I needed the closeness. He laid my head on his shoulder and went on. "When they rescued you, they sent you home. But you couldn't be that kind of a healer, so you found another way."

"Psychiatry."

"Because you still want to heal them," Tristan said. "You never give up, Miles. You're as brave as any healer I know. Braver. My friend Cormac—I wish I could take you to him."

"Amaranthines need healers?"

"We can be hurt, Miles. Or killed."

"I thought you were immortal."

"Only if we live a boring life. He'd teach you what I can't. You'd probably teach him a thing or two. But he'd have nothing but admiration for you and what you've done."

"I wish—"

"Shh. You don't have to say anything," Tristan said. "Where I come from, you'd have a companion."

"Like an assistant?"

"In a sense. Someone to keep you from killing yourself trying to save someone else. I can't imagine how you manage to do this alone."

"There's no other way to do it."

"If I—if you had a companion, he'd tell you what happened wasn't your fault. You did what you had to do so you could survive. And he'd be glad you were back."

I lifted my head from his shoulder. "You didn't know me before."

"Then I'm glad you wound up where I could find you."

He was so close. I'd been calmed before, soothed by his nearness. Now I felt more stirring in me.

He put two fingers under my chin and drew me close enough so our breaths puffed together, close enough for his warmth to radiate over my mouth in the instant before he kissed me.

The crisp sweetness of apple soda flavored his mouth, and I fizzed like the bubbles that rose when the bottle first opened, cold shivers and hot tingles chasing over my skin where his warmth didn't press against me. Dizzy, I opened my mouth wider, and he pulled me tight against him.

We'd been headed for this moment no matter how I tried to turn my back on it, to deny the stupid part of me that didn't care he was heartless, didn't care that Amaranthines never loved, didn't love. And now, with his hand cradling the small of my back, I didn't care either. I didn't care for anything but more.

We shoved bright cushions aside, and I rested my head on a padded bolster. A pillow lay awkwardly under my ribs, and I didn't care. Tristan's braid fell over his shoulder and pooled in the curve of my neck as he stretched over me. I caught his tie in my fingers and pulled it loose, pinching his collar button open. His heart beat hard in his chest, and he shivered. A warm feeling spread through me. He might be an Amaranthine, but I was enchanting him.

"Miles," he gasped. "We need a bed."

"No, we don't." I didn't want him to stop, not even for the half minute it would take to fly upstairs. I pulled him back down to undo another button, to feel his skin on mine.

It was as good as magic. It was magic. I let it seep from my fingertips when I touched him, and Tristan gripped me tight even as he shuddered. I did it again, again. I'd never touched a lover with magic. I had never been myself, even in those most private moments. Always hiding, never free.

Freed, I dragged him down for another kiss.

And then he lifted his head to the sound of the knocker on the front door.

"That could be Alice." Tristan's hair slipped loose of his braid. His shirt collar and tie were undone.

I probably looked as rumpled, but I sat up. "I'll put the water on."

We left the chaise cushions on the floor as we went our separate ways.

Miss Farmer perched on the edge of an oval-backed chair, hands nested in her lap. She wore her Restday best, and a scrap of lace netting peeked out of the bag at her feet. She was wide-eyed and frightened at calling on a house with no women.

"Tea, Miss Farmer?" I made a show of pouring my own cup, using the cream as well as the sugar even though I preferred it black and sweet. "Tristan will be with us shortly. He gives his housekeeper two days off. We should have thought . . ."

Her gaze flicked from my rumpled hair and hastily straightened tie, and she offered a timid smile. "I interrupted you."

There's a smart girl. If Tristan were staying, I'd suggest he and Miss Farmer become investigative partners. She would be better at it than me.

"Miss Farmer," Tristan said, and she nodded over her rattling cup, bark-brown curls shivering. "I hope I haven't kept you waiting?"

He set a notebook and pen next to the tea and sat beside me again. Alice suppressed a sigh of relief as his hand rested on my knee.

"I came because I didn't want anyone else in the newsroom to know. They would have . . . asked questions."

After experiencing a curiosity of reporters all trained on me, I didn't blame shy, uncomfortable Alice for wanting to avoid such scrutiny. "We'll have questions too. Is it about Nick's book?"

"Yes. Nick Elliot was writing a book about the witch asylums."

All my suppositions shattered. He wasn't writing about the war? He was writing about witches? What was Nick talking about, then, when he said the soldiers deserved to know?

Tristan set his teacup down. "Do you know why?"

"He was obsessed," Alice said. "He read everything about testing and trial, going back fifty years. He kept it a secret—Cully Miller knows her department is full of reporters dreaming of the city desk or current affairs or investigative reporting, even though writing a column is steadier money."

"Not nearly as much glory as breaking a major story," Tristan mused. "Do you know why he was so interested in witches?"

Because he was one himself, of course. But Alice didn't know, and I wasn't about to tell her. She looked down at her knees, pressed demurely together and covered in sober gray gabardine. "I think it had to do with his mother."

"Why his mother?"

"She was examined and found to be a witch. There was a notice in the *Star* years ago. Applebranch twelve, in the fourteenth year of Queen Constantina's rule."

The year I had run away to trade seven years' service to the Queen for medicine. I reckoned in my head. "Nick couldn't have been more than—"

"Thirteen," Alice said. "He came here to live with a guardian. He used to live in Bywell before his mother was committed as a patient."

Tristan glanced at me. "Miss Farmer, do you know if the other towns Nick visited had witch asylums?"

"They all did. Goldenwood Asylum in Norton, established in the thirtieth year of King Nicholas's rule—"

She watched me wrinkle my brow and took pity on me. "Forty-one years ago. Clarity House in Bywell, construction completed at about the same time. They were all built around forty years ago. May I use your notebook?"

She had round, beautiful writing, and she listed each town Nick had visited, the name of the asylum, and the year it was opened.

"Did you ever see his manuscript?"

"I'm sorry, Mr. Hunter." She rubbed at an ink smudge on her fingers. "He never let me see it. I only saw his notes on the construction of the six asylums, and the enormous amount of money approved to build railways to those towns, even though they were remote and expansion of the secondary lines had to wait while Aeland built trains to nowhere."

I shut my jaw. Every schoolboy learned of the dotty idea of an aging king who didn't understand transportation planning. But the asylums built at the ends of those lines at the same time?

They had never taught us about the asylums in school.

My next thought chilled me: What if it wasn't dotty?

Tristan squeezed my knee. "Miss Farmer. I think you were wise in telling us this, and in keeping it a secret."

She looked hopeful. "Do you know what it means?"

Tristan shook his head. "Not yet. But I will."

He escorted Alice out, then returned, plunging past me into the room he used as a library. I stood at the threshold as he hunted through his collection.

"Where is it, where is it, how could it disappear, the damned thing's huge—ah! Miles. Come and look at this."

"This" was an atlas opened to the page illustrating a map of Aeland. He waved a hand over the expensive plate illustration. "Where are these towns?"

I shook my head. "They're nowhere. Tiny little places, and even the railway didn't grow them."

"Who wanted them built?"

"The King," my schoolboy reflex said. "No. He had advisers. The Minister of—"

My mouth went dry.

"Miles?"

"The Minister of Transportation and Infrastructure."

"Which is . . . oh."

"My father. Grandpa Miles was still the Chancellor. Father was Minister. He still holds the post."

I had thought it was Sir Percy. I could blame him for the war, but did Nick's death lay at another suspect's feet? Father could be part of it. If he hadn't wanted those trains running to nowhere, they wouldn't have been built. Would my father kill to keep a secret?

I didn't really have to ask. The correct question was: Would Grace? Father had been too sick to rise from his bed a week ago. He'd been easing her into the business of taking his place. The man with the mustache could be Father's man, but he could just as easily be Grace's.

Tristan handed me the atlas. "Find those towns, Miles. Please."

I scanned the pages, but they were fly-specks. The only one

of any size was Bywell, near the center of the country. But the book had an index, and soon the map bore red dots circling the land—not quite on the borders, but close. Why would Father want asylums there?

Tristan frowned at it. "Why build there?"

"Distance from home environment—"

"I remember, Miles. You told me. But why this far? Do they all hold witches? What else is out there? I need to know, and I can't find out."

I said what I'd been avoiding all this time. "You can't stay."

"I can't. The Grand Duchess will act as if I needed to be retrieved. I expect there will be searchers looking for me on the other side of the stones, and if they cross over to find I'm not imprisoned or incapacitated . . . Well. Would you want your crown prince displeased with you?"

I didn't want him to go. "Annoying a prince is a bad idea."

"Grand Duchess Aife will take a lot of soothing. She doesn't like it when her favorites are away for too long."

"You're a favorite?"

"Ever since I saved her life." He touched the page, turning it to a map of Kingston at least ten years out of date. "If I come back . . . will I find you here?"

"Here? In Kingston?"

"In this house," he said. "Live here. I've leased it for two years. There's money in the chests; I certainly won't need it."

I hesitated. I didn't live at Mrs. Bass's house because it was all I could afford, but out of inertia. Finding a flat on the west end took more time than I had, working at the hospital, and if I didn't move, Grace would move me. I had a sum in my bank account that could cushion the cost of Mrs. Sparrow, but Michael? I didn't need a driver. It was an impractical idea. But I felt welcome in this place, welcome and at home.

"Live here, Miles. Let me think of coming back to you."

"I—"

"Please."

I wanted to. I wanted to be here. "I will."

Tristan's smile warmed my face, now caught in his hands and tilted to meet his mouth. "Miles."

The knocker rapped four times, sharp and loud.

I stepped back.

"A pox on whoever that is," Tristan declared, striding across the floor to look out the parlor window. "Twice and twice again! It's your sister."

"Grace? What would—oh, no," I groaned. "She wants me to attend the premiere of the social season."

"What fortuitous timing," Tristan muttered. "I'll send her away, if you wish."

I sighed. "Let her in. I think I know what she has planned."

"I wouldn't ask, Miles, but it's so important that people see you before the vote."

Grace still looked a little pale, but she could still make that face that made me feel terrible for denying her something she really wanted. "What vote is that?"

"The First Ring is holding a vote over who leads the ritual. Sir Percy has convinced his factions that the position of leadership should not be assumed by inheritance." Grace's lips were flat, her jaw set hard. "I'm sorry, Miles. I need all the advantage I can get. That means putting you on display."

And it would tear me away from Tristan's side. The Return was an all-night party with no consideration for the sleep of the working man. The Hundred Families didn't pursue occupations or trade, so why not stay up all night?

Tristan would be gone by tomorrow night. I wouldn't be here to say goodbye. I'd be with Grace as she sung in winter as

our father's proxy, as the successor to the Voice. With her prodigal brother returned and brought properly to heel, she would
step higher in the eyes of the Invisibles, secure her hold on the
power she'd been born to take.

The secret power preserved by Nick Elliot's death.

"I haven't anything to wear."

Grace nodded at the carriage. "We'll have to fetch your uniform."

Of course. It was the perfect costume for this little drama. I
sighed and held out my hand. Everyone would stare anyway, why
not stand out as a cardinal amongst crows?

"I can't stay until dawn. I work. You will have to leave early.
Say you're kenning the air. It'll make sense, if it's a storm year."

"I forget you don't sense much in the air."

"Enough to guess when I need an umbrella." I turned to
Tristan. "I'm sorry."

"We have our duties," Tristan said. "You still have the key.
Wake me when you come back."

TWENTY

The Return

We have to leave early," I said for the tenth time.

I'd left my watch on the nightstand next to my bed. I should have brought it with me despite custom. The rest of the Hundred Families had no care for the hours spent in celebration, but the hospital expected me with the sun.

We bounced and vibrated in the carriage as I tried to keep things ordinary. I closed my eyes, mentally scanning every conversation I'd had with her. She was better at keeping secrets than the Grace I remembered. If she wasn't, she probably had told Father about me before I'd gone there to heal him. If she was, I could be riding in a carriage with an accessory to murder . . . at least. My heart pounded. Was my sister a murderer?

She might have orchestrated our meeting at the benefit, come to the hospital to keep a closer watch on me than the follower she'd set on my trail. Was it Grace, or my father?

I had no trouble imagining my father sending an underling after Nick Elliot. Telling that same underling to follow me. It smacked of his style, of pulling on puppet strings and making them dance.

But Grace would inherit at his death. The money, the property . . . the power she craved so badly.

Clear skies greeted us as we stepped from the carriage. Returning families strolled into the Hall perched on the tip of the Western Point. Curious eyes glanced back at my jarring scarlet tunic, and mouths sprang into slack-jawed surprise at my face. Here I was, returned. A hero of the war come home, settled into his place two paces behind the sister who really counted, the sister who would be their Voice.

What would she do to ensure her place?

I pushed the thought down and followed Grace into the hall.

Whispers and shock followed me into the five-sided ballroom at the center of the hall, the crowds parting like theater curtains to make a path to the dais at the western point where a gilt and violet throne rested.

An empty throne. Her Majesty had descended. We were late.

Grace stood up straight, turned her head a fraction to the left, then right. Silence rippled to the edges, catching the musicians up in it.

Silence, until a woman in red stepped into the cleared floor. "I'm right here, my girl."

We bent our heads and knees. Queen Constantina's scarlet gown was heavy with autumn-turning leaves beaded and embroidered so thickly at the hem I wanted to hear them rustle and crunch as she came closer, hand extended for Grace to kiss.

"Rise, both of you. Dame Grace. Sir Christopher."

I nearly looked for my father before I stood and bowed over her hand, then looked into her eyes.

Queen Constantina had been beautiful as a young woman, but maturity made her arresting. Her age rested easily on fine bones, her even, golden-toned skin soft on a face that laughed, and frowned, and lived. A fortune of diamonds, topazes, rubies, and emeralds draped over lean shoulders and curved collarbones.

Golden oak leaves crowned her upswept black curls, threads of silver glinting without apology.

She reached out to touch my medals, lifting each one and feeling the profile of her own face. I wanted to close my eyes when my copper coin rested on the pads of her fingers, to pull away as she peered at the broken shackles on its face.

"So that's what you did, Sir Christopher. You ran off to join the Service. Tell us why."

"Arrogance, your Majesty. I joined the surgeons to use my gift."

"Majesty, Sir Christopher has a knack for healing. He wanted to use it," my sister explained.

"Do all Secondaries have such, or are you special?"

"Some might, ma'am."

"And now you've returned to your true duties?"

You could lose your tongue for lying to the throne. "Ma'am, I work as a doctor."

Her dark painted brows came down. "Will your work interfere with your service to me?"

"No, ma'am." My tongue was dry. "I won't allow it."

She nodded. "I am curious about the other Secondaries. You have a useful gift. Perhaps the others do, too."

Warmth flooded me. A useful gift. Feet shuffled behind us, and warm ballroom air sucked into a hundred gasping mouths.

I couldn't help smiling, so I ducked my head and tallied the score: one for Grace.

The moon had shifted its place along the panes of the ballroom's roof, from low in the southeastern corner to toeing the borders of the southern face. It was ten o'clock? Eleven? High time to leave, if I had my say. I'd had enough staring, enough lying, enough guessing at what hid beneath politely veiled curiosity. I was sick of the smell of beeswax and perfume, the taste of champagne gone flat, the ache of my smiling face.

But Grace was gone, and as far as I could see, so was the First Ring, the mages with the strongest power, positions in Parliament and Cabinet, and the expectation of deference from everyone they met. All the Callers and Links of the First Ring were probably shut away to argue over which of them would sing in winter.

Grace needed it to be her.

I squinted through the glass roof at the moon and tried to reckon the time. Once Grace freed herself, I would insist on leaving. She'd negotiate for another hour. I would go to work groggy and stupid, if I could sleep at all.

The music was pleasant, but untroubled by the fervent energy and joyful bounce of dance hall melodies. Couples glided across the elaborately inlaid floor, their steps crossing over the five petaled roses and circles that mapped out exactly where Storm-Singers stood while working their manipulations. I stood on a rose, the place where a Storm-Singer skilled at shaping the whims of the sky would direct the pooled energy of five magicians who stood on the inlaid circles surrounding the Caller.

I had learned that much as a child, attending my sister while Father taught her how to stand at the center of every mage in the room, how to catch every thread weaving peace into the sky, how to conduct the efforts of the hundred and fifty-six mages into safety for the thirteen million citizens of Aeland. Lightning might strike, rain might fall, but it was all carefully managed.

It was important work. Vital, necessary work. But I had hoped to never see this room again.

"Sir Christopher?"

I turned around. "Call me Miles. Please. Sir Christopher is my father."

She was a girl, at least ten years younger than me, dressed

head to toe in creamy white silk and lace. She tilted her head up to look into my eyes and clasped her gloved hands together.

"I can heal too," she said, so low I had to watch her red-painted lips to understand. She wasn't the first Secondary to tell me about her gifts, but she was the first healer. And too young for me to speak with privately.

"It's a useful gift," I said. "Did you attend with your mother?"

"My brother. He's in the Second Ring. We're from Red Hawk." The name tripped in my memory. Red Hawk, the northern town with a train station and an asylum.

"I would like to meet him."

She glanced at a knot of young men who laughed too loud and drank too much. One as golden-haired as she was caught us looking and raised his glass. He didn't move to join us.

What were manners, these days? He had a responsibility to her. It wasn't proper. I kept staring and he left his cronies, snatching up another saucer of rose-gold champagne on the way to us.

"Sir Christopher Hensley." He stuck his hand out. "Richard Poole. I see you've met my sister, Celinda."

"He prefers Sir Miles," Celinda said.

"It's good to meet you both. Miss Poole tells me you're in the Second Ring. You must be talented."

"Weather up north is a wild horse," he said. "I was quelling storms as a child."

He'd go far if he had the right connections. But Poole was a name I knew only faintly, so I guessed not.

"My sister has a lot of strength," he said. "And she's handy with her little trick. I haven't been sick in years. Do you like her?"

I blinked. "We've only just met, but I am charmed."

"Perhaps you two should dance."

Celinda colored prettily. "I have daydreamed about dancing at the Return."

Trapped. "Shall we dance, Miss Poole?"

I hadn't often danced with a partner in my arms, but she didn't seem to care about my amateurish technique. She sparkled in her maidenly dress and demure pearl jewelry and glanced at my medals, intent on the copper one.

"Was it terrible?"

"It was."

"You're so brave to have done it," she said. "My cat died."

What? "I'm sorry."

"She was old. She had a lot of pain; she couldn't move much. She died on my lap. I cried, and then I—" She glanced left and right, one corner of her lip tucked in her teeth before staring up at me with round eyes. "I wanted to know what killed her."

Oh. "You did a death examination."

She nodded. "I want to be a doctor. Do you think I could?"

"You have a great deal standing in your way."

"But you did it."

"I did. But consider what I did. I ran away. I joined the Service in exchange for my education, and ended up in a war. You could join the Service, but you'd need permission."

She bowed her head. My bold moves weren't so easy for a gently bred daughter of the Royal Knights. She could, if she rebelled. I couldn't encourage her to do so.

She raised her head, her face intent. "Do you think I'm pretty?"

"I—Miss Poole."

"I think you're handsome," she said. "And brave, and you know so much about healing. We could have powerful children."

Oh. Oh. "I never planned to marry," I said.

"I don't mind," she said. "Becoming a doctor would be enough. Would you . . . would you have your sister speak to my brother?"

Speech deserted me. The dance ended. We applauded the

musicians, who paged through music to find the next song. I brought Celinda Poole back to her brother.

"My card," he said. "I'm home on midweek."

He took his sister and steered her through the crowd.

Miss Poole was the first young lady to make the approach, but the gates opened to miss after miss and dance after dance with women of a marriageable age. All of them whispered their gifts to me. All of them wanted a way to pursue mastery of those gifts, and with my own history, wouldn't I be a tolerant husband?

It broke my heart and set my head on fire with anger. I didn't want a wife. I tried escaping them by leaving the ballroom, hoping I would spot Grace before she buried herself in another meeting or friendly talk, but they pursued me in the progress around the continuously refilled buffet.

The eldest Miss Lawson regaled me with all the latest in the cinema when a man interrupted with an elegantly extended hand. He gave me a measuring look that scanned the polished toes of my shoes to my carefully slick-combed hair, an inspection I apparently passed, by his easy smile. "I'm Raymond Blake, and I'm tired of waiting for your sister to cut herself loose."

"Mr. Blake." I bent my head in greeting. "The Edenhill hotel is a triumph. I can hardly wait to see what you'll do next."

"I've no plans to take on a design until after the wedding." He turned and gestured at me to follow. "Walk with me."

We left Miss Lawson behind.

"You're popular," he said. "I think every eligible Secondary girl has tried to make your acquaintance."

"It's a bit shocking," I said. "I never planned to marry."

He arched an eyebrow at me. "Unimportant. What do you think of Elsine Pelfrey?"

She'd stepped on my feet. "She was charming."

Raymond scoffed. "Her chin's a mile long and she has a sinus condition. But her father is the Station of the Southeast. She's your best choice."

The wine in my belly curdled. "Politically."

"He's on the fence. Secure the Pelfreys and Grace will be the Voice. Dance with her again."

Raymond walked away and left me staring after him.

I knew Grace was free the moment I saw Sir Percy Stanley enter the room. Queen Constantina had gone home long since, and the moon had made it to the southwestern face of the glass roof. The musicians were on their second meal break. The sky would purple with dawn before I made it back to Tristan's.

But first, I had to endure an odious, greedy, heartless martinet. Sir Percy Stanley headed straight for my scarlet tunic, his face red. "So. They've tamed you, have they? You're in your proper place."

I blinked. "I'm bound to Grace, yes."

His narrow-eyed look matched his sneer. "Estelle ran away. Your doing. When we found her again she drank poison. Your fault."

Because I'd planted the seed of rebellion in his child, by having the audacity to leave my place. "Estelle . . . Stanley? I don't believe we ever met."

The red deepened. His nostrils opened like a bellows, his outraged breath stoking rage. "Insolent. No proper Secondary would dare. I don't believe you cowed, Master Christopher. The others are befuddled by you charming the Queen with your medals instead of understanding you never belonged in a war in the first place."

"I enjoyed meeting Her Majesty," I said. "I've had a most welcoming Return. I've danced all night and met every charming young woman here. Do you suppose Miss Pelfrey likes poetry? I've been thinking of the stars in her eyes."

Cruel, if Elsine ever heard of it. But it made Sir Percy's jowls tremble, and the petty satisfaction at my insinuation felt good. But if I pushed him too far, his clenched fist would swing, and Secondaries didn't have the right to hit back.

He'd have to apologize to Grace though.

"Ah, Sir Percy." Grace appeared with Raymond Blake, her smile full of good cheer. "How good of you to greet my brother. Raymond took the time to introduce himself earlier, and from what he says, Miles didn't have a moment to feel lonely."

"Your feet must be tired, Miles. All that dancing."

"Dancing until dawn is a skill I look forward to refining, Mr. Blake."

"Surely you have time for one more?" He cast a meaningful look at Miss Pelfrey, standing alone at the edge of the floor set out for dancing, dreaming of turning on the five-petaled motifs inlaid on the floor. She caught my glance and waved, blushing as I smiled in return.

If Sir Percy grew any angrier his hair would set on fire. My pleasure at vexing him sank. I laughed today, but Grace's pleasure at my popularity nagged. She could arrange my marriage. She had the right. And if an alliance cemented her place, she'd do it.

She'd do anything it took.

"I think I should save my energy for all the calls I've been invited to pay," I said. "Grace, do you want to stay? I can send the carriage back for you."

"I'm ready to go," Grace said. "Have a pleasant evening, Sir Percy."

I held my tongue until the carriage rolled along the red road back to the King's Way. "What part of 'I have to work in the morning' did you decide was trivial, Grace? People blunder without enough sleep. I hold lives in my hands!"

"We held a debate," Grace said, "over who would sing winter in tomorrow. Three rounds of voting. I won by one vote. One vote, Miles."

Not the support Grace was hoping for. That wasn't even the support she should have had. She was weary, her body shaking along with the carriage.

"Have you eaten?"

"I thought going to work on time was the top priority?"

"You should have eaten."

"I'll manage," Grace said. "Did you dance with Elsine Pelfrey more than once?"

The question jarred me right down to my toes. "I didn't dance with anyone more than once."

"Good. Her father voted with me. We don't need her. What do you think of Laura Burleigh?"

Laura Burleigh? What is this? "Grace. I never planned to marry."

"We need this." Grace gritted her teeth. "My alliance with the Blakes isn't enough. The Burleighs would double our alignment with the Pelfreys, and Miss Burleigh isn't at all hard to look at."

A cold whisper shivered up my neck: *I don't know this woman.*

"Don't favor anyone yet," Grace said. "But get used to the idea. You'll be a married man by the Feast of Lights. I'm sorry."

The pronouncement rocked me in my seat. "I will not."

"You must, Miles."

"Grace, don't ask me to do this. Not when I already agreed to help you, not when—"

"What? When you want your heartless Amaranthine? His kind don't have the same feelings we do, Miles. You amuse him. That's all."

"We're not—"

"He's fascinated you. So you'll stay where he can use you. What does he want from you? He made you a bargain. They all do."

I bit my lips together and counted. "He's my friend."

"Do you think he loves you?"

I flinched. "I know he doesn't."

"Miles, he can't. You know the stories. We fall in love with them. They leave. We break."

"He's never done what you believe."

"Tell me you don't catch your breath when you look at him."

I looked down at the floor, at the space between us.

"Miles." Grace said it gently. "I won't lose you again. I won't. Not to one of the heartless. Not as long as I can breathe and fight."

"He's my friend."

"How did he befriend you? How did you meet him?"

I looked out the window. "We're not going back to the city."

"Where would you go? Your boardinghouse is locked. We're nearly home."

"Grace—"

"You'll be gone before Father wakes up."

"No."

"Harry's been up all night," Grace said. "He can get to his bed all the sooner instead of making him drive all the way to the Edenhill."

"Halston Street isn't far—"

She cut off my protest with the chopping motion of her hand. "Miles, I can't. I can't trust him. Please don't ask me to."

She couldn't trust Tristan? I couldn't remark on the irony. "I trust him. He's never given me reason not to."

"What are you implying?"

"That you told Father about me."

She flinched as if I had slapped her. She looked away. "He already knew, Miles. He knew and he never told me, and then he asked me if you were happy. He knew all along."

"Did you set me up?"

"No! I didn't. I swear."

"How did you expect to explain his partial recovery? Did you think he wouldn't notice?"

"I—"

I seized her hand. Her heart beat faster than normal. Her breaths were shallow. Adrenaline cruised through her bloodstream. All heightened from the stress of the argument. "Were you going to tell him about me?"

"Yes!"

Her tense muscles eased with the confession. "I knew I couldn't keep you a secret after that. I was going to make him understand I swore not to bind you. I needed you to consent and to trust me. I tried to tell him, but he wouldn't hear it. I never wanted him to do that to you, Miles. I swear."

I could feel her relief at telling me as if it coursed through my own body. "All right."

She sagged.

"One more thing," I said. "Do you know Nick Elliot?"

She blinked. "Who?"

Her heart still eased its rhythm. She breathed freely. Puzzlement reigned on her face. She didn't even know who I was talking about.

That only left Father. And whatever was happening to the soldiers. They needed the souls, Nick had said. What souls?

The souls Tristan searched for.

Who needed them?

"Miles, who is Nick Elliot?"

"Don't worry about it," I said.

"Is he important?"

"He is to me," I said. "I just wondered."

"Are you angry with me, for telling Father?"

"Yes."

"He already knew. But I could have tried to lie."

"Grace, you and I both know what would have happened if you'd tried to lie to him. He would have had the truth—after he made you feel like the worm under his boot."

"I haven't told him about your Amaranthine. And he has no reason to ask. But he will want to know where you slept, if not in the dower house."

Blast. She knew exactly how to manipulate me, after all this time. I sighed and laid my head against the padded backrest. "Fine."

Grace smiled, looking relieved. "I ordered it cleaned, but the stovepipe is cracked. You'll have to come in the house for breakfast."

"And I suppose you have something I can wear to work?"

"Of course," Grace said. "I've taken care of everything."

The dower house smelt of verbena and oil soap. The walls were plaster and paint, a soft blue trimmed in white and gilt. Ancient furniture bore the fanciful carving of my great-grandfather's day, and the bedstead stood heavy with dark carved wood. The mattress, the linens, and the pillows were new, treated with perfumes of lavender and roses to aid sleep.

I fell on the bed and slept.

A servant I didn't recognize woke me with a cup of chocolate and presented me with clothing. Suits, tailored from black and charcoal and smoke gray, with hand-eased shoulders and the shine of silk woven with wool. Cotton shirts with tiny stitches had the most fashionable of rounded collars, the brocade ties silky and thick. Gleaming black shoes rested on a rack.

Back in the bosom of luxury, with finery all around me and the morning toilet of a gentleman of means.

Grace had planned this all along.

"The smoke flannel," I said. "The sky-blue tie."

It was meant to tempt me.

"Are you my father's valet?" I asked.

"Second footman, sir."

"What's your name?"

"William, sir."

I sat back in a leather grooming chair and let him shave my face, dozing off a little.

As temptations went, I couldn't fault Grace's choice. I hadn't lived in such comfort in years. A different man strolled out of the dower house and down the short path to the glass doors of the breakfast room.

Here was my coffee, hot and black. My beloved oranges sprinkled in pink sugar, strawberries in double cream, pink rounds of cured pork and scrambled eggs stuffed in warm golden rolls. It was like being a boy all over again, only I didn't have a book open to the left of my plate so I could devour words along with my food.

Something squeaked in the corridor outside the breakfast room. I set my spoon down and watched the door, willing myself not to bolt out the glass doors to the grounds. It could be Grace.

The squeak sounded again, and I named it as the breakfast room door opened: an ungreased wheel.

Mr. Wren was still the butler. Grace might be shorter than him, but only by an inch, the frame of the tall, lean man I grew up with now stoop-shouldered. He pushed my father to the chairless place at the head of the table. I'd taken a seat halfway along the length of a table for twenty. I stood up, napkin poised over my plate. I'd eat at the hospital.

His aura was like Grace's, like tarnished silver set in sunlight. The growths in Father's lungs were small, but numerous. He took a deep breath, and it didn't explode into a coughing fit. I had done a good job. Father laid a hand over his chest in response to a flare of pain. I could have quelled it, but Mr. Wren was watching.

And if I were honest, I didn't want to.

"You were right to become a doctor, Son."

I gave him a stiff bow. "Thank you for saying so, sir."

"And you were right to believe I wouldn't have let you. I was a fool."

What?

"I believe you deserve an explanation. Sit down."

I obeyed, but I couldn't believe my ears. I was right? Father was wrong? Was it raining cats outside?

Mr. Wren warmed up my coffee, leaving a copy of the *Herald* at my elbow.

"Thank you, Wren," Father said. "I'll be content here. Enjoy your breakfast in the kitchen."

Mr. Wren's head came up in surprise. "Sir?"

"I'll make my son pass me the salt. Go on."

"Thank you, sir."

Mr. Wren left us in privacy. The moment the breakfast door closed, Father opened his hand. The salt shaker flew into his grasp. I left the paper and sipped my coffee, waiting.

"Secondaries are ignored," Father said. "Their gifts go untrained because they're not the right gifts. But they're still magic."

I didn't turn around to look out the window. "Quite a change in opinion."

"You defied me." He smiled, showing the even front teeth of handmade dentures. The bowl of his spoon came down on the tip of a boiled egg, cracking it. "I couldn't believe you'd done it. But something kept me from hauling you back. I knew where you were."

I blinked as if Grace hadn't told me already. "The whole time? And you left me there?"

He nodded. "I thought you'd come back. Life is hard when you don't have money. Living in a single room, eating crab. I thought the romance would wear off."

"But I didn't."

"You didn't. You made the best of your gift when everyone told you it wasn't worth anything. You have strength, my boy. Strength and courage, and it took me years to see it."

I wanted to pinch myself. My fingertips drifted over the tablecloth, tracing the outline of a fan-tailed bird while Father told me how he'd followed my career. He named my achievements. He'd read all the papers I'd ever published.

He praised me, but he'd forced me to consent to binding. He had killed my mother. And whatever Nick had written about witches and asylums would surely point the finger at Father, for his part in it forty years ago.

I had never doubted my father would kill to keep a secret.

"When did you change your mind about Secondaries?" I swallowed coffee, took a bite of cooling egg-stuffed rolls.

"I couldn't get out of bed before you came."

Ah. "I didn't heal you."

"But I have more time. We can hold the Voice's seat. I haven't appeared before the Stations in weeks. Grace won't mind if I sit in on a deciding to show them all what having you back has done."

I checked the date on the morning edition of the *Herald*. *Laneeri Delegation to Sign Surrender*, read the headline. It should have said, *World Turned Upside-Down*. "My healing is an advantage."

"Miles, your healing is the key to saving this family. If I'd let go of backwards beliefs, seen your potential . . ."

"You agree with Grace? You think Secondaries should exercise their gifts?"

Father scooped out cooked whites and perfectly runny yolks onto his toast. "It's such a waste. Thinking of the Secondaries as nothing more than the raw power they provide for us, when they're so much more useful."

Useful. All my disorienting, incautious hope burst on the pinprick of that word. I was useful.

I knew better. Why had I forgotten?

I stood up and dropped my napkin on the lace tablecloth. "I hear the coach. I'm due at work."

"Of course," Father said. "You'll be drained after the ritual tonight. Grace opened up the dower house. Was it comfortable?"

"William was very efficient."

"It hasn't been redecorated in a century."

"It's well preserved."

"It can be yours."

Never. "I have lodgings, Father. But thank you. Pleasant breakfast." Useful. I was a tool, not a son.

I wouldn't forget again.

TWENTY-ONE

Suspended

Beauregard Veterans' might as well have been eight miles away, even though it stood right across the street. I jumped out of the carriage and sent the man back, joining the thin crowd gathered around a constable with white-gloved hands forbidding us to pass.

"Look, I'm a doctor at Beauregard. Right there." I pointed over the policeman's shoulder. His throat was prickly with infection, and I stood back a bit.

"I understand, but you'll have to wait until the procession passes." He'd said it to other people who thought they were worthy of an exception, people who waited with tight jaws or stalked off to try a different route.

What if I went ahead? There wasn't a rope. I could just dash across, no harm done—

"Anyone who tries to cross gets a charge of obstructing a diplomat," the policeman said.

I stepped back. "It's a diplomatic procession?"

"It's the Laneeri," the policeman said. "Come to sign the surrender and swear as subjects to the Queen. We're an empire now."

This last he said with his chin high.

Flutes and drums echoed up the street. My head turned with the rest, and I breathed in a hint of burning sweetwood, carried on the wind. Dots of blue moved down the King's Way, those at the front drumming a marching rhythm slow as a funeral step.

Well, I supposed it was. I looked on and tried to blink the spots from my eyes as the people dressed in shades of blue came closer. I wasn't seeing spots, but witchmarks hovering around the heads of the musicians.

Those in the front wore robes of the palest blue, the hems swirling around their ankles as they slow-marched. The flautists played a tune that fought back tears, suppressed a keen of mourning. It made my back shiver. The robes became darker, going from dawn to noon to dusk to night, and the stars around their heads became denser. These were sky-priests, the dominant spiritual faith of the Laneeri, and every last one of them was a witch.

They glanced at me, flicking their focus back to the road ahead if I made eye contact. They could see my witchmarks too. I examined the procession and held down a yelp of surprise when I realized none of the priests had the infection.

Shouldn't there be some among them? The delegates walked in the center of the procession of priests, garbed in white robes bordered with red. All their faces were bare of the makeup upper-class Laneeri wore, their usually ornately plaited hair left loose to flutter at their ankles, and none of them had the infection either.

How did none of them have it, when the infection had spread to so many of the homecoming soldiers?

There could be a hundred reasons. If I could run tests on a Laneeri . . . But that wouldn't happen. I watched the priests with their witchmarks, their heads bowed in defeat, their minds clear of the infection.

What protected them?

They marched to their weeping flutes and death-toll drums, sweetwood smoke billowing from censers swung to consecrate the air. They would walk to the palace. They would stop before the throne and kneel. One more humiliation, as if all the death they'd suffered wasn't enough. After a ceremonial imprisonment, they'd sign the surrender and become Aeland's vassal, completely defeated.

I could feel sorry for them, even after what they'd done to me. It had been a terrible war, but they had been outgunned from the start, even with magicians helping their efforts. The fight had never been fair. Desperate people commit terrible acts.

It was as close as I could get to forgiving them.

One of the priests turned her head and surveyed the crowd who stood muttering. A spiteful little smile hovered on her lips as she locked eyes with me.

She watched me a moment longer, then turned away, dismissing me as unimportant. Not the gesture of someone who had been utterly humiliated.

That look was sly. It was smug. It knew something I didn't. The other priests glanced here and there as they played their flutes and swung their incense. I tried to follow their gazes, to reckon whom they looked at.

Soldiers. Out of uniform, some with mustaches shaved off, all of them with infection clouding their minds.

Did that mean they could see it too?

Police allowed the people down the block to cross once the procession had passed. I turned to check the policeman beside me. He signaled our permission with a beckoning hand and a nod. The people who had had to wait crossed the street, or mounted their bicycles and went about their business.

I ran to the hospital. I climbed the stairs to my office two at a time.

People passed me on the stairwell, but no one said good morning. A nurse stopped on the landing when she spotted me and retreated to the second floor, though I knew she was one of the Mental Recovery staff.

Had she been avoiding me?

The idea was ridiculous.

I rounded the third flight of stairs and Robin rose from her seat on the stairs, her eyes wide.

"Miles." She opened her hand, and the stairs lurched under my feet.

She offered me a perfectly rolled cigarette.

I couldn't breathe.

Footsteps scrambled up the stairs, and a hospital page panted for breath. "Nurse Robin? They need you. I've been looking all over." Then he saw me and his eyes went round. He backed up, plainly afraid. Of me.

She rose to her feet. "I'll be there in a minute. Gallbladder," she said. "A fast surgery. I hope I'll be out in time to see you."

The page darted frightened glances at me. "I'm sorry, please don't be mad, but they need Nurse Robin."

I took the cigarette from her and slid it into my breast pocket. "What happened? Why is everyone jumping out of their skin?"

As soon as I said it, I knew.

The page dashed down the stairs in a panic.

Robin turned worried eyes to me. "It'll all work out," she said, and left me staring after her.

This couldn't be happening. Not now. I climbed the rest of the stairs. My office key rested in the pocket next to Tristan's, iron and bronze chiming as I reached for them. Gouges of bright bronze shone in the nest of tiny scratches around the keyhole to my office. The door lever rattled and pushed deeper than it used to.

I knew what I would see before I pushed the door open.

Someone had ransacked my office. I counted the volumes of
Richardson's Abdominal Surgery Encyclopedia. All eight volumes
were there. So was my crystal whiskey set, empty, dusty, and
untouched. My filing cabinet had been disemboweled. Stray paper carpeted the floor, files and records trampled on by leather-
soled shoes. But what made my guts swoop was my vandalized
desk, every locking drawer broken open.

My belongings were tumbled back into the drawers, uncaring of the order. My tortoiseshell pen rested there, along with
the wristwatch I'd meant to have mended. I opened the drawer
I kept locked.

The journal detailing what I knew of the infection was gone.

I lifted scattered papers, feeling for the book, but no luck.
Thin transfer paper crackled under my fingers, and though it
was glued to my desk by dried green ink I knew it was the form
detailing the contents of my medical bag from Lost and Found.

I cleared papers away from my blotter.

The white-handled knife was gone.

So was the pendulum, snatched from the corner of the
drawer where I'd left it. The boline, the pendulum, the journal
detailing Gerald Grimes's and Bill Pike's condition . . .

Crosby. It had to be.

Dr. Matheson stood in the open doorway. She inspected my
fine clothing with a quick eye.

"Dr. Singer."

Dr. Singer. Not Miles. "Dr. Matheson."

"I wish to speak to you in my office."

Tools of witchcraft I could explain away, but the journal?
What could I say about that? What could I do?

Chin up and take it, that's all I could do.

"Good idea. Mine's rather a mess, I'm afraid."

Dr. Matheson didn't smile. She turned around and left me

to follow. She didn't look back or speak to me on the trip downstairs, and crossed her office in long strides.

"Close the door and sit down."

Pendulum, boline, and book were the only objects on Dr. Matheson's blotter.

"Dr. Crosby broke into your office yesterday after some hearsay from a new patient," Dr. Matheson said. "Do you know a man named James Wolf?"

I'd saved his life and his leg in my last day at the mobile hospital. I'd been so tired I could barely pick my feet up. So tired I never heard them coming.

"I had a patient by that name."

"He claimed you healed him with magic and stole his soul as payment."

Water stains marred the corner of Dr. Matheson's ceiling. She'd trained a wandering plant on the wall rather than have the corner repaired.

Dr. Matheson nodded. "It's quite ridiculous, I agree. But it drove Dr. Crosby to find these."

I waited.

"Crosby's been suspended pending board examination," she said. "As are you."

"Dr. Matheson?"

"I have to suspend you both. But I'd like to know what these are."

"A letter opener," I said.

"Obviously. Crosby said it was a silver-bladed knife for collecting spell items."

"It's a letter opener. And the stone on a chain is a pendulum. I use it as a visual focus for mesmerism, which I use on patients to help them manage pain and sleep."

"Miles, I've read the book. It's interestingly worded."

"I used the patient's language to describe what they believe lurks inside them."

This was the weak spot. I'd written what I saw, blending my magical sight and medical knowledge. It didn't make sense to write it that way, not clinically, and not scientifically.

"The accusation of witchcraft is already all over your wards. There was no stopping it. Multiple doctors have looked over Mr. Wolf's scars from the surgery. I've seen them too."

"I imagine they're extensive."

"They're astonishing," Dr. Matheson said. "He should have died before you had a chance to finish half of it. But he's alive, and he can walk. He's told everyone who will listen you're a witch."

"And they believe him."

"We can solve this." Dr. Matheson leaned over the desk.

"How?"

"Get examined, and we can dismiss this."

Oh.

She meant a witchcraft examination. They held the patient suspected of witchcraft in a room lined with copper, questioned them, tripped them up in crossing lines of inquisition. I knew how to answer. I could answer.

But I couldn't withstand that much copper. Even the lines carrying aether were enough to irritate, a fly you couldn't quite swat away from your head. Witches begged to be let out of examination rooms. I had hated the way it drained me the moment I stepped inside one, back when I was still in medical school.

Copper was the real test. Someone could claim to sing down the wind and talk to the dead all day, but if they weren't broken by the copper in the walls, they were just deluded.

Dr. Matheson spoke into the silence. "Dr. Crosby will be dismissed once you clear the examination. It's only a single day.

You could go to Kingston Asylum today, and be back on rounds by midweek."

I'd never make it a full day in a testing room.

It was over. I was ruined. I couldn't dismiss the rumors without doing as Dr. Matheson said. My reputation was nothing, just when my patients needed me most.

Unless I could use wealth and power to bully the matter out of my way.

I leaned back in my seat and drummed my fingers against the chair arm. "I think you had better suspend me. I'll hire an advocate for my board hearing."

Something desperate flitted across her face—something that made the cords of her neck stand out. "It's the easiest way to put Dr. Crosby's accusations to rest. Prove you're not a witch, Miles, and he can never try this again."

"I will not. This is ridiculous." I beetled my brows together, slung out my jaw, and let Dr. Matheson have the outrage she expected. "I'll hire an advocate."

"Why won't you take the test, Miles?"

"I have a social engagement with my sister tonight."

"You won't do the examination because you're going out with Dame Gr—"

She covered her mouth.

Now it was my turn to lean in. "You knew already."

"You look alike. You have the same eyes."

"So it was a lucky guess?" I shook my head. "My invitation to the luncheon. I'm too low in the hierarchy to be invited, but you insisted. Why?"

Dr. Matheson held my gaze. "Your paper on battle neurosis in *Psyche* was greatly admired by a noted philanthropist."

No one read a medical journal for amusement. I connected the dots: Matheson had told my father of my achievement, and then my father had hatched the plan to put me and Grace together. "Tell me who wanted me invited. And introduced to Dame Grace."

"Sir Christopher Hensley," she said. "Your father, I realize now."

She had spied on me for a father curious to see what I would do with freedom. "And what did he offer? Your promotion?"

Dr. Matheson's eyes flared wide for an instant. "Patronage."

"Is that all he wanted? Just invite me to a luncheon?"

"He wanted to know how you were doing."

"And do you think he'll be pleased to hear I've been accused of witchcraft? That instead of firing my accuser and supporting me, you want me to subject myself to examination?"

"It would remove all doubt—"

"You don't have enough power with the board to wipe this off."

Her explosive sigh made her shoulders deflate. She bowed her head. "Of course I don't. I'm not the head of Medicine yet; I don't assume the position until the first."

"Support me, Mathy. Recommend Dr. Crosby's dismissal and support me when I walk in there with an advocate, and I'll help you. If—"

She lifted her head, lips parted and eyebrows high. "If?"

"Did you order all the bodies removed before leaving for the luncheon last week?"

She glanced away.

"You did," I said. "How could you? He'd been murdered."

"He said you didn't need the distraction."

"But to destroy Nick Elliot's chance at a police investigation—"

"He was going to take the money off the table." Dr. Matheson's fists tightened until her knuckles whitened. "I couldn't. Do you know how badly we need money? How much it costs to aetherize, even with the subsidies?"

"Murder, Eleanor! You obstructed justice!"

"For my future, and yours!" she said. "For the future of this hospital! Do you even know how much more money in donations we have this year?"

"At least another five thousand," I said. "And Nick Elliot paid the price!"

"His murderer might never be found. I know. But you didn't have a suspect. You only had his word that he'd been poisoned."

"Because you destroyed the body. And looked the other way. For a *patron*."

"Without one, the care of thousands of veterans would stretch thinner and thinner." She swept loose tendrils of hair away from her furrowed brow. "We've been trying to stop an arterial bleed with finger plasters."

"But to let his killer go free? Because I was the one who was out for a smoke? Eleanor. What happens the next time my father wants a distraction cleared from my duties?"

Anything my father wanted, that's what. I wouldn't let go of this one. Nick had learned secrets Father didn't want getting out about the asylums and witches. It was his bad luck that it had been me Nick had found.

"What do you think, Miles?" She looked weary and slump-shouldered with the true weight of a deal with my father. "I'll do it."

"And if I were to leave the hospital, or be dismissed, you lose your money."

"Everything depends on you remaining part of this hospital."

"I know. I'm sorry Dr. Crosby spoiled that for you."

"If your advocate doesn't convince them—"

I nodded. "I don't want to leave."

"But if the board isn't convinced—"

"I know." I couldn't sit here all morning. And I couldn't just skulk out the door. I had to get onto the Mental Recovery Unit. "I'd like to explain to my patients."

"You can't." She shook her head. "You're suspended."

"They have a right to an explanation from me."

"Or you could be manipulating your patients as pawns in your reinstatement struggle. I'm sorry, Miles. I can't let you."

"Just for a few minutes."

"If I have to, I'll have guards escort you out. Leave quietly, Miles. I mean it."

I had to get down there. I had to look at the infection one last time, and figure out why our soldiers had it, but the Laneeri didn't.

"Fine," I lied. "Let me gather a few things."

I was suspended. I had no privileges, couldn't practice medicine, couldn't see my patients. I was to descend these stairs and walk out the door.

Hang that.

I crossed the lobby and followed the corridor to Mental Recovery, passing the ladies' dressing room. Robin emerged, dressed in boiled gray cotton. "Miles."

"Robin. I have to go."

She caught my sleeve. "I wish I could do something—I'm sorry. For all of it. And I'm sorry about Bill, too. You must be worried about him."

Bill? "What do you mean?"

Her head rolled back in frustration. "Mathy never told you. Of course she didn't. You'd never leave quietly if she had."

"What happened to Bill?"

"He had an acute stress attack. He's in a safe room. It was a bad one."

I took her shoulders in my hands. "How bad?"

"He was agitated all weekend, and then he stole a metal sock needle from the crafting group."

My insides swooped. "Did he attack someone?"

"Worse. He snuck off to the surgery floor, found an aether dock, and jammed the knitting needle inside it. He's aether-burned. He wouldn't let go of it, they say. Held fast and screamed 'get out, get out' until someone pulled him away. They're aether-burned too."

Aether burns could be terrible, reaching deep inside the body. It was a sickening way to die. "So he attempted suicide?"

"It was his delusion. He'd gotten bad. I snuck a look at the duty logs—"

"You're not supposed to do that."

"Crosby went on a rampage," Robin said. "I had to know why, and not just from rumor. Bill kept saying, 'I have to get him out' and 'he hates the light, that's the key,' but Crosby noted it down as agitation from your mistreatment of him from doing a spinal draw so high on his back. But after they sedated him, he woke up and started yelling in Laneeri about how you were a witch. And the new patient, Mr. Wolf, told everyone about how you used magic on his leg—"

There was no time to waste. I had to see Bill for myself. "Which safe room?"

"He's in B. I looked in on him. They'd sedated him— Miles! Wait!"

I ignored her and ran.

The lights flickered in this part of the ward. I ran down the empty corridor and skidded to a stop in front of safe room B, a heavy door with a peephole at eye level slid to the open position.

Bill lay inside cocooned in heavy canvas restraint. They

didn't use those until you woke up out of sedation and were still wild with unreason, ready to do violence to yourself. But what was worse was the infection, spread all the way down to fingers and toes.

Robin plucked at my sleeve. "You've seen him. You can't help him now."

Bill's lips curled back in a snarl. All he could see was a shadow over the little door. Perhaps if he saw me, if we talked . . .

"Come away, Miles. Don't torture yourself."

"I'm going to talk to him."

"Miles—"

I pulled the door open. It smelled of woolen padding on the floor and walls, of body sweat, cooked flesh, and—someone hadn't taken him to the lavatory in time. Or he'd done it on purpose.

I stepped inside, the floor sinking under my shoes. "Bill. I came as soon as I heard. Are you all right?"

"Witch."

He spat the word, a sharp, ugly bit of Laneeri.

I stood where I was, showed him empty hands. "They put you in this room to keep you safe. Because you were trying to hurt people. Do you still want to hurt people?"

"I'll kill you. We'll kill you all."

"What's he saying? Is that Laneeri?"

"So you're still violent." I had answered in Laneeri, so I switched to Aelander. "Let's talk about what made you so angry."

"Don't use dog-talk, killer."

I blinked, but I kept on. "Why don't you want to talk to me in Aelander?"

"Stop it."

"Answer me."

"Filthy Aelander. Murdering witch. Necromancer. You deserve death."

What was this? I should have read the chart before barging in here. "Why?"

He didn't answer. I tried again, in Laneeri. "Why?"

"Because you're murderers. Soul-eaters. You have to be stopped."

"And you're going to stop us."

This was—I didn't know what this was. It wasn't Bill. It was a different person, as if someone else moved and spoke with Bill's body. I had to do something. Could I manipulate the infection? I'd folded Gerald's into tiny nonexistence. What would happen if I made the body fight it, like a virus?

I moved closer.

"Miles, stop!"

Robin again. Still looking out for me. "I want to try something."

I knelt beside Bill. He tried to bite me, but I put my hand on his forehead. He thrashed about violently, jaws snapping, but my attention was on the infection . . . wait.

I touched the edge of it with my power, and the whole mass flinched. As if it were one thing, but that didn't make sense.

"Miles, you can't," Robin pleaded. "They'll know. They'll examine you. Leave him. You have to go."

I looked up. "You believe the rumors?"

She took my hand. I blinked—first that Robin touched my skin, her hand radiating warmth. Then at her, for her placid, terribly ordinary aura fell away, revealing the strong soul-light of a witch.

"Robin," I breathed. "You're—"

She let go, and the illusion of ordinariness snapped back into place. "I'll explain later. We don't have time to argue. You have to get out of here. They're coming."

Running footsteps echoed through the corridor. Robin was

right. I didn't have time to argue. But Bill needed me to solve this.

All the men did. I kept working.

I couldn't break it up. I had folded it when I helped Old Gerald. The edges resisted me and Bill thrashed, trying to free himself from my touch.

"Miles," Dr. Matheson said. "You are suspended."

"One moment."

I caught an edge. It tried to pull from me. I pulled back, and it rose from Bill's body into the air. I kept pulling, bit by bit, as if I pulled a tapeworm from a patient's intestine. Like a parasite. Like . . .

"Miles. I am ordering you. Step away from the patient."

I ignored Mathy, caught in understanding. It was a soul. This was a possession.

I pulled harder, dragging it out of Bill's body. Bill screamed in rage and pain. He thrashed and bit his own tongue, blood spraying in a mist from his harsh breaths.

It came loose all at once, torn out of my hands and—east. It went east for the fraction of a second where I could see before it vanished.

Hands caught me under the armpits, hauling me away. Bill coughed, struggling. His hair was wet with sweat, plastered to his forehead.

"Doc?" he asked, and coughed again. "Doc, what happened?"

I settled my feet under me and yanked free of the orderly who had dragged me out.

Bill's voice cracked with fear. "Why am I in here? What happened?"

Dr. Matheson's back was stiff as a board. She turned to look at me, face white as paper.

Bill had been mad. I'd touched him, and he'd returned to reason.

She took a step back, out of my reach.

"Eleanor."

"Not one word, Miles. Get your advocate. And don't come back without him. Escort him out," she said, and she turned away, hurrying into the safe room to kneel by Bill's side.

The orderly dragged me away. I had to get back there! I had to understand what I'd done. I pulled, trying to get free of his grasp.

"Come along now, Dr. Singer."

"I have to go back."

"Dr. Matheson told me to escort you out. Go quietly, or the police will get involved."

If they caught even a whiff of the rumors about me, they'd have me in an examination room in a blink. The talk would spread wider.

I quit fighting and walked with him. I had freed Bill. I couldn't help the others, but I knew where I could find one more.

TWENTY-TWO

E. 3125 Trout Street

It took thirty minutes on the train and a walk north to an address on Trout Street: 3125, a narrow house teetering up two stories, painted yellow and surrounded by garden. Old Gerald's home might have needed paint, but the order and beauty of his little yard was a tribute to his craft.

I stood at the front door and knocked for the third time. The porch still had screens up, the furniture suited for company in the last sunny days before Frostnight. They'd put up shutters tomorrow, or doubled glass if they could afford it.

I peered through the lace curtains for movement. No one came. I couldn't have come all this way for nothing. Someone should be here. Marie at least should be home.

Unless she was shopping? They couldn't grow everything in their resourceful little garden, and she'd had no help keeping it up while Gerald was away. I'd passed a Swanson's on the way—would it do any good to go and look for her?

Perhaps there was an outbuilding. A shed. A little glasshouse made of salvaged windows to shelter delicate plants late in autumn and early in spring. I rounded the house, careful to step on the flat stones paving the narrow way between the house and the fence, with garden planted even here. Squash rambled on the ground; hops grew up the side of the house.

There was a glasshouse built along a fruit wall, but it was empty. Gloves lay discarded on the grass, and a basket holding cut herbs and late vegetables spilled over the back garden path, as if someone had quit the garden in haste. Fresh earth lined the print of a left foot, but no right.

Young Gerald had been out here and had gone into the house. I followed up the back steps into the screen room meant for the comfort and privacy of the family in the summer heat and breathed in the tang of blood. Too much blood. Had Young Gerald hurt himself? I dismissed it. There was no blood trail leading into the house. It came from—

No, no.

Inside.

I pulled the screen door to the house. The kitchen door was ajar, and it stank, oh it stank, too rich and rotten and wrong.

I pushed the door open.

Young Gerald lay on the floor, eyes open and staring. His blood pooled underneath him, shimmering wet and thick but dark on the edges. I lifted his wrist, touched his waxy face.

He was cooling off.

A woman's legs lay visible in the next room, one shoe gone, a tear in the sole of her stocking. Marie?

I sidestepped Young Gerald's blood.

Marie. Her blood soaked the threadbare carpet under the dining room, her hands sliced in defensive wounds.

What would the *Star* call this? Bloodbath?

Nausea gathered in my stomach, though I'd seen worse deaths, more grievous injuries, knew the rotting meat smell of drying blood. I crouched to pick up her hand, to press against the stillest part of her wrist.

Here the link between the infection and Kingston's domestic

murders. Thousands had these parasitic souls. My patients had been telling the truth about there being another person inside them, instead of a constructed "other" who committed the terrible acts of war. I hadn't told anyone my fears that the soldiers who killed their families had the same condition as my patients, keeping my precious secret until it was too late.

These deaths were my fault. The others too, but especially these. I smoothed Marie Grimes's hair out of her face, then cursed. I was disturbing the scene of a crime, leaving my footprints everywhere, my fingerprints, fooling about with Mrs. Grimes's hair—I knew better.

The floorboards creaked as I passed through the dining room and into the front parlor.

A creak answered me from above. Another. Heavy footfalls pounded across the second floor. A boot stomped on the straight, narrow stairs with a hollow thump, and Old Gerald leapt for the floor, landing in a crouch.

He came at me with a bloody knife, the blade reversed in his grip. I picked up a parlor chair, aiming for his face as I swung it.

He ducked and dove for my legs. I leapt backwards, landing on Marie's arm. I dropped the chair in my scramble to keep my feet—if I fell, I'd be dead.

The chair fell on Old Gerald's head with a thump. Too bad it wasn't a little heavier. He kept his grip on the knife, scrabbling to push the chair away.

I scrambled backwards, my shoe coming down in Young Gerald's blood. I couldn't take a Laneeri in a knife fight. I needed reach. I needed a sword. Something. I spied a mop and grabbed it, swinging the head in Old Gerald's face. Water-soaked strings knocked him off balance.

My heart pounded. I had one chance.

I rushed him, shoving him over the dining room table. I groped for his free hand, caught it, and flexed my power.

He choked as I closed his airway, knife arm swinging wildly. I reached into his mind. *"Sleep."*

The knife tumbled to the floor.

I released his throat. Breath shuddered through Old Gerald's mouth and nose while I peeled the dried blood soul out of his body, pulling it away. I had figured out the trick of divesting Gerald of his invader, but again the soul yanked out of my grasp as if it were sucked away. Eastward once more.

I shifted my weight and stopped as my foot nudged into something. I looked down.

I stood on Marie Grimes's hair.

I stumbled backward and half tripped on the mop. Gerald lay on the table, legs dangling, arms outspread. He snored softly. I couldn't wake him yet. A soft touch on his hand pushed him deeper, and I crept past him and his wife's body, climbing the stairs to the bedrooms above.

Please be at school. Please be at school.

Gerald and Marie's bedroom was at the front, a knitted counterpane spread over the bed wide enough for two, more needlework decorating small pillows and the tops of the bureaus cramped in the space. One corner of the bedspread was turned up and all the drawers spilled open.

He'd been in here searching. I backed out of the room, turning to the first closed door.

My stomach roiled as I pushed down the door lever, opening to a tiny room with a narrow bed under the window.

It was bare, but an army bag leaned on the wall next to the tidy dresser. Young Gerald's room. I moved on.

Old Gerald had two boys, Jamie and Sam. They must have shared the room at the back, the door shut tight. The floor creaked in front of the door, a bright sign painted with both their names.

I closed my eyes and swung the door open.

Please.

Two beds on opposite walls. A braided rug in between, scattered with a boy's toys. Balls and music crank boxes, high-tailed horses and soldier men, bright and wooden and clean.

Clean.

I landed on my knees.

A crash sounded from downstairs, and a yelp of surprise turned into a horrified cry.

"Marie?"

Gerald was awake.

I dashed down the stairs.

Gerald held Marie in his arms. He rocked her dead body, sobbed in her hair, tried to smooth it out of her face, tried to keep her head from wobbling back and opening the slice at her throat.

"Gerald."

"Go away."

"Gerald, it's Dr. Singer."

"Go away."

"Do you remember anything?"

"Leave me alone."

I moved closer. "Do you remember—"

"I killed her. I killed her."

"*He* killed her."

"It doesn't matter," Old Gerald said. "She's dead."

"I have to get the police."

"Get them. I don't care."

"Gerald. Jamie and Sam weren't here. Your children are alive."

He didn't seem to hear me.

I searched for a telephone. They were well-off enough to own one, and I picked up the receiver.

"It says here in the paper!" a woman exclaimed. "That's why

all the columns have been a repeat. He was murdered! Oh, poor Mr. Greenthumbs."

"Excuse me, please," I interrupted. "I need the line."

"Who's there?" a different woman asked.

"Miles Singer. I'm a doctor. I need to call the police."

"The police!" the first woman exclaimed. "Right away."

They hung up, freeing the line for me.

I stood in the front parlor. I'd scuffed blood on the carpet. Blood stained my trousers, my coat. Gerald sobbed brokenly behind me. The telephone rang, rang again, and a voice answered.

"Kingston police, Gray Mountain."

A click. Someone had picked up their phone. They'd get an earful.

"We need officers at 3125 Trout Street East." I gritted my teeth against the prickle of copper so close to my ear. "I'm afraid there have been two murders."

The moment I hung up, the phone rang again. I let it shrill, dashing back to the kitchen to retrieve my bag and kneel next to Old Gerald. "The police are coming. Gerald. You don't remember what happened. You understand me? You don't remember." I opened the water-stained bag and quested inside for a bottle and a dosing cup.

"What does it matter?"

"You weren't yourself when you did this." Did he wake from a terrible dream? Had he been a helpless passenger all through it, unable to stop his body from attacking his wife and his friend? It didn't matter. Gerald Grimes had been shattered. The pieces of him still held Mrs. Grimes's body, her limbs sprawling at immodest angles. He rocked her corpse, stroked her disarranged hair.

He stirred himself when the bitter tang of laudanum bloomed under his nose. "I deserve to hang."

"No, you don't. You aren't responsible. Do you understand me? You weren't in your right mind. I'll tell them. I'll say it in court. Because it's true. Drink this."

He took the cup and swallowed. Old Gerald sighed. "Laudanum?"

"Yes."

"Give me the rest," he said. "So I sleep forever."

"I can't do that, Gerald."

The hum of voices grew. I stood up and looked through the lace curtains. Women milled in the street, buttoning woolen coats and tying bright scarves over house dresses against the chill. Some smoked. All of them looked at the house, brows wrinkled with worry.

They scattered like pigeons when the first police officer arrived, answered his questions with worried looks.

Gerald's head nodded, the tonic already taking effect. I eased my grip, and he stayed sitting up, though he wobbled. "Wait here."

I unlocked the front door.

A chorus of gasps greeted me as I stepped out. A few women screamed, falling among the others in a faint.

The police constable was white-lipped, knuckles tight over the handle of his truncheon.

I blinked. "What's the matter?"

"Stay right where you are!"

"Of course," I said. "I was about to invite you in. What's wr—"

I looked down. Blood dried on my hands and cuffs.

"Oh."

I put my hands up. "I called you. I came to call on my patient."

"Who are you?"

"Dr. Miles Singer. I'm a physician at Beauregard Veterans'. Gerald Grimes was my patient there."

"He a soldier?"

"Yes."

His eyebrows rose in the middle. "He in the war?"

"Yes."

If anything, the constable looked even paler. "Is he dead?"

"Sedated," I said. "I'm lucky to be alive."

Cry-bells rang, coming closer.

"That'll be the body wagon," the constable said.

A woman gasped in horror.

The arrival of backup bolstered the young man's morale and he climbed the stairs. "You can put your hands down. Don't go anywhere. We'll have questions."

Other policemen followed him, including one bedecked in more brass than I usually saw on a patrolman. A sergeant—probably the supervisor of the men who gathered here recording the grim business of murder.

"You're the one who called?"

"Miles Singer. I'm Gerald's doctor."

He signaled to a constable and beckoned him over. "Tell me what happened."

"I was coming to call on Old Gerald as part of my conditions for releasing him from Mental Recovery at the hospital."

"Mental Recovery? So he's mad?"

I winced. "Mr. Grimes was suffering a full break from reality when I arrived. It was in this state of unreason that he killed his wife and his friend, Gerald Martin."

"And how did you survive?"

"I talked him down once I subdued him."

He looked at me again, impressed. "By yourself."

"It wasn't easy."

"Still. If he's like the other one, you're formidable." His nod of approval was deep enough to be a bow. "Was he talking in Laneeri? When he was having this break from reality?"

"Yes," I said. "He was distraught when he realized what he'd done. I sedated him. He's suicidal."

"What possessed him to do this, Doctor? Why do they—? Their wives. Their families. What happened over there?"

"War," I said.

The sergeant shook his head.

There were more questions, and from them I learned Terrence Pigeon wouldn't speak anything but Laneeri, and he was in a safe room in Kingston Asylum.

They wanted me to tell them what was happening. They wanted me to tell them how to fix it. I couldn't.

A constable offered me a ride up the hill to Birdland, certain my bloodstained clothing would cause a disturbance if I took the train. I pedaled in his sidecar, bemused.

"Do they help? The people you arrest. Do they help you pedal them back to jail?"

"A lot of them do, Doctor. Even the ones who fought me. You'd be surprised. Sometimes it's a relief to get caught."

I decided to concentrate on pedaling.

He went to the door with me to explain to a horrified Mrs. Bass I had been assisting the police with a crime. I dashed upstairs to remove my gory clothing. I didn't know if I could get the blood out of my Service coat. I had a spare, shabbier than this one. It would have to do.

A change of clothes and shoes came with me on the cab ride back to Tristan's. Children swarmed over the long black car in front of his door, hovering close but not quite daring to touch the curving wheel wells or the leaping stag ornament on the car's nose.

Tristan and Grace alone was trouble brewing.

I ran up the steps and through the door, listening for raised voices or a sign they had come to blows.

Grace set down her teacup and twisted in her seat, glaring at me. "Where have you been?"

"There's no time for interrogations."

"We both went to the hospital to find you," Tristan said. "We heard about the imbroglio with that doctor accusing you of witchcraft."

"I worried you'd been arrested." Grace's voice shook. "You weren't here, Mr. Hunter didn't know where you'd gone—"

"Stop," I said. "Grace. Have you been paying attention to the *Star*?"

"We don't take the *Star,* as you know."

"The murders. Soldiers from the war murdering their entire family. Have you heard of them?"

"You were talking about it yesterday," Tristan said. "Was there another?"

"One of my patients," I said. "I'd been working on a problem some of my patients had. I thought it was a disease, but I was wrong. I was so wrong. . . ."

"What is it?"

"They're possessed," I said. "I'm not sure how. But what I saw inside them wasn't an infection. They were right all along—there was someone else inside them bent on killing."

Grace looked confused. Tristan went pale. "Are you certain?"

"I've seen two of my patients in this condition. I pulled the cloud from them, and they returned to normal."

"A cloud," Tristan leaned closer. "Like a mass of insects?"

"Yes."

The slap of Grace's palms on her knees drew my attention back. "What are you two talking about?"

"My patients—"

"A spell," Tristan said. "Necromancy."

The word froze me. "Necromancy?"

"Of course it is."

"What are you two talking about? Miles, what's this about a spell?"

I swiped my hand through my hair. "Grace, can you see magic on people? Can you spot a witch?"

"I can," Grace said.

"Come. Look out the window."

We gathered at the small panes of the parlor's window. Halston Street carried plenty of traffic. Delivery wagons dotted the road, taking advantage of lightened bicycle traffic before the afternoon rush filled the street. Even more children surrounded Grace's car, not quite daring to touch it. A man rode into the intersection, and I pointed. "Do you see?"

"See what?" They said together. The man with a bicycle loaded with fresh vegetables rode out of sight.

"Blast. There was one. There's another!"

"I don't see—"

Half his body was swathed in red-brown muck. "With the bowler hat and the green tweed jacket."

"The awful green tweed jacket," Grace said. "I don't see—"

I grabbed her hand and pushed into her power. "Look."

"Miles. How—"

"I learned it from Tristan." I put my hand out, and Tristan took it. I eased out of Grace's power, and Tristan let me in, let me show him what I saw.

He felt warm in a way Grace didn't, and anxiety dripped into his middle, tensing his stomach. Grace had only felt curious and frustrated until the leap of insight bolted through her.

"Miles, I can still see it," Grace said. "There's another."

Tristan touched the window as he pointed east. "And a third, walking out of the haberdasher's."

I withdrew and was only myself again, standing between my sister and my friend. "Do you still see it?"

"Yes." His voice was grim. "It's as I learned of it from Cormac. Those people are all tethered to the soul of a dead person. The necromancers used it as a way to stay young."

I knew this story. "Trick a person into killing you by hand or blade, touch them as your body dies—"

"And your soul attaches to them so you can take their body for your own. Miles. It's the Revenge of Lucus." Grace's face was chalky.

Tristan cursed under his breath. "How many soldiers are like this? I've already seen five."

"From what I saw at the Homecoming? I gave up and counted the ones who weren't possessed."

"How many?"

"Thousands. Tens of thousands," I said. "They're all going home. All over Aeland. If they rise up all at once—"

It hurt to think of it. More families annihilated across the country, thousands of men who should have been trusted heroes suddenly monsters. Aeland would be devastated.

"When?"

"I don't know." But I knew. The Laneeri delegation sat in ceremonial imprisonment in the royal penitentiary for three more days. "The surrender. The sky-priests who came with the diplomats—some of their most senior members had a dozen or more stars around their heads. And if they cast the spell . . ."

Grace went pale. "The Queen's in danger."

"Unless she has protection."

"This is . . ." Grace covered her stomach with one hand, breathing too fast. "Excuse me. I'll be—"

"Upstairs, the door directly across from the landing," Tristan said.

She rose to her full height with a little sway. I moved to catch her, but she steadied and left the room. The door to the comfort room clicked shut, and water ran.

Tristan pressed his lips together. "Why did the Laneeri cast this spell?"

"Revenge," I said. "One final attack to throw us off their backs. They can't be happy to be conquered."

"All good reasons," Tristan said, but he frowned at the ceiling. "Can you think of another?"

"No," Tristan admitted. "I'm trying to make it fit into my mission, but I'm not sure how the pieces go together. Maybe Aldis—that's my counterpart in Laneer—maybe he succeeded and learned where the souls are going."

I remembered what I saw when I freed Bill and Gerald. "East. They're going east. I don't know why, but that's where they're going."

The door separating the kitchen from Tristan's study slid open. Grace paused on her way through the room, peering at the books and objects stored inside a hutch meant to display the good china. "Is that a skull?"

"I relieved a fraudulent witch of it when I first came here."

She nodded and turned away. "What . . ." She bent over the atlas, still open on Tristan's blotter. "Why have you drawn a summoning pentacle on this map?"

Tristan frowned. "A what?"

Grace came into the parlor with Tristan's atlas. "The north, the east, the southeast, the southwest, the west, and the Caller in the middle, to gather five into one. That's how we stand in ritual when we sing in the seasons."

"Miles told me you used hundreds of people in the rituals."

Grace nodded. "Including the Secondaries on the borders, yes. A hundred and fifty-six Invisibles, an equal number of Secondaries. But the Stations and the Voice stand this way. The shape makes a difference."

"So could you go to these places and make a summoning pentacle of your whole country?"

"With enough power, but it would take . . ." Grace looked up. "Thousands. Tens of thousands, and I'm not sure if it would be possible. Why?"

Tristan and I looked at each other.

Grace stood up straight. "What's going on here? Why are you here, Mr. Hunter?"

Tristan stood up. "It's a long story, best told over drink. Wine or whiskey?"

We had whiskey, chill on the tongue and warm over our hearts. Grace lounged in the wingback chair, while I leaned against the sloped back of Tristan's fainting couch. Tristan waited for us to settle, then explained about his fruitless search for the souls of the dead. Aeland had no ghosts, but the tradition of witches guiding the lost to the Solace was long faded. He told Grace about Nick Elliot, and meeting me.

"So Nick Elliot was investigating asylums in these towns," Grace said. "Asylums where witches are held. Why?"

Tristan pressed his lips together. "I don't know. But a summoning pentacle gathers power?"

"Yes. Don't you use them?"

"Amaranthines don't go in for group magic." Tristan poked the map. "I have to go to Bywell. That's where Nick's mother was sent. Maybe he managed to see her. Maybe she can tell us what's happening in those asylums, what they're making her do."

Grace's cup halted on the way to her mouth. "What they're making her do?"

"Dame Hensley," Tristan said. "Your laws and methods scoop up every witch you can find and distribute them to points along your country's borders in this particular pattern. Do you believe they're held to weave baskets?"

She turned her head, white-lipped. "You have a point. So you mean to delay your return."

"I'm so close to the answer," Tristan replied. "There are stones near Bywell. I can pass through those. I don't want to break into the royal park and get chased around by guards again."

"*Again?*" Grace asked.

Tristan waved his hand. "A tiny misunderstanding surrounded my arrival to your realm last year. Anyone could have done it. I would have apologized for the fuss, but they were shooting at me."

Grace fought to keep her expression sober. "What do you mean, the stones?"

"There's a ring of stones covered in spirals on the palace grounds. It's a gate."

Grace went bug-eyed. "The King's Stone is . . . a gate? And you Amaranthines can just pop in and out of it whenever you please?"

"It's not easy, even on stable lands." Tristan offered a second round of whiskey. "What I did at the Kingston stones was downright heroic. If I travel to Bywell, and go through the stones there—"

"How were you going to get there?"

"I have a coachman."

"But we'd have to get into the asylum."

"I might be able to hide us," Tristan said. "I'd be useless if we wound up in trouble. Hiding us and moving at the same time would use all my power."

Grace fidgeted in her seat. "Or . . ."

"Or?"

"I'll take you," Grace said. "My car isn't comfortable, but it's far faster than a coach."

"That doesn't get us into the asylum," Tristan said. "But I thank you."

"I can get us into the asylum," Grace said. "The Benevolent Society funds every rural asylum in the country. We practically own them."

"We can find Ann Elliot. Find out what's being done to them."

"The asylums are the next lead," Tristan said. "I need to bring answers with me when I go home."

"But what about this . . . possession?" Grace asked. "If it's making soldiers murder their families . . . they have to be stopped."

"It'll take more than the three of us." I licked my lips and went on. "We'll need the Invisibles."

"We'll need Secondaries." Grace's expression took on excitement. "If they help save Aeland, this will show the Invisibles exactly how their treatment of fellow mages has hindered our progress."

"So that's how you see them," Tristan said. "Not as tools, but people."

"We're all tools, Mr. Hunter. The Invisibles are merely the ones the Crown knows have a use."

"You *are* people, Miss Hensley. In particular service to your Queen, but still people. How will you tell the others?"

"Tonight, when we sing in winter. Everyone will be there. I'll gather the First Ring and tell them. Miles, you'll need to explain, but you know everyone."

"Sir Percy will be a problem."

Grace's mouth shifted to one side, and she nodded. "Sir Percy's always a problem. But the other four will be sensible. We'll talk to them tonight, and go to the asylum in the morning."

"Can you wait another day, Tristan?"

"I'll have to." Tristan shrugged. "Better to be a day late with the answer. Aife will temper herself if the mission's complete."

TWENTY-THREE

Black Beads and White

Grace's car made my head pound and my skin crawl. It ran on aether, and the active power it took to make the heavy black vehicle move down the street had me squinting against the pain in thirty seconds.

"How do you stand it?"

"It takes a good hour to get a carriage ready," Grace said. "It's a sight worse than aether lights, isn't it? Too bad it's already a relic."

It was a beautiful relic. The front panel was carved from rich, golden wood made more interesting with dark knots. The thick leather seats were hand-tooled with frond-like leaves, and brass trimmed the dials and gauges arched around the driver's wheel.

Only the wealthiest could afford such a wonder, and most of those would have to endure the pain of being near so much aether and the copper to run it. I gritted my teeth and watched the smooth black road that fed the little branches leading to one jaw-dropping house after another.

I was ready to get out and walk by the time we passed the gates to the hall where we'd celebrated the Return. A golden carriage rested directly in front of the door. We dashed across the trampled heads of violets in our rush to get inside, tracking them with us as we went.

I ran to the Hensleys' private suite while Grace ducked inside the glass-domed room where I'd danced with a dozen young women. I changed into a Secondary's robe, white embroidery on white wool with square-cornered sleeves. I didn't have the knack for the looped button fastening, and my haste only made it worse.

Voices hummed and murmured beyond the tiny chamber where I dressed. Grace had gone to gather the Stations to hear our warning. I would have to tell the Stations what I'd seen, and withstand their questions. Grace didn't know enough to handle their scrutiny.

It would be like explaining the particulars of a difficult medical case, or arguing one's findings in front of peers. I'd done that often enough. This would be no different. But a handful of people couldn't make so much mumbling noise.

I emerged from my little dressing room and stopped short. Two dozen people glanced over their shoulders and dismissed me with a shrug. Grace had gone to find the five people who led the magic at their Stations, but they'd brought their immediate Link Circles.

This was no brief conversation between leaders. This was a deciding, a gathering big enough to decide an outcome by vote. Grace stood at the front of the suite, leaning against the hearth. She ignored the black glass bottle on the carved table facing the gathering. She was the only one not in her vestments. I was the only Secondary in the room.

"Be on your way, boy," an older woman said to me. "We have business before the ritual."

"He's the one who has business with you," Grace said. "Miles, come up."

Tiny clicks sounded as I wove through the lounging knots

of people, as if they were counting with a string of beads. Grace leaned against the mantel, giving me an encouraging smile.

From the front of the room, the entire First Ring stared impassively at me. I knew some of these faces. None of them looked back at me with warmth or encouragement.

"Tell them what you told me," Grace said.

I folded my hands into the sleeves of my Secondary's robe. This had been a mistake. I shouldn't be wearing a reminder of my inferiority for this.

"We haven't much time," I said, "so I'll get straight to it—Aeland is in danger, and Queen Constantina might be attacked at the signing of surrender at the end of the week by our own men."

Some people looked disbelieving. Others frowned.

"I work as a psychiatrist at Beauregard Veterans' hospital. Most of my patients have battle fatigue, a condition we are still working to understand."

Too many eyes rolled to the ceiling when I said battle fatigue. Many didn't believe in it, or in melancholy, or in chronic anxiousness. But I had to go on. I had to give them something they could connect to. Maybe they'd seen it themselves.

"How many of you have the trick of being able to see mages, or auras around a person?"

Grace hissed a warning, but downturned mouths and crossed arms scolded me. Invisibles didn't admit to having Secondary tricks.

"I misspoke. My apologies. How many of you have family members or friends with the trick?"

A few hands went up. Few enough so I could count them, and a few more when others saw the admission.

"They're about to be vital to the Queen's protection. I have this trick myself. I will describe what I can see, so you may ask your household if they have also seen people who look like this."

I described the miasma to them, and a few people widened their eyes. They'd seen. Hope spread from my chest to warm my cold hands. Some of them had seen.

"I didn't know what I saw. I thought it was a disease, since my trick is healing. But I was wrong. It's not a disease."

I took a deep breath and went on. "It's the effect of a spell binding the soul of a Laneeri to the body of the soldier who killed them. Gradually, they possess the soldier's body, and then attack their families, and then anyone who gets close to them. There have been four such murders reported in the papers. I witnessed the fifth today."

People shifted in their seats, glanced around to check the reactions of others. All of them saw Sir Percy Stanley, arms crossed and mouth thin with disapproval, glaring at me with narrowed eyes. I sought those who had recognized the signs I described. They sat so, so still.

"One thousand soldiers will stand at rest while the Laneeri who came to Aeland sign the surrender. Of those one thousand, some will be possessed, bearing ceremonial arms in the presence of the Queen. An attack there could end in disaster."

Now voices rose up in alarm. Invisibles shouted questions one atop the other. But Sir Percy stood up, and raised his hand for silence.

The room settled down.

"That's enough," Sir Percy said. "Miss Hensley, we've all seen this opera before. You waste our time with this? You let your Secondary run entirely too free."

I couldn't let him deny it away. I addressed the First Ring, as if he'd asked for clarification. "It's not only whichever thousand are attending the surrender. Tens of thousands of possessed men have gone home to their families all over Aeland. The slaughter of their families alone will devastate the country."

Murmurs rose. The mages who could see auras turned to their neighbors, their whispers urgent. But Sir Percy barked a short laugh.

"This is absurd. The revenge of Lucus the Witch-King is a story, Master Miles. An entertainment. Grace, I knew you were too young to take on the responsibility of the Voice, but not even a moony schoolboy would believe this."

"What I tell you is true." I let my voice fill the room, but I didn't shout. Shouting was for the powerless. "But even if you need more proof, can you afford to ignore my warning? At least tell the Queen and increase her protection—"

He chopped his hand sideways, his face red. "I said that's enough."

Every one of the Invisibles who knew averted their eyes from me, shook their heads. One bit her lip and stood up.

"We should look into this," she said. "Sir Percy, I have the trick he's talking about. I've seen what he described."

"Did your Station leader ask you to speak, Dame Joan?"

She raised her eyebrows. "Are we in formal attendance? I thought this was an emergency meeting."

"I can see it too." Another Invisible stood up, beak-nosed and long-faced. "And I've read the papers. Every one of those killers was a soldier, back from the war. Sir Christopher might be mistaken, but I don't believe he's lying."

More voices murmured.

Sir Percy rolled his eyes. "Are there any more Links with Secondary tricks who believe this Secondary's story?"

Grace stepped up to stand beside me. "I can see them too. I believe my brother. He's seen thousands of soldiers with the condition he reports. We can't afford to ignore him."

Voices stilled as one of the men in the heavily embroidered robes of a Station stood up. "This Secondary ran away from his responsibility, joined the army under a false name, and had to be dragged back to his duty." Johnathan Blake was a tall man, and the gathering turned their attention to him in silent respect. "How do we know he's not inventing a threat to make himself important? He clearly doesn't know his place."

I went cold. Grace's future father-in-law had risen to question her. The ground crumbled out from under us.

My sister answered him with a steady voice. "My brother is an accomplished healer and a war hero. His choice to make the most of his gift is the only reason we have advance warning. Without him, this attack would be a complete surprise."

Sir Johnathan took on a considering look, and opened his mouth to speak again.

"Enough! We're late for the ceremony." Sir Percy raised his fist, making something inside it click.

Clicks answered him, double handfuls of fists clicking. Not beads.

Voting balls.

"I have no confidence in Dame Grace Hensley's competence to stand as the proxy Voice of the Invisibles," he said. "I move we vote."

Johnathan Blake rose to his feet. "There's no time to vote. The ritual—"

"—Is too important to leave in the hands of someone we can't trust. I thank the stars she never had a chance to learn the Cabinet's true secrets. We vote, and we vote now."

Sir Percy marched to the black glass bottle, and his vote fell in with a plink. His followers crowded the bottle before he'd settled in his seat, smug as he watched the First Ring file to the bottle and drop their votes inside.

It was done in under two minutes. Some of the Ring wouldn't even look at her when they cast a ball inside. Sir Percy nodded toward the bottle, unable to keep the triumph off his face.

"Count."

Grace's mouth was thin as she picked up the bottle and up-ended it.

A shower of black balls. A flash of white. But not enough. Not nearly enough.

Sir Percy spread his arms wide. "Dame Grace Hensley is no longer the Voice in proxy. By custom, she is demoted to a Link in the Third Ring, if there is a place for her. Does anyone have one?"

No hands went up.

It was over.

Grace stood motionless as everything she'd worked for burned to ashes. The First Ring filed out of our family suite—was it even ours anymore? The Hensleys had centuries of power behind them, measured in the permanence of this suite's decoration. Portraits of my father, my grandfather, and my great-grandmother stared down at us from the walls.

I had expected argument, but I hadn't expected Sir Percy would be so petty he would ignore our warning—

My warning. Grace had let me do the talking and stood aside. That wasn't what Invisibles did with their Secondaries. Maybe Father had realized what a wealth of tools the Invisibles had discarded, but the others didn't share his insight.

Grace had been completely ousted from the Circle. She wouldn't even be in the lowest-ranking position there was. I put my jacket back on, leaving the robe crumpled on the floor.

Grace still hadn't moved.

I came closer. "Grace. We have to figure out what to do."

She blinked, still looking at the portrait of Fiona Hensley.

"Grace." She couldn't crack on me now. We had a massacre to stop. "The Queen is here."

Now she looked at me. "No."

"Grace, she's in danger."

A muscle in her jaw jumped. "But now, you don't have to ever attend the major rituals. You don't have to marry anyone. The Hensley legacy is broken. And that works out in your favor, Miles."

Her words drenched me in cold. It did. She was right. "This is a disaster, Grace. Do you hear me? I didn't do this. Why would I?"

"Your freedom," Grace said. "We took your freedom. This is your revenge."

"Grace. It's not. This is the last thing I wanted. I should have insisted you speak to them. Of course they wouldn't listen to a Secondary."

Grace tilted her head and watched me.

"I wouldn't let Aeland burn because you bound me."

She breathed again, letting it out in a shaky sigh. "You wouldn't. You only think of yourself after taking care of everyone else. What do we do?"

I headed for the door. "We tell the Queen."

"They won't let us anywhere near her," Grace said, but she followed me to the door and across the wide corridor where white-robed Secondaries gobbled selections from the buffet. They eyed us, muttering to each other as we passed.

Word had already spread.

I kept going around to the north end of the hall, opening the doors to the summoning chamber where we had danced only the night before.

We made five steps across the ornately inlaid floor before Invisibles stood in our path.

"You've been ousted. Please leave."

I burned to say something, but I'd already made that mistake. I looked toward the throne, where Queen Constantina spoke to Sir Percy. I stared at her, wishing I could Speak into her thoughts. She wore a dove gray silk gown, diamonds draped over her collarbones like snowflakes caught permanently in the light. They dazzled from across the room.

Please look at me. I repeated it in my mind. I used my will to push the thoughts out to her. *You're in danger. Please look at me.*

"You're ignoring a mortal threat to the Crown." Grace kept her voice down. I wished she would shout, but she'd never break the façade of control. "Defending the Queen stands above all. Sir Percy may have forgotten, but I haven't."

Sir Percy spoke, tucking his hands into his robe, then letting his hands fall to his side as if he wasn't sure what to do with them. Queen Constantina didn't quite sigh, but she flicked her gaze away and it skipped over the crowd, landing on me.

One eyebrow rose. She cocked her head, intent on me and my sister, the only people besides her not in ceremonial garb. I made the most pathetic entreaty of my face, and prayed for her curiosity. Sir Percy followed her gaze to me, and his face darkened.

With a gesture, he sent his Links to deal with us and spoke to the Queen, who turned her attention reluctantly back to the new proxy Voice.

Sir Johnathan spoke again. He had a chin like Raymond's, narrow and pointed. "Please leave."

"You're so certain my Secondary is wrong?" Grace demanded. "You're willing to wager lives on that? Are you?"

The other glanced to her partner before saying, "You let your Secondary tell us something straight out of an opera."

"So you're going to ignore it?"

Sir Percy's Links marched up and blocked my view of the Queen.

She didn't look at me again.

"Yes. Don't make us force you, Miss Hensley. Take your Secondary and leave."

A robed Invisible in the simpler robes of the Second Ring

broke out of the crowd. Raymond. He took Grace's hand and folded something inside it.

"Sorry."

He melted back into the crowd.

Grace opened her hand. Grandfather's engagement ring rested in the valley of her palm, the emeralds so deep a green they were nearly black.

She closed her hand into a fist. "Miles. Let's go."

I followed her into the night, bracing myself against the car's skin-crawling effect. "We don't have enough time to ask for an appointment."

"We're sunk," Grace said. "We're now uninvited from the surrender signing, too. Only those in the Circle are attending."

"There must be something."

"There might be. If they won't listen to us, maybe the Amaranthines can help. We go to the asylum with Tristan, and ask his Queen."

"Grand Duchess."

Grace waved the correction away. "I'll go into the stones if I have to. Sir Percy Stanley can't blackball *her* for telling wild tales, can he? We get her help, Miles, and pray we get it in time."

Grandfather's engagement ring rattled on the lipped shelf in the middle of the car's console as we drove away.

"I'm sorry, Grace."

She glanced at the ring and shrugged. "I didn't love him."

"Even so."

She shook her head, and the round cap of her hair swayed. "Forget about Raymond Blake. It was political. He had a lover."

"A Secondary?"

"Richard Burleigh."

Sleet bounced off the hood of Grace's car halfway through Halston Park.

"What the deuce." Grace flipped a switch, and a rubber wiper cleared the windshield. "Sleet? During a ritual? They have to be singing in winter by now."

"Maybe this is how?"

"The ritual's supposed to be done under the stars, Miles. Somebody blundered."

"Or Sir Percy's skill isn't up to being the Voice."

Grace's smile was unkind. "How embarrassing. Poor man."

She exhaled—a slow, calm breath—inhaled, and sang. My hair stood on end, from my scalp down my arms. Grace was strong. How much magic could she do on her own? The fall of sleet slowed, and stopped.

"No sense getting your coat wet," Grace said. "I'll let it go once you're inside."

"Aren't you coming in?"

"No." Grace stroked the fur cuff of her coat. "After all that, I want to be alone. I'll be back early, so get some sleep."

"How will you explain leaving in the morning?"

Grace waved her hand. "I'll be gone an hour before he wakes up. The next time he sees me it'll be in the company of Amaranthines."

"Initiative. Father likes that." But not too much. "Grace . . . we don't know what we're going to find at the asylum. And I don't know if he would encourage us to go there."

She tightened her grip on the steering wheel. "What are you saying?"

If we kept the whole secret, we'd leave the Queen without a last line of defense. "Tell him about the Laneeri's spell and the soldiers. He can talk to the Queen, arrange her protection, at least. Don't tell him we're going to Bywell, or anything about the asylums. Or Nick Elliot."

He could protect the Queen. He would protect her, and he could make Percy look like a power-hungry idiot. He might have taken the proxy from my sister, but Father was still the Voice.

"Why not?"

I couldn't tell her all of it. "I think we're about to stumble onto a state secret with these asylums. He might forbid you. And then we couldn't ask the Grand Duchess for help, because it would be an act of diplomacy somewhat beyond your authority."

"I have no diplomatic authority. I see your point. I won't tell him the part about the asylum."

I pressed my lips together. I shouldn't leave her to deal with this alone. "Maybe I had better go with you and explain."

"Miles. Walk into that townhouse and enjoy a night of privacy," Grace said. "I'll handle Father."

My jaw hung open. "Grace . . ."

She shrugged. "Tristan and I had a talk. I'll be here in the morning. Make pancakes."

I took a breath of fresh, cold air and let myself into Tristan's home.

The lights were dimmed, but I knew Tristan's narrow foyer well enough to kick out of my shoes and put my own hat away, dry thanks to Grace's show of magic for the sake of my convenience. A faint smell of hot chocolate hung in the air, and rinsing water drummed into a pot in the kitchen.

"You two are back already? I wasn't expecting you for hours," Tristan called through the half-open kitchen door. "I thought of something while you were out, Miss Hensley."

I cleared my throat. "Tristan, Grace isn't—"

He slid open the door and stopped, staring at me on the front door mat, hanging up my coat.

"Grace isn't here. She'll be here in the morning."

His eyebrows rose. "Interesting." His hair was loose down his back, freed from its usual plait. He'd removed his tie, the top buttons open to expose smooth golden skin. "What happened?"

"They kicked us out. Voted Grace out, sent us packing."

"They didn't listen."

"Grace wants to ask your Grand Duchess for help." I came to a stop before him. "Would she?"

"If it means your people will be indebted to her . . . she might. But I wouldn't guarantee it." He lifted his hand, then stilled, as if he didn't quite dare. "Miles."

"What is it?"

"You're here."

"Should I go?"

"No. Stay." His hands trembled as he set them in mine.

I raised them to my mouth and kissed his knuckles. "You didn't enchant me."

"Like in the stories," Tristan said. "I never did."

"You're shaking."

"I am. Isn't it silly?"

I turned his hands over to kiss the palms, tracing the calluses of his sword hand. "You're nervous. I didn't think you felt—"

"Shut up, Miles."

He wound his arms around my neck and let me carry him upstairs.

The birch log in Tristan's fireplace fell with a shower of sparks. I propped myself up on one elbow, prepared to brave the goosebump air to tend it, for the master suite's radiator stood cold and useless between two tall and drafty windows draped in silver and violet damask.

Tristan caught my arm as I slid out from under down-filled quilts. "No."

"The fire's dying."

He burrowed under the blankets and I laid another log atop the coals, closing the chain curtains meant to keep sparks from landing on the thick carpet. My face and arms were heated from the fire, my back chilled from the draft seeping around the curtains.

I didn't feel lost to infatuation, and I should have. I smiled at the blanket-covered hump in bed. I should be enchanted twice over, and I wasn't.

It would hurt when he was gone. But it would only hurt.

"What are you smiling at?"

"How you'll howl when I put my cold hands on you."

"A precious memory to bear in my heart." Tristan flipped the covers back. "Come here. Don't tell me what time it is."

Morning was too soon, anyway.

He curled around my cold back, his chin on my shoulder. "I'll do everything I can to come back."

"I know."

"Miles." He pushed me onto my back so he could see my face. "It might take some time."

"It's all right. You have to go home. You have to report, and you're the heir's bodyguard. You don't have to explain."

He hunched his shoulders. "Yes, I do. Because I know what the stories say. Some of it's true."

"Like how you can't—"

"How we can't love," Tristan said. "How we lock up our hearts so they can't be hurt?"

If I put my hand up, it would touch his chest. "They do."

"We don't put our hearts in caskets for safekeeping, Miles. But mortal lives span seven or eight decades. Powerful witches live ten or eleven, and then they die."

I licked my lips. "Tristan, how old are you?"

"Concerned I'm robbing the cradle? I'm fifty-one."

"You look twenty."

A pillow landed on my face. "Flatterer."

"All right, twenty-five. But you don't—you don't die? And I will."

"An Amaranthine never forgets the ones they loved. They go on with the memory, forever. Until they are killed." His hands feathered along my face. "Miles. I will never forget you. Never."

TWENTY-FOUR

Frostmonth

Frostmonth dawned with a silvering sky. It clouded gently, suggesting enough rain to plaster golden orange leaves to the street and clean the salt and seaweed from the air. I looked out the parlor window at streets empty as a held breath, warming my fingers against a cup of black coffee.

"She'll come," Tristan said from behind me.

"I know," I said, but I turned my head to watch the west again.

Tristan's hand traced gentle circles over my shoulders. I turned to draw him close, leaned to kiss the corner of his jaw. We stood together before the parlor window, but I wasn't watching the street any longer.

The low rumble of an engine drew nearer, and Tristan drew his head back. "Look."

Grace, in her long black car. She pulled up to the space in front of the townhouse and waved up at the window before she let herself in.

"Pancakes, you said?" Tristan stepped away, leaving my left side cold. "I'll heat the griddle."

Grace followed Tristan into the kitchen. "Do you think your people are looking for you?"

"I'm sure they are, but no seeking spell has touched me yet," Tristan said. "And the longer it takes, the bigger the response we can expect."

"Will they really send a war party for you?"

"I am . . . indispensable to the Grand Duchess. She's waited a year and a day for my return. Best to assume they're coming in heavy numbers."

An army of Amaranthines headed right for us. Tens of thousands of soldiers possessed by dead Laneeri, bent on retribution. But breakfast would keep us on our feet if we had to use magic, so Grace and I got in the way trying to help. Tristan banished us to the kitchen table, where we guzzled coffee and ate what he brought us.

I cut my pancakes with the side of my fork and ignored Grace's grimace at my working-class behavior. "How did Father take the news?"

She used a knife, and her every gesture was precise. "He's going to see her Majesty when he wakes up. He's convinced."

"You make it sound easy."

"I told him what you told me, I told him what I saw myself, and he trusts your talent. Miles, he really does love you."

That was no comfort. Maybe he did, but it didn't matter. Whatever we found in the asylum would likely shred our relationship beyond repair. I shrugged and drained my coffee. We could still succeed. Grace would win her place back. Secondaries would win more rights, more dignity. Raymond Blake would regret jilting her. Maybe they'd reconcile.

And maybe enough people would join her side so I wouldn't have to make a dynastic marriage.

Oh, Miles. Still selfish. "Do you know what you'll ask the Grand Duchess?"

"No idea. What if Tristan's prediction isn't correct and she's not there?"

"I guess we go with him to find her."

"She'll be there." Tristan finally sat beside me, his plate piled high with round golden pancakes, sweet syrup, and half a pound of sausage. "I'll eat fast," he promised, and set to his breakfast with an unseemly quickness.

We left dirty dishes behind with apologies to the absent Mrs. Sparrow and braced ourselves for the ride to Bywell.

Grace pushed her car to the limit, the press of our own speed rocking us back against the seats. How thrilling to travel so unimaginably fast, faster than a horse could gallop, long past the time a horse would collapse and die from the strain. Forty miles an hour, the velocity gauge read. Faster even than a train.

If only it hadn't made us feel so ill we barely spoke, trying to keep our breakfasts down. If only we weren't racing to find the truth Nick had been killed to keep. If only the evidence pointed to someone other than Father.

He was above justice. They'd never arrest him for murder and I knew it. But that wasn't reason to give up. Tristan still didn't have the answer to the question he'd been sent to answer—where were Aeland's dead going? I remembered the path of the two souls I'd pulled from Bill and Old Gerald, slipping out of my grasp and out of sight. To go where?

East. East, toward Bywell.

Grace drove around a bend in the narrow road. "I think—yes. That's it."

She pointed out the window. The asylum was graceful white plaster, with tall windows and rambling wings, hemmed by scarlet-leafed shrubbery and cheerful yellow mums. To the eye it was serene, peaceful and composed. A black iron fence standing twelve feet high bordered the long, rolling lawns and mature oak trees, the points atop the bars long and sharp.

"Friendly," Tristan said.

"Welcoming," I agreed.

"Can you feel it?" Grace asked.

"I can't feel anything sitting in this car—"

But my hair stood on end, and the air tasted of the heavy pressure in the second before lightning.

It was thick with power.

"What is that?"

Tristan squeezed my hand. He craned his neck to look at the sky, and his voice was small with horror.

"Souls. They're pouring into the building. Can you see them?"

"No," I said. "Show me."

A minute later, I wished I hadn't asked. "Oh, gods."

They sped through the air, headed for the asylum. They went in.

None came out. A force tugged at me, and pulling away from it was like the struggle to keep iron from a magnet. It wanted to pull me inside the asylum, and with every step the pull grew stronger, like it would pull me from my body and make it fly into whatever hungered behind those clean white walls.

Grace showed the gate guard her identification, and the guard ran out to open the gate for us, touching the brim of his uniform cap as we drove along the curving path to the asylum's front doors.

"That was easy," Grace remarked, and a chill ran up my spine.

"I'm going to be sick," I said, and Grace braked. I stumbled onto the leaf-scattered lawn before the asylum and tried to breathe in air that didn't taste like screaming.

There wasn't any to be had.

"It feels wrong," Grace said. "My skin's crawling. What are we going to find in there?"

"Horror," I answered, wiping my mouth. I didn't want to go in. I had to. I headed for the asylum's front door, Grace on my left hand, Tristan on my right.

Guards waited for us inside. Grace held up her identification and they fell back.

A man walked into the lobby, headed right for us. He wore a fine suit under his doctor's white coat. "May I help you?"

"You may," Grace said. "Dame Grace Hensley, Dr. Miles Singer, and Sir Tristan Hunter. We're here to see the facility. My brother is particularly interested."

"I'm a psychiatrist." The air was thick with a horrible, helpless gravity. My muscles trembled to hold me upright. Every limb was drawn down and slightly ahead of where we stood. Grace's jaw was stiff with effort. Tristan grabbed my shoulder and squeezed.

"*Psyche*. You wrote about dissociative memory episodes and their treatment in veterans with battle fatigue."

I swallowed. "You know me?"

"I recognize your name. I wrote an article about the commonality of delusion among witches, and I noticed your observations about veterans. . . . You aren't here to talk about that." The doctor pasted on a smile before turning to Grace. "Dr. James Fredman. I'm at your service. You're here to show Dr. Singer the asylum?"

"And to satisfy my curiosity," Grace said. "I'd like to see the results of our investment."

"Of course. Please, come in."

He unlocked a door for us, and led us into an aether-lit corridor. He ambled toward a staircase made of golden oak. "Dr. Singer, I suppose you're interested in our patient care?"

"I am," I said. "I want to see the witches."

He stilled mid-step. "They're here, of course. We're an approved facility for the care of patients with magical aptitude. We've kept them as comfortable as possible, given the circumstances—"

Grace cleared her throat. "Not that way, if you please."

Dr. Fredman halted again, one foot on the stairs. "I'm sorry?"

"Take us to the basement," Grace said.

"Where you keep the witches," I added.

He swallowed. "Patients are on the upper floors."

He knew exactly what I meant.

Grace shook her head. "It's definitely coming from below. Come on." She walked briskly across a five-armed star inlaid in the floor. "We've no time to waste."

Grace had locked onto the source of the collection of power, and she navigated her way through service hallways, back stairs, and wrong corners. She ignored Dr. Fredman's demands to stop and explain herself, his protestations fading to agitated utterances of "Ma'am!" and "Please, stop."

He finally fled, calling for guards when Grace led us down three flights of stairs and straight into Hell.

Hell was a deep, wide room with bare stone walls and the smell of unwashed hair. Fifteen people sat chained into a circle inlaid on the floor in copper. Sigils and curves spread across the floor in one unbroken line, as complex as the inlay on the floor in the Hall of the Invisibles.

Grace sucked in her breath. "It's a Calling Circle."

Tristan shut the door behind us. "Like the Invisibles use?"

Her nod was tight. "The way they're . . . chained up, they're arranged in Stations, with one Caller and two Links. They're moving the power into the center."

None of the witches looked up as we entered. They sat opened to the power coursing through their bodies, funneling it into the heart of the Circle.

"Can you feel it?" Tristan asked.

He didn't mean the souls, exactly. He meant the sense of their movement. They pooled in the center of the Circle, then were forced out along straight lines stretching out past my perception.

How could they stand it? It was worse than the copper-lined rooms used for examinations. I wanted to run away from here until my legs gave out. How long had these people been coerced into this?

"It's the copper," I said. "Miles of it, probably. Like railway, shuttling the souls along to—where?"

"Power stations," Grace said. "It's aether."

I stared at Grace in horror. Aether? Our lights, our wireless, our telephones and machines, our cinema projectors and passenger trains ran on . . .

Oh, Solace. Oh Guardians, forgive us.

"We have to break it." Tristan looked sick. And furious. He covered his mouth, tense with the need to shatter something. "Stop it."

"How?" Grace asked. "How could we break it?"

"Start with the witches. They have to be part of it."

"They're channels, like bound Secondaries," I said. "That's all they're doing. The souls pass through them and into the copper. This is what aether is. This."

"Yes," Tristan said. "The Amaranthines will . . . I swear I'll protect you, Miles. Both of you are safe from them. When they learn what your people have done . . ."

Grace raked her fingers through her hair, grabbing a handful. Her throat went tight, the cords on her neck standing out. "It's always been from souls. All along."

"Yes." I paused next to a woman who stared at me with un-comprehending eyes, who watched me test her bonds.

"Try this." Tristan handed me a handcuff key.

I looked at the key, and then him. "Really?"

He shrugged. "I expected chains. No one's here willingly."

Clever Tristan. I tried it in the shackles. It fit. I popped the locks holding her.

"Can you stand?" I asked her, and helped her up.

When I moved to the next prisoner, she followed me. She watched me unlock the man's cuffs and help him stand up. He moved into a corner, as far from us as he could get.

"The power's fluctuating," Tristan called. "It depends on the witches."

I moved on to the next prisoner. The woman followed me, a new light in her eyes.

"You're going to be all right," I said. "I'm Miles. What's your name?"

"Ann."

"Are you Ann Elliot?"

Her eyes were wide. "Did Nick send you?"

Her hopeful look stung me in the heart. "He did."

It was true.

"Everyone's going to be all right, Ann." I said. "No one is ever going to lock you in this Circle again."

Ann followed me all the way around, reluctant to leave me even when I rejoined Tristan and Grace. Tristan watched me with shining eyes, but Grace covered her mouth in horror.

"It doesn't feel like this in the Circle. This feels like—" She shuddered. "Miles, I was wrong. I was so wrong—"

Her knees landed on the copper-inlaid floor with a thump. She buried her head in her hands. "What have we done?"

"You didn't know," Tristan said. "I'll tell the others that only a few understood what they had done."

"I should have known." Grace turned her face up to the ceiling. "I should have questioned. Miles. Miles, I'm sorry."

"I know," I said. "But you didn't know. Now we can—"

"No," Grace said. "You don't understand."

The door clicked open. Ann clutched at my arm.

"Miles, I am so sorry," Grace said, and Father walked into the room.

He stood tall, my father. He walked with a cane across the sigil-laden floor. Guards spilled into the room to flank him. The guards moved to seize us, but paused at Father's quelling hand.

"You may go, gentlemen. Thank you for the escort."

Reluctantly, the guards left. One man stayed by his side, an ordinary-looking man with a well-groomed, curling mustache. He remained until Father gestured at him to go.

I knew him. The man from the hospital. The one we had chased through West Kingston, the man who had stolen my bag, who had followed me, who had bribed his way into delivering Nick Elliot's poisoned groceries.

Tristan moved to shield Ann, who cowered behind me. My heart was lead as I looked at Grace. "You told him."

"Grace has always been faithful," Christopher Hensley said. "She didn't know you had stumbled onto the truth. She didn't want to believe it was true. So she asked me."

"And you didn't tell her." My heartbeat pounded in my ears. I wanted to grab Father, put him in those shackles, make him feel what Ann had felt. "How could you do this?"

"Look at the wider picture, Miles. It's terrible to have to carry in your heart. But you can bear it." He planted the tip of his cane and leaned on it as he took a step closer. "Think of Kingston. Think of all the people blessed with fine weather and the

C. L. POLK

wonders of aether. Count the millions who thrive because of our great works."

I shuddered. "Look at the fifteen who suffer in here. What do you say to them, Father?"

"That the needs of the many are paramount."

"Then take their place."

He gave me a patient smile. "Miles. Does a general fight with the infantry?"

"Then put the Invisibles in their place." I flung my arm toward that awful ritual circle. Souls clogged the air, and I fought to breathe through it. "If the needs of the many are so important. Since it's for the good of the country. Like the war against Laneer."

"Laneer won't need all of the aether they could produce."

"You started a war! You sent thousands to kill—for what? For gadgets?"

Father thumped the floor with his cane, his lips pressed in a tight line. "For the advancement of our people."

"That's the real reason for the Laneeri War. To set this up and take their souls too. That's why they're out there, isn't it? Possessing our men, ready to slaughter at the surrender. Anything to stop this . . . abomination."

Father leaned on his cane. "I didn't expect their resistance, but it doesn't matter. The Invisibles are guarded. The royal family is under protection. The reserve has been ordered to muster."

If I could vomit again, I would. "You truly don't care. They'll kill anyone they find. Innocents. While you're behind royal guard and your high walls."

"I can count the costs, Son." He stepped forward, leading with his cane again. "Thousands will be killed by the possessed. Millions will suffer if you break the summoning complex."

If I break it? I could break it. How? "Did Grace tell you about Tristan, while she was betraying me?"

Grace looked agonized. "Miles—"

"She didn't want to tell me about your witch lover." Father shook his head. "You should have known better than to share our secrets. He'll have to die, of course."

Tristan bared his teeth. "You want my death, mage? Come and take it."

I held up a hand and Tristan didn't lunge, but he quivered with wanting to. "He's here because the Amaranthines noticed, Father."

Father blinked and looked at Tristan more carefully. "The Amaranthines?"

My sister hadn't told him everything, then. "They'd assumed that Aelanders had all died until they noticed the decreased flow of souls from Laneer. If you'd left it alone, they would have gone on assuming we had been wiped out."

Tristan loomed, taller than the rest of us. "What you have done is unspeakable. Run back to your Queen, and prepare her to beg us for mercy."

"Father, he's not bluffing. The Amaranthines will go to war with you over this."

"Let them come," Father said. "You don't see the full scope. Ten deaths increases our power a hundredfold. Our greatness will continue."

The blood in my veins turned to ice. I locked my knees to keep standing. "Our greatness? Or yours? You'll do anything to keep this power. Believe anything. But it's wrong, Father. It's monstrous."

Rage propelled me—not forward, but back.

I stepped inside the Circle, felt the souls around me. With no witches to channel the power along the copper lines to the aether stations, the souls pooled inside the boundaries, filled it up.

They had nowhere to go.

It clicked into place. I understood.

They needed somewhere to go.

"It ends now, Father. It's finished."

The souls of Aeland's dead clamored around me. The well filled as I searched for the way to free them. The raw power in the air scalded me, dug under my skin, squeezed my breath. It was worse than the car, worse than the testing room.

Tristan grabbed a handful of air and Father flew back, hitting the wall hard before slumping to the floor. He groped his way up, his hands in front of him and his eyes wide but unseeing.

"We have to hurry." Tristan stepped over the line and took my hand. "They'll pass through you."

"I know," I said.

We joined our power together, his meeting mine. "I'll open the way."

I took a deep breath.

"Wait."

Grace stood at the edge of the circle. I shook my head, and tried to give her one last smile. *Goodbye, Sister.* "I have to do this, Grace."

"I know," she said. She raised her hand. I stiffened as the tension of the tether between us went taut for an instant; then I staggered as the tension vanished all at once.

She'd freed me.

"Mind if I join you?" She stepped over the line. "You'll need a Caller."

TWENTY-FIVE

The Liberator

I stretched out my left hand, and she took it.

Grace sang out to the magic, Called the souls. Tristan unraveled the space in the center of the room, opening it to bright light and a sound like a thousand hooves pounding the earth. I saw the threads of energy Tristan bent, and I filled in the flimsy spaces between with the starry light of my energy, knitting them together like healing bone. The souls came to Grace's Call, cramping the air around us.

I staggered. Linked like this, I knew Tristan's power and Grace's. Above us in the unseen sky, cold air bulged, heavy with pressure. Clouds.

I could feel what Grace could. I stretched my senses along the copper on the ground. It screeched along my nerves and radiated from the complex sigils into straight lines joined at hubs a half mile distant, following parallel to the iron railway to the border towns with asylums.

It was vast. It was years of work to build. We had to stop the souls' helpless attraction to the network and set them free. Moisture coursed down my lips, and when I licked them I tasted blood.

Father stretched out one hand to the edge of the Calling Circle, and drew it back as if he'd been burned.

Grace held me upright. I heard her sob as I coughed, a fire-blossom of red bursting from my lips. But she Called the souls who passed through me. She never stopped.

A woman screamed. I couldn't look for the source. The lives of Aeland poured into me, their memories smearing into mine. I was born, learned to walk, went to school, worked, loved, had children. Hunted, gardened. Memories passed through me, tossing me about.

I wept to hear a symphony perform *Abianta* when I was sixteen, knowing I would never sit on a stage and play. I felt the warm leap of joy when the prettiest girl I'd ever seen said she'd be my wife.

I didn't know how much longer I could stand.

Ann hovered on the border, wringing her hands as I swayed. I couldn't spare her a nod, a smile, a promise she would be safe. But she ventured into the Ring, flinching at the power, and clutched at my shoulder. She opened herself up and channeled her power through me. I could stand up straight. My nose stopped bleeding. The burning in my chest subsided.

The pale green light of her soul left her body and bound itself to me. Freed, her soul fed more power through me, enough to join to Tristan's gateway from here to his realm.

Ann's body lay at my feet. One of the witches I'd freed came closer and carried Ann's corpse away, then laid his hands on my head and gave me his power.

When he died, a third witch stepped forward. A fourth.

Father shouted at me, but I couldn't hear his words. The thundering sound was louder now, the faint shouting nothing compared to its rumble. He struggled to come closer to us, battling against blindness and a high wind Grace had woven to keep him back. I cried as the barber cut my russet hair short, because I was ten and no longer a little boy. Grace's voice was hoarse, but she kept Calling. Tristan held the passage open, but his power flagged.

I gave them some of the strength gifted to me by the witches who had moved their predecessors aside to give their lives before mine, each one another starred soul floating around my head. Some of those seventeen souls flickered feebly, giving everything to the last.

A thousand voices roared. Horns blared, calling again and again. My grandmother put her hands over mine and taught me to knit. And still I worked to strengthen the gateway Tristan opened, tracing the threads and hardening them.

My vision swam, darkness growing on the edges of my perception. I didn't have long. The lacelike sigils on the floor were joined by simple straight lines cutting across the land, branching off smaller and smaller to cover the land . . . like a circulatory system.

"Miles," Tristan said. "Do you see them?"

I didn't know what he meant, but he had his eyes closed. I shut mine and let a picture of the aether network blossom in my mind, too big to really hold all of it in my head, but through his senses I saw what he did.

Souls like stars. A galaxy of them in Kingston, and smaller blobs marking other cities, other towns. Tristan showed me a soul that was twinned, the second one dried-blood brown and spreading to take over.

I reached, and peeled the parasite soul free. It sucked into the aether network and sped toward us. With all the power I commanded, peeling the soul loose was easy as a thought.

I found another. And another.

"You can't do it one by one!" Grace shouted. "There's no time!"

She was right. But how? I could see those angry souls now,

red stars in the sky, only uncountable. Like grains of sand on a beach—

Like a virus.

And I knew what made the invading souls different from living ones.

One of my star-souls extinguished. Ann, kissing the fine colorless hair of her infant son. Another winked out, dancing in a square with his newly wedded wife. Nick, ripening an orange in a glasshouse. Another faded, and this one stopped my breath.

"No. Mother, no."

I fought to unravel her link to me, but she poured the last of her power into me, the last touch a kiss to the crown of my head. A hole tore through my chest, the ache unbearable. I wanted to keen for her loss, to drop the whole web of magic, to fall to the floor and weep.

Thousands of tethers reached for the invading souls, moved by my healing magic. I sent out the lines, and they found their targets and pulled them into the network, making it stronger.

I learned to play the spirit-flute. I helped my brother get ready for temple, drawing a wooden comb through his shining blond hair. I sat with my hugely pregnant cousin and held her as she wept over a message saying her husband had been killed in battle. I bowed my head as a sky-priest lay a spell on me and all the men of my village. We picked up knives and left for war, covered in their blessing for our sacrifice.

They passed through me too, the Laneeri souls. I saw what had happened to them, how they had fought and died, how their sky-priests had known what the Aelander army had built in the territories they conquered, how they'd kidnapped priests and novices and imprisoned them in the death engines. I understood why they fought so relentlessly to stop us.

But their revenge would have made the soul machines stronger.

Father was right. Every death made the aether network brighter. We were draining it, but we couldn't stand here forever. Souls had found their way to the Solace before this gate was built. We'd have to break the aether network.

But how?

The asylums linked to power stations through the copper lines. The witches Called the souls; the copper coils in the asylums sucked them down. We had to shut down the main lines, and then the souls would either come to the gate we had fashioned or find their own way.

"Grace."

She saw it too. "Help me."

I gave up my power and Grace seized it, working at all five junctions simultaneously, even though they were miles away from where we stood. Grace took all the threads of power and made them into what she wanted. Clouds mounted, huge and dark with moisture. Cold air rolled in underneath.

She made a finger of her will and pointed, and thunder cracked overhead, rolling like kettle drums. The next strike made the lights go out, flashing twice before half the bulbs relit.

The power thinned around us as Grace called lightning down. One by one, each spoke of copper line broke, not just in half but into pieces.

But she had to drop her wind spell to do it, and Father stepped into the awful radiance inside the circle, his silver-bladed knife in one hand. He raised it over his head and brought the blade down, sinking it deep into Tristan's chest.

It staggered us all. The pain made our link falter, and Father reached for the power, trying to take it from us.

Tristan clutched the handle and drew it out. Blood poured from the wound, spilled out of his mouth.

"No!"

Tristan didn't let go of my hand. He raised his head and held onto the gate he'd made. He'd hold it until he died, the last thing he would ever do.

No. I fused the nick in his lung closed, held the thick artery shut, and sealed it.

"Let go of the gate!"

He shook his head. "No."

"You'll die!" My heart beat too fast, too painful. But we had done it. The seal on Tristan's artery held. Blood flowed through it without leaking. It throbbed, but he'd live.

And then I couldn't breathe. Beside me Grace choked, her free hand grabbing at her throat.

Father. He stood in the Circle with us, the bloody blade still in his fist. "Stop this."

I gagged on my answer. He couldn't wrest control of the Calling from Grace—from the link we three had made, the bond blending us and our power. I could stop Father from suffocating us, but if I let go of Grace or Tristan the link would break. The gate would collapse.

But if we blacked out, it would anyway.

Grace reached out and grabbed Father's wrist. His bare wrist, pulse beating wildly under Grace's fingers. Blood moved through the veins in Father's skin. His lungs filled with the air he denied us. Rage and terror poured out of him, a desperate howling denial of what we had done to destroy everything.

I reached out through Grace's body and touched Father's heart. I held it in tight bands. I squeezed it and made sure it hurt. He staggered and landed on his knees. I squeezed harder. He pulled on Grace's grasp, trying to free himself.

My throat unblocked, and I breathed in the damp subterranean air tinged with human effort and the smell of spilled blood.

I squeezed again, and Father clutched his chest.

But Grace let go of his hand and pulled us away from the gateway, staggering and bloody-nosed. She narrowly avoided the ebony hooves of a velvety black horse—no, white—no, piebald—ridden through the gate by a woman who held a horn bow in her left hand, ready to draw and loose the arrow poised in the fingertips of her right. Another horse like smoke and silver followed, ridden by another woman with her golden hair bannering out behind her, a horn poised to her lips.

A dozen riders poured out of the gate we'd made. The archer slipped off her saddle-less horse and rushed to Tristan. A man dressed in white knelt beside me, uncaring of the blood spraying from my last desperate breaths.

"Help them," I gasped, and everything went black.

I wasn't dead.

Instead, I breathed around jagged tears in my throat and licked dry lips. I was in a tent heated by a brazier. Heavy blankets pressed me down, and when I shifted in the layers of bedding I knew I was naked.

"Hello?" My voice was a croak. I coughed and tried again. "Hello?"

No one answered me. I tried to sit up, and just pushing the blankets aside took enough of my strength that I had to rest before I could go on. I staggered across the tent and knelt before a hand-carved wooden trunk. It wasn't locked, but I didn't—

What sort of clothes were these? I pulled out a silver tunic. It was long enough to cover me to my knees, and covered in embroidered ivy vines. Wasn't there anything I could wear in here?

I pawed through silk and suede, wool and velvet. I had to rest after I removed from the cedar-lined trunk clothing fit for a children's tale. I was heaving for breath and covered in twinges, aches, and trembling weakness by the time the trunk stood empty, and I never found any trousers. I considered the heap of discarded finery and searched for the least embellished garments I could wear.

A blast of cold air swirled into the tent. "You shouldn't be out of bed." The man in white headed straight for me.

"I'm fine. Where's Tristan? Is Grace alive?"

"You're a healer," the man retorted, "so you are the worst sort of patient. You are not fine. I barely saved your life. And you will not die because you haven't the sense to stay in bed and let your body heal."

"I can walk," I protested, as he steered me back into bed. "What about Tris—"

"You can lie down and rest. You can stop giving me trouble. And don't you dare even try to heal yourself."

"How did you know—"

"Because healers are idiots," the man said, "and I should know. If you manipulate your energy to heal yourself, you will undo the web I've cast over you, and *then* you will collapse and die. You're about as strong as a candle in a breeze, and you will not die by your own foolishness."

"You sound like Robin," I grumbled.

He settled the heavy blankets over me. "Do you respect Robin?"

"Robin's the best nurse I've ever met."

The healer touched the blankets, and warmth bloomed from them. "Good. There is someone who wants to see you. If I let him in, will you stay in bed?"

"Is it—"

"Tristan? Yes."

"I—that's kind of you," I said. "I'm Miles."

"Cormac."

"I'm glad to meet you, Cormac." I licked my lips again, and Cormac helped me sit up and drink water, clean and icy cold.

"Stay sitting up." He piled more pillows up behind me, and I sank into them gratefully. "You'll only have a few minutes before you need to rest."

He opened the tent and admitted Tristan. He rushed past Cormac and kneeled beside my narrow bed, catching my hand. He pressed my knuckles to his lips and closed his eyes.

"Tristan," I said. "It's all right. I'm not dead."

"You don't know how close you came," Tristan said. "We sat by you for days, keeping you alive."

"How long?" I asked. "Where are we?"

"We're at the stones of Bywell," Tristan said. "We couldn't move you any farther."

"What day is it?"

"Frostmonth eight."

It had been a week. "Are the Amaranthines angry? Was there an attack on the Queen? Are we at war?"

"Furious, no, because you saved nearly every man possessed by the spell, and not yet." Tristan stroked my hair. "Don't worry. Grace is doing her best."

"Grace? She's all right?"

"We're both fine, Miles. You need to recover." He leaned in and kissed my brow. "Do what Cormac tells you. Don't try to speed up the healing. The fact you got out of bed and managed to toss your clothes all over the floor is a testament to his skill."

Those were my clothes? Oh. "Tristan." I licked my lips again. "What do you mean, we're not at war yet?"

"The Solace and Aeland are waiting to see if you live," Tristan said. "Sir Percy is calling you a traitor. Grand Duchess Aife has declared you the Liberator. Intruders have been shot trying to cross into the camp."

Assassins, he meant. "I'm going to live. Tell them." As I said it, I realized that it might be easier to prevent war if I died. "How many soldiers rose up?"

Tristan shook his head. "Scattered incidents. Nothing like what it could have been. "

I shut my eyes. "The people?"

"The power's out everywhere. There are lost souls all over the country. Aeland is reeling in shock."

I kept my eyes shut. They needed me, and I wasn't there for them. "Father?"

"Is in Aeland's diplomatic party. He's demanding to see you," Tristan said. "No one will let him near you. Grace has deserted the Invisibles and is in our camp. Do you want to see her?"

"Yes."

"After you rest," Tristan said, and leaned down to kiss my dry lips. "She'll come to the Solace with us."

I struggled to sit up. "What? I can't go to the Solace, Tristan. I have to stay here."

He kept his hand on my chest, pushing me back into the fur and cushions. "You can't touch magic for at least the next month. If I could show you the web keeping you alive—"

"But you can," I said. "You can see it, right?"

"Yes."

"Then show me what it looks like."

"I shouldn't."

"I need to understand this. Show me."

Tristan nodded, and a latticework of green light sprang to life over my hand. The threads were thin as a hair, crossing each other in a network that mimicked the complex branching of my veins, my nerves, the fiber of my muscles, right down to the marrow in my bones.

"How . . . ?"

"Cormac's a genius."

I turned my hand this way and that, able to see the full depth. It was stunning. It would take power—too much power. "How is it maintaining? What's powering it?"

Tristan held my hand. "Me."

I shook my head and the tent spun. "You didn't."

"I did. I bound myself to you. It was the only way." Tristan lifted my hand, now free of the illusion, and kissed it. "I'm eating like a horse to keep this web going."

"I owe you my life."

Tristan shrugged. "My life is yours."

"As soon as I can, I'll release you."

"I know," Tristan said. "But I'd ask you to do it again."

"How do you mean?"

He covered my hand with both of his. "Amaranthines do bond sometimes."

"Really? What do they use it for?"

"Marriage."

I couldn't speak. All the pain I endured melted in the warmth that played over my skin.

"Marry me, Miles. Spend your life with me. And whatever we do after this, let's do it together."

"We can do that?"

"We can. Our people do." Tristan kissed my hand again. "Say you will."

I had no idea what had happened in the week I'd lain insensible. The power of aether was gone, the Invisibles in the hands of a man who counted me as his enemy.

But Tristan would stand by me through all of it. I propped myself up on one elbow and freed my hand to touch Tristan's face. His true face, ethereal with inhuman beauty, but it didn't drag me down into enthrallment. It was him, the truth of him, and it hardly hurt when I smiled.

"I will." I clenched his hand, and his happiness spread from the center of his chest to his fingers, wrapped around mine. "I can feel you."

"Part of the binding. Do you mind?"

I didn't mind. Joined with him, I was free.

ACKNOWLEDGMENTS

So many people had a hand in helping me through the process of writing and producing this book. I'm going to miss some, I just know it.

For Tom. You are my rock, and I leaned on you all through this book. Thank you.

For Bear. You never doubted that I could do this, not once, and you are a mighty vanquisher of brain weasels. Thank you.

For AJ. Everyone needs a scientist asking them questions about your book. Yours always made me think. I can't believe how many times you read this thing. Thank you.

For Liz. I was hoping for feedback on what to fix. What happened next was totally unexpected, and led directly to this moment. Thank you.

For Kim. You were right about the opening scenes, and you wouldn't let me take one more step without being sure I knew my characters. Thank you.

For Caitlin, Justin, Carl, and Irene. I'm still amazed by how much you like this book. I think we made a good one. Thank you.

Thank you so much, drowwzoo. You kept my head on straight, you read my draft, you told me to suck it up and send another query. To Isle of Write, my friends, thank you for entertaining every idle, random question I came up with. To #rwchat, and all the writers who helped make a space where I found I wasn't alone, that everyone experiences all the ups and downs of writing.

And thank you, reader, thank you. I'm so pleased that you're here.

Shell Arkell

ABOUT THE AUTHOR

C. L. POLK wrote her first story in grade school and still hasn't learned any better. After spending years in strange occupations and wandering western Canada, she settled in southern Alberta with her rescue dog Otis. C.L. has had short stories published in *Jim Baen's Universe* and contributes to the web serial *Shadow Unit*.

CPSIA information can be obtained
at www.ICGtesting.com
Printed in the USA
LVHW03s0255090918
589573LV00003B/360/P

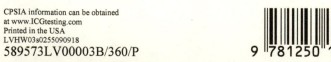